ELLIS ANGELS
ON THE MOVE

Making A Difference In Brooklyn

A Novel by Carole Lee Limata, RN, MSN

Dedication

In memory of my mother-in-law,
Eleanor Bartoli Limata

Table of Contents

Part One

Ellis Island

This story begins on Ellis Island, the place where many American stories first began.

Located at the tip of New York Harbor, Ellis Island was the initial stop for immigrants entering the United States in the early Twentieth Century. From 1892 to 1921, when Ellis Island first opened as an immigration center, almost 10 million people from foreign lands registered there before entering the United States. During that time, there were few admission restrictions. However, the Immigration Law of 1924 established strict quota guidelines, permanently restricting immigration.

Changes were in the air for the nurses and doctors who worked at the 750-bed Hospital on Ellis Island during the summer of 1924. Although Ellis Island remained open until 1954, the number of immigrants passing through the registration center dropped dramatically when the new law was implemented on July 1, 1924.

Chapter One

∾

August 4, 1924
12 Noon

Nursing Angels, ladies-in-white,
Work all day into the night.

The early morning summer rain came fast and furious, splattering upon the roof tiles and pelting the window panes of the hospital until they shook and clattered. It lasted until noon when all evidence of the downpour quickly dissolved as the gray clouds parted, revealing the sun to shine down upon Lady Liberty and Ellis Island. The squall cleansed the walkways leading to the hospital entrance and recharged the air. Outside, the birds returned to their singing. Inside, within the hospital walls, another storm was slowly brewing as the *ladies-in-white* coped with an unexplained *increase* in patient census.

On Ward 240 South, the young nurse stocked the top shelf of the instrument cabinet with an assortment of shiny scissors and sterile clamps in a variety of sizes. She was closing the cabinet's glass door when she heard a knock on the ward window. She turned to see Jimmy, one of the many messenger boys from the Ellis Island Registry Room. Jimmy opened the ward door with one hand. With the other, he pushed a tall, wicker wheelchair into the room. An attractive, freckled-faced woman, no more than twenty, sat in the chair. She appeared to have been recently washed and scrubbed from head to toe. Her feet were bandaged.

"Afternoon, Miss, this here's your next patient. Miss Ida said to bring her to you. She said she's full up on the North Wing."

"That's correct, Jimmy. I came ahead to ready the ward. We're opening it for new admissions today. The charwomen wiped down the walls and tables with carbolic this morning. The matrons finished making up the beds only minutes ago."

"A good thing that is, because there's surely more comin' behind me. This here's Miss Elsbeth Ferguson."

"Welcome, Miss Ferguson. You're our first patient this afternoon. Do you speak English?"

"Of course, Miss. I'm from Wales, I am. I speak the King's language."

"These here are her papers." Jimmy said, as he handed the nurse the patient's admission papers which contained everything she needed to prepare the medical chart. Jimmy turned to leave, "See you later, Miss!"

"Thank you, Jimmy."

"You ain't seen the last of me, for sure. I'll be back with more patients for you."

The nurse looked down to examine her patient's bandaged feet. She wasn't aware of the slight frown of concern on her face.

Elsbeth Ferguson watched her carefully. "I don't know what all the fuss is about, Lady. Don't think my feet were as bad as all that. I was walking on them all right 'til the docs stopped me and started poking at them. Now, they say they won't allow me into the country until they're fixed...or maybe never at that...and my poor Callum. They put him in the clinker, they did."

Bending down to take a closer look at the woman's bandages, the nurse observed for swelling or redness in her patient's legs. She quickly read the admission details "...abrasions and burns noted with laceration on right toe requiring six sutures."

She chose the first bed on the window wall of the ward, anticipating that the light from the window would help when the time came to change her patient's bandages. She assisted the young woman into bed, and asked, "How did this happen, Miss Ferguson?"

"Lost my shoes, Lady, on the boat coming over."

"Oh, I'm sorry to hear that. How awful for you to lose your shoes on the ship. Did they go overboard?"

"No, nothing like that, Lady, my Callum took them...lost them in a gamble...gambled away all our money, too. Now, between these feet and my Callum, we're in for it. We are. They're talking about sending the likes of us back to Wales...not allowed to come to America with no money and no shoes."

"I'm Miss Angie. I'm sorry I didn't introduce myself sooner. I'll be your nurse today."

"I never thought I'd be getting this royal treatment. This here's a nice place, Miss Angie, everything being so clean. How long you think they'll let me stay before they'll be sending Callum and me back to Wales? Soon as I stepped foot in America, they did their inspection and chalked me up, but I do have to say that it was kind of them to give me a nice bath. I surely was a manky girl. Must admit that was good of them, don't you?"

"Yes, of course. Who is Callum?" Miss Angie asked.

"That would be my husband, Miss Angie, Callum Ferguson. We're married a year come October. He made good money in Wales, but was never any good at holding on to it. Always gambling it away and dreaming of coming to America where, he says, the streets are paved with gold. Callum brags he'll be rich in no time, no time at all, given all the opportunity in America. For two years, I worked at Miss Devenshire's sweet shop. I saved my money, I did. Hid it from Callum, and saved up enough for a wedding dowry chest. It paid for our passage tickets. I even had some left over to give the doctor as payment for our vaccines. Now, we are worse off than when we started...with no money and in a bit of trouble to boot."

"Is Callum being held at the Registry Room?"

"Yes, they put him in that prison of theirs. I saw him in the pen with the others."

"They are detaining him for a hearing. They will give him an opportunity to tell his story. You've been admitted to our hospital to prevent infection of your sutures."

"Don't know what all that means, Miss, as I told you, they'll be deporting me soon."

"They don't deport people for losing their shoes, Miss Ferguson, but you may have a problem if you have no money. There is a minimum amount of money required for a person to be granted admission into the United States."

"Why is that, Miss Angie?"

"To show that you are not a vagrant, and that you're earnest in coming to this country to begin a fruitful life so you won't be a burden to others. Twenty-five dollars is all they ask. That's plenty for room and board until work is found."

"Well, if it's money we need, Callum will find a way to get the dough. He will. I am sure of it."

"You're not saying that he would steal, are you?"

"No, Miss, my Callum never stole nothing from nobody. He's a good man, he is."

"Perhaps, you have a relative in this country who can post a bond for you."

"No, we don't know anyone here in America. I wish we did, though. That would be good."

"I could submit your name to the IAS this evening, Miss Ferguson."

"What's that, Miss? Sounds like trouble to me."

"The IAS is the Immigrant Aid Society. There are people here who assist immigrants at the hospital. They could help. I will, too. After work tonight, I'll look through the Donations Depository for a pair of shoes for you. Your shoe size looks about the same as mine. Are you a size five?"

"Size three, Miss."

"I believe that converts to the same size. The United States has a different sizing system. I'm certain I'll be able to find a pair of shoes for you. Now, I'd like to take your temperature. I want to…"

Miss Angie was interrupted by another knock on the door window. She turned to see Jimmy, once again.

"Excuse me a moment, Miss Ferguson. I'll be right back. There's another patient coming in."

"Sure, Miss Angie. I ain't going nowhere."

Miss Angie opened the door, and held it open as Jimmy wheeled in a patient on a gurney wagon.

"Mrs. Jana Mertens," he announced. "She's lookin' a bit unhappy."

Plump Mrs. Mertens lay on the gurney wagon crying her eyes out. Tears rolled down her chubby cheeks and bounced off her pillow. She wiped them with the handkerchief that she gripped in her hand. "Why is she crying, Jimmy?"

"Had an operation on the ship four days ago, Miss Angie. That's all I know."

Angie looked directly at her patient and asked. "Do you speak English, Mrs. Mertens? Are you in pain?"

"No. No. Ik speek Nederlands…mine babe boy…Jordy."

"Did she have a baby with her?"

"Don't know, Miss Angie. Where do you want her?" Jimmy asked.

Miss Angie pointed to the bed beside Mrs. Ferguson. Jimmy helped her transfer the patient from the gurney to the bed while Mrs. Mertens continued to cry.

"Oh, she is so upset. When you return to the Registry, Jimmy, request an interpreter to come to South Wing."

"Will do, and just so's you know, there's still more patients coming. This situation seems all balled up to me, Miss Angie, with the Commissioner announcing *less* immigrants coming after July. Why are so many patients coming through?"

"This sudden increase in patient census is baffling everyone. I promise to ask Sister Gwendolyn about it. Maybe, she can solve the mystery."

"Well, if the big boss lady can't figure it out, Miss Angie, I'm not sure anyone can."

8

Chapter Two

❧

August 4, 1924
1 PM (13:00)

Somewhere along your journey, you know you'll never part.
For when you love each other, love lives within your heart.

Nurse Angie Bosco took vital signs on her patients, and recorded their TPRs: temperature, pulse and respirations. She started a new TPR flow chart for Ward 240 South. Next, she searched the admission papers of Mrs. Jana Mertens for information that would help her care for her post-op patient. The ship's doctor had submitted detailed notes of an emergency appendectomy performed at sea four days earlier. The nurse found the physician's order for pain medication to be given Q4H, *every four hours.* There was a notation in the chart that Mrs. Mertens had been given her last dose at 08:00. She was overdue to receive her pain medication.

"I know about Mrs. Mertens," Elsbeth began. "She was with her little boy on the boat until she got sick with bad stomach pains. Then, I see the ladies on the boat caring for the little tyke, passing him off to each other, and taking turns feeding him. Seems he got a case of the cooties from their kids. The guards took him to the cootie room when we got off the ship."

"That would explain things a bit," said Miss Angie, giving Mrs. Mertens a reassuring pat on her shoulder before she left to prepare an injection of pain medication.

In the cramped space of the small utility room, Angie unpacked a sterile kidney basin. She removed a glass syringe and plunger from the syringe drum. Using sterile forceps, she selected the appropriate size needle for the syringe. She placed these in the basin. Next, she unlocked the medication cabinet and signed for the withdrawal of one morphine tablet. She lit a Bunsen burner, and melted the morphine tablet in one-fourth of a teaspoon of sterile water. She carefully prepared the syringe, and drew up the medication into it. She carried it to her patient in the sterile basin.

When she returned to the ward, Jimmy was waiting for her with another patient. "This is Miss Dunne, Miss Angie," Jimmy said, giving her the admission papers. "She broke her arm."

"Thank-you, Jimmy."

As Jimmy turned to leave the ward, he said, "Looks like you might be needin' more help soon, Miss Angie, 'cause there's still more patients coming along."

Help came in the form of Sister Gwendolyn Hanover, Superintendent of Nursing. While Miss Angie admitted twelve more patients throughout the afternoon, Sister Gwendolyn rolled up her shirtsleeves and went to work. After passing late lunch trays and assisting patients with their meals, Sister distributed bedpans and took another round of TPRs.

Miss Angie assembled the patient charts, reviewed the physician's orders, and prepared color-coded treatment and medication cards. While Miss Angie distributed medications, Sister Gwendolyn organized the treatment cards and began dressing changes. The two worked fast and efficiently in this manner until supper trays arrived.

While Miss Angie was completing her charting, Sister Gwendolyn interrupted. "It's getting late. I must go now to prepare my Supervisor's Report. Don't forget to order your supper before you leave the hospital. You've had a busy day, Miss Angie. It's time to eat and rest."

Soon after, Miss Ruth, the night nurse, and Betsie, her nurse's aide, arrived on the ward, ready to receive the evening report and begin the night shift. After reporting the day's events, Angie tidied up her desk and left. She hadn't eaten since breakfast. It was 8 pm, and she suddenly felt hungry.

Her first stop was the Hospital Lobby where she filled out an FRF, a *Food Requisition Form*, to request a late supper that would be delivered to the Nurses' Residence Cottage. Her next stop was the Central Administration Office where she completed an IAS form to request financial assistance for Mrs. Ferguson. She tucked the form into their mail slot in the door.

Returning to the Lobby, Angie used her house keys to open the door of the Volunteers' Donation Depository. A strong stench of camphor and carbolic blasted her as she entered the tiny space. Filled, from top to bottom, with boxes of winter clothes, the room housed wool dresses, jackets, coats, hand-made woolen scarves, hats, and mittens. Angie noted that everything a person did not need during the warm month of August was there, packed and ready for distribution in the fall. Miss Angie searched through the open bags and boxes for a pair of women's size five shoes. The air became stifling hot. Beads of sweat formed at the back of her neck and wet her hair. Angie felt herself getting overheated and in need of fresh air, forcing her to abandon her mission before it was completed.

Quickly locking the door, she rushed outside to rest on the steps of the hospital building. She breathed in deeply, thankful for the cool evening breeze blowing from the harbor. As she sat, an idea popped into her head. She stood up, hurried back through the Hospital Lobby, and turned toward the Children's Ward on the North Wing. There, she found Miss Rose. Angie shared her plan with her. Miss Rose agreed with Angie, and gave her the go-ahead to return.

Angie returned to Ward 240 South.

"Back so soon? Did you forget something, Angie?" Miss Ruth asked.

"Ruthie, I've come back to walk Mrs. Mertens. She has a physician's order to ambulate to prevent pneumonia. You might be too busy to find time this evening."

"That's thoughtful of you, Angie, and your timing is perfect. I gave Mrs. Mertens her 20:00 meds a short time ago. They should be kicking in about now."

When the nurses approached Mrs. Mertens in her hospital bed, she looked up at them with misty eyes. They helped her out of bed. Miss Angie held her elbow and walked slowly with her. At the end of the hall, Angie opened the door and walked through a short passageway. She knew that Mrs. Mertens didn't understand English, but that didn't stop Angie from talking. "You see, Mrs. Mertens, you need to walk to get well. The more you walk, the better you will feel. In fact, I have a notion that you will feel even better if we walk a little further. Let's go down this hallway to see what we find."

The nurse walked with her patient through the North Wing until they came to the Children's Ward. The women stopped to look in the ward window. Miss Rose was inside, and waved to them. She pointed to the first crib. No further explanation was needed for Mrs. Mertens immediately spotted her chunky little toddler sleeping peacefully in his crib. Reassured that her baby was clean and well-cared for, Mrs. Mertens stopped sobbing. She smiled for the first time that day. Angie couldn't help but smile, too.

When they returned to Ward 240, Miss Angie took Mrs. Merten's pulse rate, charted the result, and tucked her into bed. As Angie was leaving, Miss Ruth called out, "Good night, Angie. Thank you for your help. Now, promise me that you will go straight to the Cottage and eat your supper."

"I'm on my way, Ruthie. Good Night! Hope you have a quiet night."

Chapter Three

August 4, 1924
9:30 PM (21:30)

*One thing that can't be bought or sold
Is the treasure of a heart of gold.*

Angie always enjoyed the short walk along the covered pathway from the Hospital to the Nurses' Residence Cottage, especially on a summer evening. It gave her an opportunity to be outdoors, if only for a few precious minutes. Angie entered the Cottage through the kitchen to retrieve her dinner tray from the hospital food cart. Sister Gwendolyn called to her from the Dining Room.

"We have your dinner here, Miss Angie. Come and join us."

Angie entered the Cottage Dining Room. The window shutters were wide open, revealing a breathtaking view of the harbor. Shimmering lights from Bedloe Island shined on *Lady Liberty*, casting silver sparkles on the water surrounding the landmark statue. Sister Gwendolyn, the Nursing Superintendent, and Miss Elsie Archer, Assistant Superintendent, were seated at a round table, enjoying the view and eating supper. When Angie sat down, Sister asked, "Where have you been, Miss Angie? I thought you would have arrived at the Cottage before us."

"I stopped at the Donations Depository to look for size five shoes for Mrs. Ferguson, but my search was unsuccessful. All I uncovered was a pair of baby shoes. If we were in need of them, they would never have surfaced."

Sister Gwendolyn looked at Miss Elsie, and then, Angie. "Is that *all* you've been doing tonight?" She asked.

"No, ummm…"

Sister laughed. "Don't worry, dear. We don't have a policy prohibiting you from taking a patient from the South Wing to the North Wing of the hospital."

"How did you know?"

Sister winked. "We have our ways."

Angie looked down. "Of course, Sister."

"Miss Angie, have you heard from Miss Adeline in California?"

"Yes, Sister, I write to her every week."

"How is her recovery from tuberculosis coming along?"

"She's getting stronger every day. Her husband, Harry, made a good decision to take her to California to recuperate. They're planning on returning to New York in the spring."

"I pray for her speedy recovery every night." Miss Elsie said.

Sister agreed. "Yes, I do, also. I pray for her, as well as, all nurses who become ill in the process of caring for their patients." Sister turned to Miss Angie. "I want to talk to you about next week. Miss Elsie and I were discussing the schedule this evening. Helene Waters offered to cover for you. You can take off the day that you requested."

"No, Sister, I couldn't. There are too many patients, and not enough nurses to cover the busy schedule." Angie looked thoughtful for a moment. "Sister, I don't understand why we are experiencing this sudden increase in patient census. Do you have any information to explain it?"

"That's the question everyone is asking. I'm meeting with the Commissioner on Thursday. I am hoping that he will have some answers for me. I want to get to the bottom of this dilemma."

"Me, too, it's a mystery." Miss Elsie added.

"Miss Angie, do you still have your meeting with Dr. Martin scheduled for August twelfth?"

"Yes, I've been much too busy to call him to reschedule."

"Excellent. Then, it's settled. You will visit Dr. Martin, as planned. Miss Elsie and I will pitch in on the wards again, if need be. We know how much you look forward to your annual visit to the Infant Incubator Exhibit. We're eager to hear all about what you learn, especially if they're incorporating new treatments into their nursing care. You must write up a short report for us when you return."

"Yes, of course, I will. Oh, thank you. I didn't expect..."

"Now, now, Miss Angie, enjoy a well-deserved day off. Like all good nurses, you work yourself too hard."

"I could do better, Sister."

"Yes, dear, all good nurses strive for their best. What do you think makes a good nurse?"

Angie did not hesitate to answer, "...her education and experience, Sister."

Miss Elsie was thoughtful for a moment. "That's true," she said, "but there is one thing more."

"What would that be, Miss Elsie?"

"She needs a caring heart," Miss Elsie answered. "If she cares, she'll see to it that no harm comes to her patients. She'll remember the little things that make her patients feel safe and secure. She'll find a way to get all the information she needs to properly care for her patients."

Sister Gwendolyn smiled. "Beautifully said, Miss Elsie." After taking a sip of her tea, she turned to Angie. "Miss Angie, about next week's outing, remember to honor our twenty-three-hundred curfew. Please plan on taking the twenty-two-thirty ferry that evening, no later, dear."

"Yes, Sister, I will," Angie promised. "I think I shall try to wake up early tomorrow morning to continue searching for shoes for Mrs. Ferguson. She will need something to wear on her feet when she goes before the Board of Special Inquiry for her hearing."

"I believe you are working the night shift tomorrow, Miss Angie. It would behoove you to rest in the morning."

Miss Elsie offered a solution. "Let me help you with your search. I'm going to the Registry bright and early tomorrow morning. I'll ask the volunteer women to check their storerooms for shoes."

"Thank you, Miss Elsie."

"Very good! That's settled. Ladies, may I suggest we finish up our supper, and get a good sleep tonight. We all have a busy day ahead of us tomorrow."

Chapter Four

❧

August 5, 1924
9 PM (21:00)

*The angels work swift and fast
To dress a wound and set a cast.*

To *float a nurse* means assigning her to a medical ward where she's most needed in the hospital. For the patient, it conjures up a picture of the professional nurse confidently floating, like a honey bee, from one hospital unit to another. Assigning a trained nurse from a well-staffed unit to an inadequately-staffed one is a sound solution to a staffing challenge.

Although every unit appears to be identical, each unit has its own characteristic flow and culture. A nurse is trained in all areas of nursing but, when she's floated to an unfamiliar ward, she must be hypervigilant, extra resourceful, and humble enough to ask questions from the aides and matrons who work there regularly.

When Miss Angie reported to work, she was floated. Angie found herself in charge of the entire North Wing: the Male Medicine and Surgery Units on the third floor, the Female Units on the second floor, and the remaining Children's Quarters on the first and second floor. The children on the first floor were all healthy and active. They had been admitted to the hospital because their parents were patients. Having nowhere to go, and no one to care for them, they lived in the hospital until their parents were well enough to be discharged.

18

The day shift nurses always included the most important aspects of the day's activities in their evening report. However, because they were so familiar with the routine of their units, they often forgot to report on the minor details.

No one told Miss Angie that she was to keep a watchful eye on the four boys who were bedded closest to the windows because, on calm, quiet evenings, they would climb out of the first floor windows to explore the docks after supper.

Miss Angie hadn't realized that the boys were missing until Miss Elizabeth, the Night House Supervisor, marched them back into the ward. They were soaked to the bone. Miss Elizabeth scolded Miss Angie. Not only had the boys escaped, they had jumped into the water. "I'm taking young Mr. Iskvan directly to X-ray. He bruised his arm when he fell off the dock. Ring up the House Officer, Miss Angie, if you would. Ask him to meet me in X-ray. Don't hesitate to send for Miss Sarah to help you shower the others."

Later that evening, Dr. Nelson was called to cast Moric Iskvan's broken arm. It took quite some time to obtain parental consent from Moric's father, a patient on the third floor who only spoke Hungarian. After searching, Miss Angie located a matron on night duty who spoke Hungarian. Miss Angie asked her to act as a translator in order to obtain the necessary consent from Moric's father.

Next, Miss Angie carefully assembled a dressing table with plaster, water, gauze, and scissors in preparation for Dr. Nelson. When he arrived, she was forced to humbly admit that she hadn't assisted in a casting since nursing school. She asked if he would inspect the table before starting to ensure that everything he needed was on the table. Dr. Nelson was kind enough to talk her through the procedure. Both the patient and nurse survived the ordeal.

No one told Miss Angie that, when she turned down the lamps and tucked in the Voros girls, the three sisters could not sleep apart from each other. Although each little girl was assigned to her own bed, the nurses had long ago given up attempting to separate them. The girls, named Rebeka, Rachel and Renata, ranged in age from five to nine. They were in the hospital because both parents had a fever when they disembarked their ship. Each time Angie came around during her routine child-checks, she found the little girls huddled together in one bed. She carried them off to their assigned beds only to find them cuddled together again upon her return. She had separated the sisters four times that evening when she finally decided to abandon the effort. Miss Angie was certain that Miss Elizabeth would take note of this during her rounds at twenty-two-hundred hours. She braced herself for the second reprimand of the evening.

During her rounds, Angie stopped to review her charting. She was grateful that the hectic activity on the wards had slowed so that she could evaluate her care plans. As she sat down, she heard her name called.

"Miss Angie, is that you?"

"Yes, Miss Flanagan." Angie walked over to the young woman's bedside. Merta Flanagan had been admitted to the hospital for severe seasickness. Her nausea and vomiting persisted, continuing for days after she disembarked the ship. "You are certainly looking quite a bit stronger, and have good color in your cheeks this evening, Miss Flanagan."

"My parents are coming to pick me up tonight. I can hardly wait to finally see America."

"Yes, I heard. I'm glad you feel better. I've prepared your chart for discharge, but I'm worried that it's getting late. Perhaps, your parents have been detained."

"Miss Angie, can I ask you a question? My…um…friend is in a family way. She arrived in New York with her mother and father last month. She was wondering what she should do about it."

"Has she seen a doctor?"

"No."

"Does she know for sure that she is pregnant?"

"Well, she thinks she is. She hasn't had her monthly visitor. You see, Miss Angie, she isn't married. She has a boyfriend in America who she needs to find. When she locates him, she is certain they will wed."

"Where does she live?"

"Brooklyn."

"Do her parents know she is pregnant?"

"No, they don't know, no one knows…only I know. You see she isn't showing or anything. I told her that she has to see a doctor to check the baby. She's afraid to go to the hospital because I heard that she could be deported. I mean, *she* heard, she could be deported."

"There are a number of free clinics throughout the city. I know of one in Brooklyn, too. She should go there to confirm the pregnancy."

"Yes, Miss Angie, that's what I'll tell her. How will I find them?"

"In the city, the nurses at the Henry Street Settlement House will help. In Brooklyn, she could go to the Sanger Clinic."

The conversation was abruptly interrupted by the night messenger who announced that the parents of Miss Flanagan had arrived, and were waiting in the Discharge Room off the Main Lobby.   Angie readied her patient.

As the night messenger escorted the young woman toward the elevator, Angie waved. "Good Luck to you, Miss Flanagan." She sighed and whispered, "Take care. I do hope everything works out well for you."

It was time for Miss Angie to review and organize her treatment cards. There were HS, *at the hour of sleep*, heat applications and a number of dressing changes. The pre-ops would need enemas and shaves at sunrise. She was relieved to find that there were no orders for urine catheters on the men's wards. Having worked primarily with women for many years, she could catheterize a woman in a matter of minutes, but the same procedure on a man presented a bit of a challenge.

When Angie finished her treatment plans, the laboratory reports arrived. She attached each report to the appropriate patient chart. When she reached Miss Flanagan's reports, she noticed her doctor had ordered a pregnancy test. The result was positive, just as she suspected. If the lab results had been delivered earlier in the day, the young woman would not have been approved for discharge. She would have been detained, and possibly deported, because she was not married.

Angie had two options. She could walk down to personally deliver the report to the Discharge Office, or return it to the lab. Angie chose the latter. She stamped the paper, PATIENT DISCHARGED, and returned the report to the laboratory, knowing that the lab slip would eventually find its way to the Discharge Office.

Perhaps, by then, Miss Flanagan would have located her baby's father.

The remainder of the night shift seemed hopelessly long, but finally, the clock struck seven. Miss Marion arrived for early morning report.

When Angie walked back to the cottage, she noticed the sun had already risen. It was struggling to shine through the dense morning fog. The coolness of the morning and the misty fog refreshed her. Although she was eager to hop right into bed, she decided on breakfast first.

When Angie finally reached her room on the third floor of the Nurses' Residence Cottage, she was tired and sleepy. A note was taped to her bedroom door.

Dear Miss Angie,

I am sorry to report that I had no success with my assigned mission of hunting for shoes for Miss Ferguson today, but, rest assured, I will continue my search tomorrow.

Yours truly,

Miss Elsie

Angie put the note on her nightstand and frowned. She sat on the edge of her bed, took off her shoes, and rubbed her feet. Angie quickly undressed, gathered her bathing supplies, and dragged herself down to the nurses' bathing room. The cool shower revived her as the water washed away the weariness of the night. She dried off quickly. Before reaching her room, she passed Adeline's room, now vacant. She remembered that before Adeline left for Palm Springs, she had given Angie a present of a gift-certificate for two pairs of new shoes. With a burst of newfound energy, Angie sat at her desk and wrote a letter to her friend.

Chapter Five

❧

August 6, 1924
9 AM (09:00)

Separation brings a sorrow and with sorrow comes the pain,
Until slowly we discover, our best memories remain.

WEDNESDAY, AUGUST 6, 1924
ELLIS ISLAND HOSPITAL,
PORT OF NEW YORK,
NEW YORK CITY

MRS. ADELINE FERMÉ STEINGOLD
TWO SUNSET LANE
PALM SPRINGS, CALIFORNIA

My Dear Adeline,

How are you? As you open this letter, I hope my love pops out and encircles you as you continue on your path of recovery. I received your letter yesterday, and was overjoyed to hear that you are feeling stronger and taking walks with Harry every evening. I imagine it is terribly hot in California this time of year. I am certain the dry summer air is exactly what you need for your lungs to heal. Isn't it just like you to talk about taking riding lessons with Harry? In my mind's eye, I can already see the two of you riding off into the sunset. Now, you will be careful, won't you? Promise me you will not get up on a horse until you're feeling sufficiently well and stronger than a horse!

Adeline, I hope and pray for your complete recovery every day. For quite selfish reasons, I can't wait until you are back in New York. I miss you terribly, but I am comforted by the thought that you are happily healing with your husband, Harry. You've been gone almost three months. Although it feels like three years, I strive to remain positive until you return in the spring.

This morning, I walked up the stairs to the third floor of the Cottage and went directly to your old room. I lifted my hand to knock like I did so many times during the four short years we were Cottage neighbors. My heart ached when I remembered your room was empty. Oh, how I miss our bedtime talks. I wanted to tell you all about work last night, and the trouble I managed to get myself into.

I have news for you. Dr. Goodwin has received the official go-ahead to open a neighborhood clinic in Brooklyn. He offered me the position of Nursing Director. I start my new job in January. There's a great deal of work to do in the coming months. The number one priority is to select the correct location. Dr. Goodwin and Father Benedetto, the parish pastor, feel the clinic should be in Williamsburg, near Nativity Church. We remain mindful that the immigrants are apprehensive of established health facilities. Therefore, a church affiliation is an asset.

My meeting with Miss Lillian Wald is scheduled for next month at Henry Street. Thank you for writing a letter of introduction for me. In her return letter, she spoke very highly of you. She remembered you worked as one of her visiting nurses from the Settlement House. You never told me they had a nickname for you. She instructed me to send "Energy Addie" her well-wishes.

Henry Street Settlement House has become a valuable community resource. I hope to learn from Miss Wald's experiences working with the immigrant population. I remember the stories you told me about your visiting nurse days. You often spoke of how frightened the immigrants became when they were taken ill. They avoid formal hospital and clinic settings for fear that they will be deported, or their children will be taken from them. That is why the visiting nurses go directly to their homes to care for them.

Dr. Goodwin and I often meet for an evening stroll to discuss plans for the clinic. He asked me to call him by his first name. After so many years of calling him "Dr. Goodwin", I find it difficult to call him "Abe". I invited him to accompany me to the Infant Incubator Exhibit at Coney Island's Luna Park. Guess what? He is coming with me. Adeline, I know you would call it a date.

What shall I wear to Luna Park next week? I desperately need your fashion advice. I have all sorts of questions for you, like...how does one quiet her knees when they start knocking on her first date?

Every time I visit Coney Island, I remember the Loop-the-Loop ride we went on together. I was frozen with fear when I saw it. You told me that was the very reason why I had to get on that ride. "Crash through your fear, Angie Girl," you told me. Your words still ring in my heart. So, that is exactly what I will do. No matter how jittery I feel about this first date with Abe, I will crash through my fear and show up.

Once we are on our way, I know I will be fine. Abe always makes me feel comfortable, and he is easy to talk to. Throughout the four years that we worked together, I knew our professional philosophies were in alignment. Now, as I learn more about him, I find him to be a truly kind, generous, and loving man. He is very polite and quite the gentleman, always holding the door open for me, and walking on the outside of the walkway to protect me from the sea spray. He is a wonderful and sympathetic listener. I confided in him that I was married for only six months before I was widowed prior to attending nursing school. Perhaps, tomorrow's outing will give us time for more sharing.

Good night, dear friend. May the Lord continue to keep you and Harry safe and sound. I am off to bed now, and sending happy healing thoughts to you in this letter.

Sweet dreams always,

Love and Kisses,

Angie

X X X

P.S. In your last letter, you asked me if I ordered my new shoes at Bartoli's Shoe Store with the gift certificate you gave me in May. I haven't found the time to go uptown, as yet, but this morning I had an idea. Two days ago, an immigrant woman came into the processing center wearing no shoes. Miss Elsie and I searched through the donation depositories. We can't find shoes for her. I've decided to give her my old shoes. I am certain this will ensure that I go to Bartoli's Shoe Store on my next day off to order new shoes.

Angie finished her letter, and slipped into bed. After her hectic night at the hospital, she floated right off to sleep. Visions of her childhood days in Sicily drifted into her dreams.

∾

Chapter Six

Castelvetrano, Sicily

August 26, 1908

Your legs begin to buckle, and you're weak in the knees.
Your tummy flops and flutters. You've caught the jitteries!

"Angelina, Angelina, come sit down. You are working too hard, Child." The Signorina shook her head and sighed.

Signorina Sirina Selinunte lived in the house that belonged to her mother and her mother's mother before her. When her mother died, Sirina inherited both the house and her reputation as a village healer at the modest age of twenty-two. When Angelina's Zia Dona heard that Sirina was in need of hired help, she rushed over to Sirina's house and paraded her niece before her. Dona encouraged Sirina to hire the young girl as her maid. However, Angelina possessed a keen interest and a natural ability toward the healing arts, and quickly became Sirina's assistant.

"Signorina, there's no time. There's still so much to do today. We must pit all these olives before brining. We collected seven baskets yesterday."

Angelina cracked open each olive with a hammer to expose the pit. She felt a bit jittery. Hitting the green targets, over and over, made her feel a little less nervous.

"I will help you after lunch. Angelina, now it is time for a rest break. I must read your tea leaves in preparation for your journey."

"I don't have the time today. After I pit the olives, I must prepare the brine."

"Come, sit with me, Angelina. I will make the brine this evening."

"You must soak the olives until their bitterness dissolves."

"Yes. After brining, I will store them. I'll add celery and onions at the very end. I learned this recipe from my mother and her mother before her. Come. Precious time is passing."

"What if the leaves speak of danger? I am frightened, Signorina. My stomach is in flutters."

"Come, Child, I have some peppermint tea for you. It will soothe your jitters. I've prepared a pouch of peppermint to take with you on your voyage. It will ease the ocean sickness you may experience."

"How will I be able to make tea when I am on the steamship going to America, Signorina?"

"Break the mint leaves with your hands, and mix them with water in your drinking cup. Muddle them with your spoon until their oils release. Then, add more water. When you feel queasy, sip the mint-water slowly. In minutes, you will feel relief. Ah, here...our tea is ready. Sit, Child. Drink your tea. If we are fortunate, mysteries may be revealed to us today in the leaves that remain in your cup."

Angelina did as she was told. After Angelina finished drinking her tea, Sirina studied the tea leaves remaining in the teacup. "Oh, my," she said, dramatically.

"Yes?"

"I see...".

"What do you see, Signorina?"

"I see a new life ahead of you across the ocean."

"Will I be happy?"

"Let me look…" Sirina lowered her voice, as she carefully examined the tea leaves once again. "Yes…I believe so," she answered.

Then, Sirina whispered. "You will meet many new people on your journey. Some you can trust, but others you must walk away from."

"How will I know the difference in the two?"

"You will find the answer deep in the pit of your stomach. Your body will tell you everything you need to know. Next week's adventure frightens you today. Your flutters come with a message. They tell you to move forward, to not be afraid, and to walk through your fear. However, there is another kind that will warn you of danger."

"How will I know which is which?"

"Danger warnings slowly begin to envelop you. Soon, you will recognize the difference in the two. With one, you must walk away quickly. With the other, you must proceed with a leap of faith."

"But, Signorina, how will I be able to do this when I'm in America? I won't have you to guide me."

"You will remember my words, Child. You won't forget them. I will always be with you."

August 7, 1924
9 PM (21:00)

Our instincts come in crisp and clear,
But we ignore them, gripped with fear.

Journal of Sister Gwendolyn Hanover

Superintendent of Nursing

Date: Tuesday, August 7, 1924

Entry Time: 21:00

Journal Notation:

We were blessed with another glorious day on Ellis Island. I couldn't have imagined a day lovelier than yesterday, but today was equally beautiful. After working indoors all week, I forced myself to go outside. I walked to the Contagious Disease Hospital to offer lunch relief to the nurses. If I didn't offer my assistance, the nurses would have missed lunch. Many of them did not take a lunch break yesterday. They've been extremely busy on the wards. To make matters worse, I know my *ladies-in-white* often skip breakfast, no matter how many times I remind them that a substantial breakfast is the proper preparation for a busy day.

The short walk lifted my spirits. A cool sweet breeze was blowing. At high tide, the water was absolutely luminous. There wasn't a trace of ocean in the air, which is quite uncommon for this time of year. August usually blankets us in a stale, heavy haze. When there is a hint of a breeze, it carries the stench of fish and factory oil from the city.

A wayward seagull suddenly swept past me in search of his buddies, who were already flying in formation, high in the brilliant blue sky. It reminded me of an article I read in the newspaper last week. Two young men took a flying machine into the air, and traveled across the ocean. In my wildest dreams, I never would have imagined such a feat. These manmade machines are heavier than air, yet they find a way to soar. A wealthy investor offered an enormous cash prize to anyone who could successfully fly nonstop from New York to Paris. If I were a young man, I might be tempted to take up the challenge. Imagine taking flight on a glorious day like today.

I'd fly across the city skyline, following the East River. At the tip of Manhattan, I'd see this tiny island shaped like the letter "E". For a moment, I'd wonder if the island was purposefully molded to create the first initial of its name, *Ellis Island*. Next, *Lady Liberty* would come into view. From the air, all would appear peaceful and quiet. Seconds later, I'd salute farewell to her as I flew into the wild blue, across the Atlantic, with nary a hint of the hustle and bustle of activity down below at Ellis Island Hospital.

Now, now, enough daydreaming, Gwendolyn, continue...

This week has been a hectic one at the hospital due to the South Wing closure three weeks ago in response to the Commissioner's July directive. At the time, I should have followed my instincts. If I had, I would not be in the predicament I am today. I had a hunch. Something told me, "Gwendolyn, not yet, wait. Don't implement the changes. Wait!".

Did I follow my instincts? No!

One would imagine that, after all my years in nursing, I would have learned not to ignore my intuition. In that respect, I blame myself, not the Commissioner, for I, too, am responsible.

The new Immigration Law was implemented one month ago. It called for severe immigration restrictions. The Commissioner estimated that, by the end of the summer, immigration numbers would fall dramatically. He further projected that the number of immigrants coming through Ellis Island could be cut in half by the end of the year. Consequently, the *old boys* had a *club meeting*, without yours truly, I might add. At that meeting, it was decided that hospital ward closures would commence immediately. Following this directive, I closed the South Wing of the General Hospital. I consolidated the four Women's units into two, and moved them to the North Wing.

Now, we are frantically reopening wards on the South Wing due to an increase in the hospital census. Instead of enjoying time off during the summer months, my *ladies-in-white* are working overtime with no extra pay.

This afternoon, I had an opportunity to meet with the Commissioner in his office. On the top of my agenda was the subject of the hospital census. I asked, "Commissioner, instead of the projected ten-percent decrease, we are experiencing a ten-percent increase in patient volume. What are your thoughts on this subject?"

The Commissioner could not give me an explanation. He stood behind his projections. According to his calculations, the hospital census should have gradually decreased as the number of immigrations declined.

Making A Difference In Brooklyn

The Commissioner's office is on the third floor of the Registry Building. After our meeting, I conducted my own investigation. I took a moment to observe the activity in the Great Hall from the high vantage point of the mezzanine on the third floor. Huge, half-moon windows on both the second and third floors flooded the large room in a pearly-white light. As I surveyed the Great Hall below me, I observed newly arrived immigrants working their way up the Grand Staircase for their initial medical inspection, the first step in the immigration process. There, doctors of the U.S. Public Health Service observed for signs of illness, walking difficulties, and the overall general appearance of the immigrants. In the past, the physician had a mere six seconds to make his assessment before he placed a chalk mark on a weary traveler, the signal for further examination.

As I looked down upon the Great Hall this afternoon, something felt amiss. Indeed, all the examinations and interviews appeared to be progressing efficiently and orderly. However, the room was strangely quiet, quieter than it had ever been before. As I studied the activity in the Great Hall, it took me only a matter of minutes to solve the mystery. Fewer immigrants meant that the doctors had more time to make their diagnostic assessments. Indeed, the answer was quite simple. The doctors were working slower and more carefully.

I took out my pocket watch to time them. They now had sixty seconds to do their traditional six-second exam. They were identifying more people to be detained. One didn't have to be Thomas Edison to figure that out.

I continued on my way. I did not return to the Commissioner's office to report my revelation.

Signed:

Sister Gwendolyn Hanover

Superintendent of Nursing, I

Ellis Island Hospital, Ellis Island

Chapter Eight

〜

August 12, 1924
8 AM (8:00)

How many times have I kissed you in my dreams,
and wished I was there beside you?
I longed, with passion overdue, that this vision would come true.

After breakfast, Dr. Abraham Goodwin returned to his room to make certain he looked presentable. He gave himself a final inspection in the tiny mirror that hung above his wash sink. At six-foot-two, he was considered a tall man who towered above his peers. Unlike his contemporaries who wore handlebar moustaches, waxed and curled at the edges, he preferred to be clean-shaven. This, along with his wavy dark hair and inviting smile, gave him a certain boyish quality. He had a handsome oval face, a high forehead, and eyes as brown as chocolate drops.

He suddenly decided that the red bowtie he was wearing suggested a certain devil-may-care attitude which he did not want to convey that day. That left him with two alternative choices: his pink polka-dot tie or a green-striped one. He settled on the green one with subdued olive and navy-blue stripes. It blended in well with his blue seersucker jacket.

He took a deep breath to calm himself, and then another. Abe Goodwin wished he could meet Nurse Angie Bosco at the ferry building with a dozen red roses in his arms to mark the occasion as their official first date. However, there were no florists to be found on Ellis Island.

Red roses, he thought, *might not be appropriate for a morning rendezvous. Perhaps, I would choose yellow roses to represent our friendship or a bouquet of miniature white roses to symbolize my purest of intentions.*

He had looked forward to this day for weeks for he always enjoyed spending time with Angie. He locked his door and stepped out onto the front porch of the doctors' quarters, a simple one-story bungalow that he shared with five other physicians who worked on the island. When he reached the bottom step, he realized that he had forgotten his hat. He returned to his room to retrieve the straw boater hat which he had placed by the door. In his haste to leave, he had gone right past it. With hat in hand, he eagerly departed for his rendezvous at the ferry dock.

Angie Bosco woke up with a strange feeling in the pit of her stomach. After washing, she spent quite a bit of time deciding what she should wear. She selected a beige cotton blouse and a brown skirt which perfectly matched her light brown hair. The mirror on top of her bureau dresser was so small that she had to jump up to examine the full effect of her outfit. Her bobbed haircut looked neat and stylish, but, after working indoors all summer, she looked far too pale. She wondered if she should put on more rouge. Even her outfit looked drab and in need of some color.

She surveyed the room. A scarf would be needed later in the evening for the cool breeze that blew on the boardwalk. She snatched up the paisley apricot scarf that was neatly draped over her chair. When she tied the ·colorful scarf around her waist, it completed her outfit. Angie locked her door, and walked down the stairs to eat breakfast in the nurses' dining room.

How can I possibly eat with my stomach in knots? I know, for certain, these flutters are the kind that are nudging me forward, telling me not to be afraid.

When she reached the foyer, she remembered she had forgotten her straw hat. She returned to her room to retrieve it.

When Angie met Abe at the ferry dock, greeting him with her big dimpled smile, Abe felt his spirits soar. The short ferry ride left them at Battery Park, the ferry stop on the New York side of the river. From across the park, they heard the clatter of the uptown streetcar approaching. They hurried to catch it. The streetcar took them to the Brooklyn Bridge stop of the BMT, *the Brooklyn-Manhattan train line*. Once on the train to Flatbush, they relaxed and settled in for the ride. Abe began to tell Angie about his family.

He was born in Brooklyn, the fourth child of an Italian-Catholic mother and Austrian-Jewish father. His parents immigrated to America when their first child was born. They came, not only for the many opportunities America offered, but they hoped for a fresh start away from the old-country attitudes toward mixed-marriages. Abe had three older sisters and a younger brother, Samuel. Once in America, all went well for the Goodwin family for many years. The family grew and prospered. His father worked as a pattern-maker. They moved from the congested Lower East Side of New York to Williamsburg, Brooklyn where the air was clean, and the sidewalks were swept daily. The Goodwins lived in an eight-family, four-story, walkup until tragedy struck. His father severed his arm in a factory accident. From then on, the family struggled. The factory owners offered his mother work as a garment worker. She often took piecework home for her children to earn extra money in the evenings. While each sister was assigned a section of a jacket, Abe was the button sewer, and a good one at that. In fact, no one could sew a button better than Abe. When money was scare, his father insisted that the money go toward buying food for the family. He felt it was wasteful to burn coal during the winter when he was home alone. He stayed in the cold during the day, and only warmed the apartment when the children came home from school. That winter, he developed pneumonia.

The train conductor called: "FLATBUSH STATION! FLATBUSH! CHANGE HERE FOR THE BRIGHTON BEACH LINE!"

Abe quickly grabbed Angie's hand. They both jumped up and out of the train. "That's the first time I almost missed a train stop in Brooklyn, Miss Angie…Angie, I mean. I was talking. I wasn't paying attention."

"I didn't notice the train station stops, either," Angie said.

When the Brighton Beach train arrived at the station, Abe and Angie sat together on a cozy wicker seat. The train quickly filled with people eager to go to the beach at Coney Island. When every seat was taken, the remaining passengers held on to the leather straps that swung from the ceiling as the train chugged along the track.

"Please, go on. Tell me more, Abe."

"Father died from pneumonia when I was fifteen. Mama didn't have money for his funeral expenses. She had no family in America to borrow from. Mama went door-to-door to almost every funeral director in Brooklyn until she found one on Central Avenue who agreed to do the funeral on credit. Mama was to pay him one dollar each week for two years. Every payday Saturday after work, she took the trolley to pay off her debt before she came home. Walter, the undertaker, had collected one year's worth of debt. He had another year to go, when he asked Mama for her hand in marriage."

"Your mother married the undertaker?"

"Yes, Walter is my stepfather. He was a bachelor, and found himself looking forward to Mama's Saturday afternoon visits. He often says he fell in love with her from the start. I remember waiting at home for Mama. One evening, I asked her why she didn't send the payments through the mail. She smiled, and said she wanted to save the cost of a stamp. That didn't make sense to me because the trolley ride cost more than the stamp.

"When they did marry, two of my older sisters were already married. There were three siblings living at home with Mama: my younger brother, Samuel, my sister, Gisella, and me. Walter insisted on paying Gisella's college expenses. She had always been an excellent student, and was excited for the opportunity to attend the city university.

"Walter moved us to Central Avenue to be closer to his work. He took Sam and me under his wing. Having high hopes for us to follow his career footsteps, he encouraged us to work with him. He paid us handsomely to be pallbearers at funerals because Sam and I were tall for our age. In addition, we received generous tips which Sam and I used to start a savings account. Looking back, I was sad and depressed during that time, grieving the death of my father. Walter's patience and support helped pull me through my grief. The only time he ever lost his temper was when he asked us to paint the coffin show-case room. We got tired and persuaded a group of our friends to help us. By evening, we had turned the walls into quite a creative piece of artwork.

"The three of us traveled to every hospital morgue in Brooklyn to retrieve the deceased late at night and into the early hours of the morning. Walter waited to do this errand until after eleven o'clock at night. We had a wonderful time together on those trips. He often stopped at the bagel factory to buy freshly-made bagels at one or two in the morning before heading home. Oh, those bagels were so soft and hot, coming straight from the oven. We couldn't wait for them to cool before we bit into them. We devoured them on the way home, but always saved some to bring home to Mama. When we were older, Walter taught us the embalming process. We assisted him with the procedure."

Angie lowered her voice to barely a whisper, "I've never seen an embalming. How is it done?"

Abe whispered back, "Blood is pumped out of a vein on one side and replaced with embalming fluid on the other. It's a fairly simple process. Sam became the undertaker, I didn't."

"Why didn't you?"

"One night, I was waiting in the hearse carriage in the parking lot of the hospital emergency room. I watched the physicians caring for their patients as they came out of the ambulances. On the way home, I confided to Walter that I was interested in becoming a doctor. From that time on, he did everything he could to encourage me to go to college, and then, on to medical school. He often said, 'It's much smarter for us to have a doctor in the family than two undertakers. Don't you agree, Mama?' Mama agreed."

When the train stopped at the last train station on the line, the train conductor called, "CONEY ISLAND, CONEY ISLAND STATION!"

"We're here already. How can that be?"

"I talked too much. Thank you for listening, Angie."

"Thank you for telling me about your family."

"Okay, but it will be my turn to listen on our way home tonight."

Angie and Abe walked past the food concessions and candy stores that lined the train station ramp until they reached the corner of Surf Avenue and Stillwell Avenue. The cotton candy and pulled taffy in the air collided with the smell of hotdogs and French fries sizzling at Nathan's. It turned into one wonderful aroma of sweets and treats.

"Smell that, Angie?"

"Heavenly, isn't it? I love those hotdogs."

"We mustn't call them *hotdogs*. Nathan insists we call them *frankfurters*. He is afraid that people will think that they are really made of... well, you know... *dogs*!"

Angie laughed.

"Let's get one tonight, Angie."

"I'd love to, Abe."

They walked along the boardwalk until they came to the Luna Park Entrance. Dr. Martin's *Infant Incubator Exhibit*, showcasing growing premature infants, was in the heart of Luna Park, Coney Island.

"It's this way," Angie said.

They showed Dr. Martin's letter to a lad stationed at the entrance booth who allowed them to enter without charge. Abe followed Angie as they passed the *Loop-the-Loop* and the *Dragon's Gorge*. After the Luna Park skating rink, they came to a large, castle-like building with a sign out front:

Infant Incubators
With
Living Infants

"We're here," Angie announced.

Angie and Abe entered through the side entrance.

Dr. Martin was waiting for them. He greeted them warmly.

"Welcome! Welcome! I am delighted to see you again, Miss Bosco," he said.

After Angie introduced the doctors, Dr. Martin shook Abe's hand and said, "I am always eager to meet with physicians, and am honored to have you here with us today. Come, I want to show you the exhibit before dinner is served. My cook has prepared a wonderful noontime meal for us."

Dr. Martin led the way as they traveled through the rooms of the pristine, hospital-like facility. In the main nursery, eight premature infants were being expertly cared for by three registered nurses. They were living in eight of the ten glass incubators which hung from the walls. A barrier aisle in the middle of the room allowed paying guests to walk through to observe the tiny babies without disturbing the nurses or the babies.

Dr. Martin explained his plan for the day. After dining, they would have an opportunity to care for the infants. He would assign each of them to a registered nurse to work side-by-side with her in the main nursery. He was interrupted by his cook, Emelie. She announced that their luncheon was ready to be served.

The meal was elegantly presented on French Haviland Limoge China, white dishes decorated with delicate baby-pink roses and light-blue scrolls encased within a gold border. Fresh lemonade was served in German Nachtman Crystal. The table was set for twelve. This included the three registered nurses who were not on duty, the three wet nurses employed to produce milk for the infants, the Nursing Supervisor Madame Louise, the Doctor, his wife, his daughter, Eva, and their guests, Abe and Angie.

Emelie had prepared fishcakes from fluke fillets freshly-caught at nearby Sheepshead Bay. The fish was so light and tasty, the meaty cakes tasted like crab cakes. Summer squash, sautéed with onions and tomatoes, and buttered mashed potatoes accompanied the dish. Warm peach crisp with creamy vanilla ice cream was their dessert. It was elegantly served in crystal dishes.

"Dr. Martin, where did you first learn to care for your premature infants?" Dr. Goodwin asked.

"I trained under Dr. Pierre Budin. We continue to religiously follow his methods. He's a pediatric specialist who studied under Dr. Tarnier. It was Dr. Tarnier who adapted the design for the incubator from chick incubators. I was fortunate to have the opportunity to work with both of them at the Maternity Hospital in Paris."

"Did you know that our daughter, Eva, was born prematurely?" Mrs. Martin asked. "She was four pounds, one ounce at birth."

Eva blushed, "Mama, must you always tell everyone?"

"As you can see, Eva is now a beautiful, healthy woman. During the summer months, she works here with us, caring for the babies. The nurses have trained her well."

"Thank you, Papa."

Abe asked, "How do the incubators work?"

"They provide a clean, warm environment for the infants to grow. Each incubator has a heater and an air filtration system. As you know, infants born prematurely do not have fat tissue to retain their body heat. They have a difficult time maintaining their body temperature. The incubators provide a constant source of heat, as well as clean, purified fresh air."

"What other challenges do these little ones face?" Angie asked.

"Their immune systems are not fully developed. The infants could easily succumb to infection. The air they breathe must be clean and fresh. The linens and diapers they use must be immaculately clean. All feeding equipment must be sterile."

Abe asked, "Tell us what you learned about feeding them?"

"The tiniest ones have a weak sucking reflex. Often, they cannot coordinate sucking and swallowing at the same time. Therefore, we use a variety of feeding methods to assist them. In addition, Dr. Budin found that mother's milk is the easiest milk for premature infants to digest. For this reason, there is always, at least, one wet-nurse on duty. Our wet-nurses provide milk around the clock for the babies."

"How did the hospitals in Europe react to the incubator units?"

"They embraced them, and implemented many of Dr. Tarnier's concepts because of their cost effectiveness. You see, Dr. Tarnier recommended grouping infants in one central location, creating a shared center of neighboring hospitals. The hospitals collaborated and pooled their resources, such as equipment and nursing care."

"What prevents American hospitals from implementing incubator centers similar to the ones in Europe?" Abe asked.

"I've observed that there is competition among the hospitals in the United States. They have yet to learn the advantages of collaboration."

Angie asked, "What are your future plans? Will you open more exhibits?"

"No, I have two exhibits now. One is here and one is on the Atlantic City Boardwalk. I have no plans to expand. My only wish is that the hospitals will work together to open a center for premature infants in the city. Should that occur, I will transfer all the babies there. Then, I will close the exhibit and return to private practice."

The afternoon was filled with learning. When it was time to leave, Abe asked, "Angie, would you like to take a walk on the Boardwalk?"

Angie didn't hesitate to answer. "Yes, I would love to."

"I'm so glad we came today. I'm pleased that I had the opportunity to finally meet Dr. Martin. I had a preconceived notion that he was exploiting the infants for his own financial gain, but I found him to be a learned man who has devoted his life to their survival."

"I agree. So many infants have thrived under his care. He has an eighty-five percent success rate with the tiniest infants."

"I was wondering what happens in the wintertime. I meant to ask him that question."

"Doctor Martin doesn't accept new admissions after September when the exhibit prepares to close. The nurses work at the exhibit until all the babies are strong enough to be discharged to their parents. During the winter, the nurses accept private-duty assignments. They return in the spring when new babies are admitted once again."

"That's very interesting. Look at the time. It's getting late. I was hoping to treat you to a relaxing dinner tonight, Angie."

"We had a magnificent lunch. Let's stay on the boardwalk, and stop at Nathan's before we catch the train."

"That's my kind of dinner, Angie. The luncheon today was very elegant. Who would think that one could live so lavishly on twenty-five-cent admission fees?"

"He doesn't charge the parents one penny for his services. Madame Louise said that the entire enterprise is financed from the exhibit fees. There were hordes of people coming through this afternoon. I started to count them, but gave up. There were so many. Apparently, the same people come, week after week, to watch the babies as they grow bigger and stronger.

"If I didn't see it with my own eyes, I would never have believed it."

Evening breezes were gently blowing. The misty air smelled of sea salt and cotton candy. Surrounding Luna Park were thousands of light bulbs in the shape of quarter moons, giving the illusion of mid-day. People walked up and down the Boardwalk, stopping to look at the ocean or to listen to the boardwalk barkers. Goat-pulled carts and a procession of real elephants, carrying paid passengers, added to the magic of the evening.

It was Angie's turn to talk. Angie told Abe about the death of her parents at an early age, and that she was raised by her aunt in Sicily along with her two older brothers and her younger sister. Her old-est brother, Giacomo, came to America first. He led the way for the others. Angie and her brother, Santino, followed three years later. Last year, Giacomo paid for her younger sister, Celestina, to come to New York to study to be a teacher. However, after a year at Teachers College, Celestina transferred to nursing school.

It was after nine when they stopped for a frankfurter and a paper cone of chunky French Fries at Nathan's. "Everything tastes so good when you're at the beach." Abe declared.

After they ate, they hurried to the train station to catch the train to Flatbush. From there, they connected with the BMT train return-ing to Manhattan. They caught the downtown streetcar to the Ferry Building but arrived five minutes too late for the 22:30 ferry. While they waited for the next ferry to arrive, Abe talked about his hopes and dreams for the future clinic. While working with the immigrants at Ellis Island, he had always worried about their follow-up care. He was especially concerned about the lack of medical services available to them, and was excited to now be able to provide a solution to their healthcare needs.

Once on the ferry, the two sat quietly, listening to the sounds of the sea. Abe reached for Angie's hand and held it.

Abe said. "I would like you to meet my family. Do you have plans for Thanksgiving Day?"

"I'm working on Thanksgiving, and, if I recall correctly, you are too. You're named as House Officer on the hospital schedule."

"Yes, I know. I always try to go to my parents after work on Thanksgiving Day. Rudwick, the Assistant Harbor Deputy, often takes a couple of us over to Red Hook in his boat. My brother picks me up there in his Hudson Special."

"Red Hook, Brooklyn? Why is Deputy Rudwick going to Red Hook at that time of night? There's nothing there by the docks, except bars and..."

"Well..."

Angie smiled, "Yes, of course, I understand. I mean...say no more."

"Will you be going to your brother's house after work on Thanksgiving?" Abe asked.

"No, there isn't time. I'll take the train uptown on Sunday to see everyone. They always plan a family dinner for me the first day I'm off after a holiday."

"Would you like to come along with Sam and me? We have it timed to perfection. He picks me up at ten minutes to eight, and delivers me to Mama at a quarter after."

"Will he pick us up in the hearse?"

"That may very well be a possibility."

"Count me in, but will we return in time for the curfew? The last ferry is at midnight, you know.

"I've always been able to catch the last ferry, never missed it yet. We leave Brooklyn at exactly eleven. Do the nurses get penalized if they come in after curfew?"

"Yes, luckily that doesn't happen very often. You see, the ferry schedule keeps us on the straight and narrow. Do you think that Sister would be able to wait up and watch the comings and goings of each one of us every evening? Poor dear, she would never get any sleep."

"Well, it's settled then. I'll tell Mama that you're coming."

"I'll look forward to it."

Abe took Angie's hand, and helped her off the ferry. He walked Angie to the Cottage, and waited until she opened the front door.

"I had a wonderful day, Angie."

"So did I."

"It was almost perfect..."

"It was perfect for me. What was missing for you?"

"This..." Abe whispered, just before he kissed her goodnight.

"Good Night, Miss Angie."

"Good Night, Dr. Goodwin."

When Angie opened the cottage door, Sister Gwendolyn peeked out of her room. She smiled as she watched Angie float up the two flights of stairs to her bedroom on the third floor.

Chapter Nine

September 25, 1924
7 PM (19:00)

What a thoughtful thing to do,
To take the time to say thank-you.

When Angie reported for the night shift, she noticed a letter was tucked in the brown leather corner of her green desk blotter. It was addressed to *Nurse Miss Angie*. The return address was from a *Mrs. E. Ferguson* on Amsterdam Avenue. She remembered her barefoot patient, Elsbeth Ferguson.

FROM: MRS. E. FERGUSON
98 AMSTERDAM AVENUE
NEW YORK CITY, NEW YORK

TO: NURSE MISS ANGIE
THE NURSE ON WARD 240
ELLIS ISLAND HOSPITAL
ELLIS ISLAND, PORT OF NEW YORK
NEW YORK CITY, NEW YORK, USA

Curiosity got the best of her. Angie put her work aside for a moment. She was about to open the envelope when Betsie, her nurse's aide, called to her for assistance. After that, Miss Marion was ready to give her the evening report. Angie tucked the letter in the pocket of her heavily-starched uniform.

It wasn't until the end of her shift, in the morning, that she remembered that the letter from Mrs. Ferguson was still in her pocket. Angie hurried to the Nurses' Dining Room at the Cottage. Eager to open the letter, she quickly grabbed a bowl of oatmeal, found a seat, and used a kitchen knife to open the envelope.

September 14, 1924

Dear Miss Angie,

I don't know if you remember me but I met you on my first day on Ellis Island when they brought me to your hospital. You said I was the first patient of the day. I remember how kind you were to me when I ended up in the hospital with my feet so sore and bandaged up. The other day I was thinking how grateful I was to you for giving me your shoes. My mother always taught me to say thank you. This has been pressing on my mind since you did that good turn for me. So, that is what I am doing now, as the purpose of this letter is to state that I am beholden to you for your generosity. My husband, Callum, asked his friend's wife to write this letter for me. I am telling her what to write. I am grateful you gave me your shoes because you didn't want me going barefoot in America.

You told me that Callum needed money to be allowed in, and you were right. Like you said, they were only looking at the money part and didn't care about the shoes part, but I was glad I had those shoes because it made me look a bit respectable and not like a pauper.

When the man came to call at the hospital, he said that my case was being presented to the Board. I was nervous going over to the Court. On the way,

I thought I would be kicked out of America, for certain. I didn't know that Callum had the dough to get us in. It seems the only thing holding us up was the money. The hearing lasted all of five minutes. Callum showed his twenty-five dollars to the judge. To my amazement, the gavel went down. We were given our landing cards right there and then. Can you imagine? All that worry, and it was over in a matter of minutes.

The Immigrant Aid people visited me at the hospital. They said that I could fill out an application and petition their people for a bond. They said the chances of making that happen were good, with the only problem being that it would take about one week. They couldn't do nothing for us right away.

In the meantime, my Callum was getting a little bored in the clinker, and he is a betting man, like I told you. So while he was waiting with nothing to do, he decided to do a little betting. They had no dice, mind you, but those fellows could think up all kinds of ways to bet…like how many raindrops got stuck to the window pain and how many minutes it would take the guard to return to the room. In no time at all, Callum had won five dollars. He learned that, for the price of a dollar, one of the Registry guards would let Callum hold a crisp twenty-dollar bill which he needed to show the hearing board. So, that's what Callum did.

After the hearing, the guard approached Callum. He offered his hand to congratulate him. As they shook hands, Callum slipped twenty-one dollars back to the guard, like they agreed beforehand. Now, that left Callum with four dollars in his pocket. Callum gave me two to hold when we got off the ferry. He held on to the other two dollars. He said that he wanted us both to have the feel of money in our hands when we set our feet down in America for the first time.

Well, there we were finally in New York, but we didn't know what to do. As luck would have it, Callum ran into a friend from home in the park. His friend took us to his apartment to meet his wife. They let us stay in the living room for ten days until Callum found a job and got his first pay. Mind you, these people shared their small space with us, even though they lived in two small rooms with five little ones. They called us their "boarders" because each night they put down boards in the living room. We made our bed on them and slept right on those boards on the floor.

After that, Callum and I were able to get a room here on Amsterdam Avenue. I was referred for a position as an upstairs chambermaid. Now, we both are working and enjoying the good life in America. Callum says that if we keep working, we will be moving to Brooklyn in no time. One day, we walked across the Williamsburg Bridge. It was beautiful on the other side.

It is my sincere hope that this letter finds its way to you because it meant a lot to me to have shoes on my feet and money in my hand when I stepped foot in America.

Yours truly,

Mrs. Callum Ferguson

Thankful for receiving the letter, Angie smiled. It made her feel good that her efforts made a difference to the young girl. She returned the letter to the pocket of her uniform, and finished her breakfast. Suddenly, she felt very tired. She climbed up the stairs to her room and went straight to bed. Sleep came quickly after her busy night shift. Her last thought was to remind herself to order her new shoes on her next day off.

Chapter Ten

Castelvetrano, Sicily

June 17, 1907

Dandelions and morning dew,
Come together in witches' brew.

"Angelina! Angelina! Wake up. Wake up. Up with you, lazy child, it's time for work. The Signorina is expecting you in thirty minutes."

Angelina's heart pounded as she lifted her heavy head from the warmth of her pillow. She had been enjoying a sweet dream when her aunt abruptly woke her, but who and what was she dreaming of? She strained to remember.

Yes, of course! Mama!

In her dream, her heart was full of anticipation. Her mother had been walking past Piazza Garibaldi, coming toward her.

A flash of candlelight interrupted her thoughts, and sadness swept over her.

She thought, *Mama isn't returning to Castelvetrano. She is gone. She died seven years ago.*

Angelina jumped from her bed and dressed quickly. In minutes, she was out on the dark street without breakfast, and without a whisper of a goodbye from her aunt. Although it was June, the young girl felt a chill in the morning air. The Signorina lived at the opposite end of the village. Angelina walked quickly to keep warm. She would have to maintain her brisk pace if she were to reach the Signorina on time.

When Angelina arrived at the Signorina's cottage, Sirina was already up, dressed and ready to leave. She looked at the clock on the wall. "Hurry, soon it will be too hot to walk in the fields. We must leave now if we are to find the cladodes before noon."

"I will fetch the baskets and meet you outside."

Angelina grabbed four baskets and her straw hat. She was out in the courtyard in seconds. She followed Sirina, single file, along a narrow, cobblestoned sidewalk until they reached the village Piazza where a group of elderly men were beginning to gather, preparing for a game of Bocce Ball. Father Salvador was working in the alleyway on the side of the Mother Church. He stopped weeding his tiny vegetable garden long enough to tip his hat and call out a morning greeting to the woman and the girl.

Angelina and Sirina continued walking until they reached the thick stone walls of the village and passed through its massive gate. There, they turned and followed a path through the meadow.

"Perhaps, we will see Santino, my brother, the shepherd boy."

"By this time, Santino would have already left with the sheep to reach his morning's destination."

Signorina Sirina looked down to see a batch of dandelions at her feet. "I can use these." She stopped to pick a handful. When she had gathered what she needed, she put them in her basket, and walked on. Angelina followed.

They walked over a mile through the meadow until they came upon a patch of prickly-pear cacti.

Sirina smiled. "There, in the brambles, I see some plump cactus cladodes popping out."

Sirina used a linen towel to break off the oval pads that grew from the cactus plant. Angelina imitated her actions. "Ouch!" She cried.

"Be careful, Angelina, these cactus spikes are very sharp...very sharp indeed. Let me pick them. Perhaps, you can pick the *ficurinnia*. Be careful, they have a rough skin, also."

Angelina carefully picked the prickly pears, the rose-colored fruit of the cactus, until one of her baskets was filled with fruit.

"That's plenty, Child. I need only a few more cladodes. Then, I'll be ready to leave."

When the Signorina filled her basket, they headed back toward the village.

Halfway there, the Signorina stopped. She spotted a cluster of fennel plants lining the side of the road. She kneeled down to cut the plump fennel roots. She filled the last empty basket with the bulbs.

"What will you do with the dandelions that you picked, Signorina?"

"We will dry the leaves to make a tea."

"What can you heal with dandelion tea?"

"We will make a tea infusion for someone who has a stomachache. It can also be beneficial to a new mother to help her milk flow."

"Once, you used it on a wart, too."

"Yes, but for a wart, you must use the sap of the dandelion when it is freshly-picked."

"What will you do with the cladodes of the cactus, Signorina?"

"We will carefully open them to release the gel inside."

"What can you heal with it?

"It is used to hasten the healing of a wound, and reduce scar tissue."

"What will you do with the pink prickly pears we gathered, Signorina?

"We will wash them, and peel back their rough skin. Then, we will chop them up, put them in a bowl, and add vino rosso.

"What will you do with the fennel bulbs you picked, Signorina?"

"After we wash and slice them thin, we will add olive oil, salt, and a little Romano. Then, we will pop them in a pan and roast them."

"How will you use the prickly pears after they are soaked in wine, and what will the fennel bulbs cure?

"It will cure our hunger, Child, for we are going to eat the roasted fennel at our noon meal, and the pears will be our dessert when we return to the cottage."

"Thank you, Signorina. When I am with you, I always learn something new."

Chapter Eleven

~

September 27, 1924
10 AM (10:00)

Her insights reveal a power and knowing.
She tells where she's been.
She knows where she's going.

By 1924, the headquarters of the Henry Street Settlement House at 265 Henry Street was not one building, as its address led one to believe, but a series of three adjacent red-brick, Federal-style buildings. The three-story houses had been built a century before when the neighborhood was once a thriving center of commerce. However, this section of the city had been quickly abandoned by the prosperous bankers and merchants who lived there when it became home to the hordes of poor immigrants coming to America. The Lower East Side was a notorious and crowded hotbed of crime, squalor and disease when Nurse Lillian Wald "settled" there. Together with her nursing colleagues, she established the Visiting Nurse Service in 1893.

During the next three decades, Henry Street became one of the most successful and well-funded settlement houses in all of New York. What began as the headquarters for a small group of nurses determined to clean up the neighborhood and nurse its citizens back to good health, grew to be the central hub of the community. By 1924, the settlement house was not only a place for healthcare, but a haven for recreation and community education. It provided something for the entire family: a safe place for children to play and learn, an educational resource for parents, and a park and playground for families to enjoy picnics and family outings on weekends. For the smart visiting nurses knew that good health came from healthy living, fresh air, sunshine and pristine hygiene. They discovered early on that improving the social aspects of the neighborhood, improved the health of its residents. The nurses not only provided nursing care, they fought for social reform as a means to improve the health of the community. The first social workers in New York City were the visiting nurses.

Henry Street was located six blocks from the entrance of the Williamsburg Bridge which connected the Lower East Side of Manhattan to Williamsburg, Brooklyn. Brooklyn was the next stop for the immigrants, both physically and emotionally. Immigrants who once lived in the filthy, crowded tenements had slowly moved across the bridge during the last decade. As immigrant families saved their hard-earned dollars and began to prosper in America, they picked up their belongings, crossed the bridge, and moved to a newer apartment and a safer neighborhood.

Although Williamsburg had everything that growing families wanted, it didn't have everything they needed. Brooklyn still needed to expand its schools, clinics, and libraries. A number of dynamic settlements houses like Henry Street sprinkled around town were desperately needed. Nurse Angie Bosco knew that if Dr. Goodwin's church-funded neighborhood clinic was to be successful in providing healthcare to the immigrant population in Brooklyn, they would first have to establish trust with the residents. Becoming an educational and recreational resource for the community was one way to do this.

She believed it would be most beneficial to meet with Nurse Lillian Wald, the founder of The Henry Street Settlement House. Angie's friend, Adeline, had once worked as a Visiting Nurse with Miss Wald. It was Adeline who taught Angie about the health customs of people coming to America from different cultures. She taught her how important community education was in maintaining good health and preventing illness. Last summer, Adeline had written a letter of introduction to Miss Wald for Angie. Angie's appointment with Miss Wald was scheduled for ten o'clock on the twenty-seventh of September.

When Angie reached Battery Park, after taking the ferry from Ellis Island, she decided to walk uptown to her appointment. It was a long walk, but the crisp autumn weather made it a pleasant one until she reached the littered streets of the Lower East Side. Struggling through the uneven cobblestones, she twisted her ankle. Her feet hurt. She was relieved by the thought that she was planning to order her new shoes the following day. Since June, she had continued to procrastinate on that errand. She wondered why she had waited so long.

This is a perfect example of what Miss Elsie and Miss Elizabeth preach to us. Angie could hear the two older women lecturing to the nursing staff. "Nurses are always caring for others, never taking the time to care for themselves. Remember to take care of yourself. Eat breakfast. Take your bathroom breaks. Step out into the fresh air at least once a day."

When Angie turned the corner at Henry Street, she was surprised to find that the sidewalk was immaculately clean. The century-old houses at 263, 265, and 267 Henry Street had been beautifully restored to their former splendor. Inviting window boxes on the first and second floors overflowed with red geraniums. The decorative wrought iron handrails shined. They appeared to have been freshly painted. Five white-washed steps led up to the heavily paneled front door. The *All Are Welcome* sign on the doorknob of the unlocked door at 265 Henry Street beckoned entrance.

Angie opened the door and entered the foyer. A young girl, who appeared to be no more than twelve, sat at a small desk at the foot of the stairs. She asked, "Are you here for the baby class, Miss?"

Angie smiled and introduced herself. "No, I have an appointment with Miss Wald this morning. I am Miss Bosco."

"Oh, yes, she is expecting you. She told me to keep a lookout for you. She's in the study upstairs, first door on the left, at the top of the stairs."

The door to the study was open. Angie found Lillian Wald waiting for her. She stood to greet Angie as she entered the room. Miss Wald appeared to be a woman in her fifties who wore her graying hair tied back in a loose bun with a slight wave on the side. Her dark gray dress looked a bit dated and old-fashioned, but her twinkling eyes and infectious smile compensated for her somewhat drab appearance.

"Miss Angie Bosco, I am delighted to meet you. I am glad you could come today. Adeline told me so much about you."

"It's my pleasure, Miss Wald. Thank you for taking the time to meet with me this morning."

"Adeline's letter stated you were planning to open a clinic in Williamsburg."

"Yes, a local church has raised funds to finance the project."

"That's good to hear. Over the years, a great many immigrants moved across the bridge to Williamsburg. Some had been evicted from their tenement apartments when landlords were forced to abandon their buildings because they couldn't meet the new fire department regulations. One of the challenges you will face is that the immigrants are fearful and afraid to seek medical help when they get sick."

"Yes, they fear they will be quarantined and separated from their families."

"...Or their children will be taken from them. You will have to gain their confidence."

"I believe that will be our biggest challenge."

"Establishing residence in the neighborhood should be your first step. I remember that it took months to find an apartment with running water and a bathtub when we first *settled* in the Lower East Side. That is how *settlement* houses were named. You *settle* here, and take up residence. Soon, you learn the comings and goings of the community.

"Back then, the immigrants would never come willingly to a clinic. The nurses went directly to their homes. We trudged through foul-smelling hallways and littered stairwells to reach our patients. At times, our only access to them was to climb up on the fire-escapes and cross over the rooftops. Gradually, the people in the community began to trust us. They came to the free classes we offered.

"A church affiliation will most definitely help you. I have no doubt about that. The bonds of trust have already been formed both by the church, and by their positive experiences at the settlement houses in the city. I will help you in any way I can. Which church is it?"

"We will be working with Father Benedetto at Nativity Church."

"I was hoping it would be a church dedicated to a lady saint so that you could name the clinic after her...like St. Mary's Health Center. Catholic women relate to their saints, but, let me see, I think *Nativity Settlement House* could be a most appropriate name."

"Miss Ward, as I was walking here this morning, I was trying to think of a name. One of the names we've considered is *Nativity Clinic*."

"Clinic is far too formal and frightening. Don't you think it brings to mind vaccinations and injections?"

"Yes, I see, *Nativity Settlement House* is more welcoming."

"Perhaps, you can add it at the end, like this: *Nativity Settlement House and Health Clinic*. My guess is that the people in the community will shorten its name to *Nativity House*."

"It sounds perfect. Miss Wald, I think you may have just named our clinic."

"Call me *Lillian*."

"Thank you, and please call me *Angie*."

"Angie, have you ever visited our settlement house before?"

"No, but I did read every one of your six journal articles. They were extremely informative."

"Thank you, would you like to take a tour?"

"I would love to."

"As I stressed in my articles, you cannot work toward the good health of the community without addressing the social and economic pressures of its population, which is often the underlying cause of illness. The living conditions developing here on the Lower East Side were not conducive to good health and wellness. In many cases, it was not directly the fault of the immigrant settlers. Location changes habits and customs. Take, for example, a peasant family from the Russian countryside. When a member of the family took ill, a fire was built. Soiled linens and towels were boiled before cleaning. Bed sheets were hung up to dry outside in the fresh air and sunshine. We know that both the hot water and the strong sun killed the germs. That was the practice in the old county, but it's difficult to continue such a routine in the cramped quarters of a tenement apartment. New and different techniques had to be quickly adopted. These new methods are not always as effective in preventing the spread of disease."

"I see, so you begin teaching basic hygiene."

"That's correct, come down the hall. I want to show you our classrooms. We started first by teaching housekeeping and hygiene to young mothers. Then, we added baby-care classes to our curriculum. Women wanted to learn the new language, so we offered them free English lessons. Now, we teach a variety of classes: Citizenship, Calisthenics, Diction, Music, Sewing, and Reading. Henry Street has expanded to seven houses. One building is dedicated to helping people find jobs and barter their talents. A local carpenter teaches carpentry. Come downstairs with me. Let me show you the park and playground outside."

Angie followed Lillian down to the ground floor and through the kitchen. "Would you like a cup of coffee, Angie?"

"Yes, please."

The coffee had already been brewed. Lillian poured two cups of coffee from the coffeepot and placed them on a tray. "It's a lovely day. Let's have our coffee outside. Help me with the door, if you would."

When Angie opened the door, they stepped into a beautiful garden. Following a rose-lined path, they stopped to rest when they reached the gazebo.

"This was one of our community projects. Access to the playground and the gardens are open to the public. It was my intention to create a garden sanctuary, a place to heal and restore."

"Sitting here, I can't believe we are actually still in the city."

"Next door, we built a playground. There were no parks and few trees grew on the streets of the Lower East Side. The streets were filled with broken furniture, mattresses, and lumber. Our young boys were getting into trouble, playing in the crowded streets that were littered with filth and debris. When we invited the schoolchildren to come after school, we discovered that they were too hungry to concentrate on their lessons. We now have a Boys' Club and a Girls' Club where the schoolchildren are given nutritious snacks, tutored, and helped with their homework. They're often here until dusk. In this building, we have childcare and story-time for toddlers, as well as, daycare for sick children and the elderly. On weekends, families come to picnic and sit outdoors to watch their children play."

"You are sending the boys and girls to summer camp in the country, also."

"Yes, I bought a plot of land upstate. The volunteers did the rest."

Suddenly, Angie felt overwhelmed, feeling a twinge of a headache coming on. She rubbed her forehead, and thought. *I'm only one person. I can't possibly accomplish all this.*

As if she read her mind, Lillian said, "No need to get overwhelmed, Angie. Relax. Drink your coffee. This center wasn't built in a year or even two years. It's the result of thirty years work. We started in 1893 with lots of help from the community. You will, too. I am going to write to Jane about you."

"Jane?"

"Why, yes, Jane Adams at Hull House in Chicago. She stays connected with all the settlements. There are over five hundred across the country."

"She is far too important to have time for me."

"On the contrary, Jane will *make* time for you. She has helped me through the years. She has become a valuable resource to other settlement directors, as well."

Sitting under the shade of the gazebo on a mild October morning, Angie was mesmerized as she listened to Lillian.

Lillian Wald continued, "I have much to tell you. Where shall I begin? Yes, in the beginning you should start small, slowly incorporating these concepts. Begin with prenatal classes. Always remember that a young mother's love will seek out wellness for her unborn child. The maternity link with healthcare is often the first link for couples. After that first bond is established, they'll bring in their families. They will come to trust you…

"You must know the community you serve. Learn the customs and habits they bring from their old countries. This will help you understand them. You will learn from the diversity of the neighborhood…

"My nurses are now doing home visits over the bridge. They have identified that childcare is needed during the day. Perhaps, we can collaborate. I suggest an alliance of some sort. They need a place to rest and write their nurses notes. If you would like, I can arrange for you to accompany them on their home visits…

"More than caring for the sick, you must care for the human condition. Sickness will prevail if something isn't done about the circumstance of poverty…

"Have another cup of coffee, Angie, you will feel better. I have so much more to tell you…"

Chapter Twelve

❧

Castelvetrano, Sicily

March 31, 1907

Syrups, ointments and lotions,
Tinctures, mixtures and potions!

When Angelina opened the Signorina's front door, the house stung with cold. She hurried to build the morning fires in both the foyer fireplace and in the cast iron cooking stove. When the fires were burning brightly, Angelina went outside to snatch up a lemon from the lemon tree and an orange from the blood-orange tree that grew in the courtyard. Returning to the house, she quickly inspected the front room. The fire had already cast a rosy glow on the tiny space. There wouldn't be much to do in the way of cleaning today since Signorina Sirina kept a meticulous home.

Angelina proceeded to prepare the morning coffee to the Signorina's specifications. On numerous occasions, she had been instructed to double the amount of ground espresso and pack it tightly into the upper chamber of the coffeepot to prepare the strongest of brews. While the coffee brewed, she lined the breakfast tray with a white linen towel. She peeled the orange and separated it. Then, she meticulously arranged its segments in an overlapping circle on a small glass dish. She placed the orange, two almond biscotti, a demi-tasse cup, and a stiffly-starched napkin on the tray, and waited. When the coffee was ready, she filled the cup with the rich espresso. She stirred in a teaspoon of sugar, and watched as the creamy foam swirled into circles of bronze and tan.

She carried the tray to the Signorina's bedroom, balanced it in one hand, and knocked on her door.

"Enter," Sirina called.

Signorina Sirina was already up, dressed, and feverishly working at her writing table. She stood to help Angelina with the breakfast tray. She was four feet, ten inches tall and a bit stout. Her long dark-brown hair had been brushed down past her waist, and had not yet been pinned and rolled in preparation for the day. Her eyes sparkled when she spoke. "Good Morning, Angelina. Did you have your breakfast this morning?"

Angelina looked down and said, "No, Signorina. There was no time."

"Well, then, you must go downstairs and prepare breakfast for yourself, Angelina. Eat it all up. I need you well-nourished. We have much work to do today. Senora Sciarrino has sent word that she will arrive at eight o'clock this morning. She is suffering from the *malocchio*, the headache of the evil eye. Greet her warmly when she comes to the door. Escort her to the study and offer her a cup of this delicious brew. Insist that she drink it while she waits. Tell her that I need a moment to sit in prayer for her continued good health. Darken the room and allow her to rest. Place a vinegar towel on her forehead the way I taught you. Remember that I need you to prepare two small bowls: one for holy water and one for olive oil. Also, you must not forget to place my silver scissors nearby. When twenty minutes pass, come fetch me."

"Yes, Signorina."

"Angelina, do you have any questions about these instructions?"

"No, Signorina, I understand. I will also begin making the new batch of cough syrup as you requested yesterday. When it is time to add the brandy, how much shall I add?"

"How much water will you start with?"

"One cup of water..."

"Let me see...six tablespoons should do it."

"Shall I bottle it after that?"

"No, let it sit and rest until noon. We will bottle it after lunch. Go now, Child, and eat."

"Thank-you," Angelina curtsied, turned and left the room.

Angelina broke a chunk of bread and cut a slice of cheese for her breakfast. After she prepared the glass bowls, she retrieved the Signorina's silver scissors from her velvet-lined cedar chest. Next, she prepared the cough syrup. To one cup of water, she added the juice of one whole lemon, a quarter cup of honey, a handful of dried mint leaves and grated ginger root. She carefully stirred the concoction. When it had thickened into a syrup-like consistency, she added the brandy. She placed the pot on a nearby table to rest.

Senora Sciarrino rang the cottage bell at exactly eight. Angelina welcomed her, and went about carrying out the Signorina's instructions. When twenty minutes passed, she knocked on Sirina's bedroom door. Signorina Sirina rose swiftly to attend to her patient. Angelina followed behind. Sirina always allowed Angelina to watch and observe while she worked.

"Malocchio! Malocchio! It's my head, Sirina, it is pounding," moaned Senora Sciarrino.

"How long have you been experiencing your headache, Senora?"

"It's been three days since I was overlooked by Marucha."

"Why would Marucha overlook you, Senora?"

"She is jealous of my looks, you know."

"Of course, Senora."

Sirina poured the holy water into one bowl, and the olive oil into another. She dipped her index finger into the olive oil and crossed the senora's forehead three times as she whispered the prayer of the malocchio. Three times again, she etched three small crosses on the woman's forehead and prayed. With dramatic flair, she mixed the olive oil with the water and stabbed the scissors three times into the bowl.

"Hurry home now, Senora, and rest."

"Is the curse broken, Signorina?"

"When you arrive home your headache will have lifted. Of that, I am certain, Senora."

Sirina escorted Senora Sciarrino to the door. She turned to Angelina with a smile of relief.

"Did you cure her of the evil eye, Signorina?"

"Perhaps..."

"What is the prayer you whispered? I could not hear all the words. Please teach me."

"This prayer can only be passed on to another on Christmas Eve."

"Then, I will be patient and wait until December. I want to know the secret of curing the malocchio."

"Child, you may already know the secret of the malocchio cure."

Angelina looked confused. "I do not understand, Signorina. Please explain."

"It is very simple, Angelina. I have come to believe that the secret of lifting the malocchio may very well be in the strength of the coffee that we brew."

Chapter Thirteen

~

October 8, 1924
10 PM (22:00)

Treasure the friends that come your way,
And the ties that have endured.
Give thanks for your friends every day,
And the bliss that they've secured.

WEDNESDAY, OCTOBER 8, 1924

ELLIS ISLAND HOSPITAL,

PORT OF NEW YORK,

NEW YORK CITY

MRS. ADELINE FERMÉ STEINGOLD

TWO SUNSET LANE

PALM SPRINGS, CALIFORNIA

My Dear Adeline,

I hope this letter finds you in continued good spirits. I've stuffed this envelope with my thoughts and prayers for your continued recovery. After reading this, take a long, deep breath. Absorb the healing powers of all the well-wishes enclosed in this letter.

So much has happened with the clinic project that I don't know where to begin. I spent an afternoon with Lillian Wald at the Henry Street Settlement House. She welcomed me warmly with coffee and a tour of the facility. Lillian *filled me, from head to toe, with a wealth of information. She has created a very active community center for young and old alike. I was impressed and surprised at the variety of free classes offered by her volunteers. The schedule includes classes in newborn care and health, as well as, ceramics, art and drama. While I was there, I observed a group of immigrant women taking English lessons. Another group was rehearsing a play they will perform at Christmas.*

Lillian suggested a name for our new clinic: "The Nativity Settlement House and Health Clinic". Father Benedetto and Abe liked the name. They believe in the settlement house concept. The success of the clinic depends on establishing trust with the people in the neighborhood by gradually developing community resources for them.

Abe and I overflow with excitement and ideas when we discuss plans for the clinic during our evening walks. Abe is very supportive and encouraging. He feels nurses are smart, independent thinkers, and should not be limited to being the handmaidens of physicians. He is confident that I will be able to coordinate the educational activities at Nativity House. I do believe he may have more confidence in me than I have in myself.

On his days off, Abe searches for a space for the clinic. He found two storefronts in Williamsburg in a perfect location. However, after touring both, Father vetoed them. He insists that we need a bigger space, preferably with living quarters overhead. Miss Wald advised us that our first step should be to "settle" in the neighborhood by residing there. It helps that Abe grew up in Williamsburg. In January, we will be "settling" in. We are looking for two small apartments. If need be, Father said there's extra room at the church rectory and the convent to board temporarily. If nothing is to be found, it looks as though I may be rooming with the good sisters.

Father Benedetto assures us more money will be coming to finance the venture after the summer. We will then hire a nursing assistant to help with the clinic work. In the meantime, Lillian advised me to seek out interested volunteers.

I often ask Father about the source of our financing. His answer is always the same. He cannot disclose the identity of the donors. I sometimes wonder if you and Harry are the mystery contributors because I can't imagine who gave Father such a large sum of money.

Please give my regards to Harry. God bless him for taking such good care of you.

Love and kisses,

Angie

X X X

SATURDAY, OCTOBER 18, 1924
TWO SUNSET LANE
PALM SPRINGS, CALIFORNIA

MISS ANGIE BOSCO
ELLIS ISLAND HOSPITAL,
ELLIS ISLAND, PORT OF NEW YORK,
NEW YORK CITY, NEW YORK

Dear Angie Girl,

Thank you for all your weekly letters and your well-wishes. The doctors say that I am doing better than expected. I feel stronger than I have in a long time. I have more energy now, too. You will be happy to hear that I have developed a ravenous appetite out here in the country. Our cook prepares wonderful meals for us with the freshest ingredients. Each meal is more delicious than the next.

Life is not exactly wild out here in the Wild West. Instead, the pace is slow and easy. Time passes quickly. I take riding lessons every morning. I walk in the evenings as the hot sun is setting and the desert begins to cool. My maids are very attentive. I have fashion magazines and books to read, wonderful weather and a beautiful house to live in. What more can I possibly desire? There is only one thing missing. Angie, in my heart of hearts, I yearn for a child. I don't know if I could ever get pregnant because of my age and my recent illness. The doctors have advised us to wait a year, but, by then, I will be forty years old. Harry is confident that we will be successful in having a baby of our own. We have also considered adopting.

I have news. Steingold Jewelers will be expanding to Fifth Avenue. Harry is going to take the train to New York next week to review the plans for his new store. It is the first time we will be separated since we married in May. He will be gone less than three weeks, and promised to return before Thanksgiving. How I wish I could accompany him, or better yet, that you could come out and visit me. It would be such fun to see you riding a horse. Alas, I know you are too busy to travel. I miss you terribly and wish you were here.

As nice as the living is in California, I look forward to returning to New York in the spring. However, I can't imagine what I will do with my time. Direct patient care is entirely out of the question during this phase of my recuperation. I would love to volunteer and work with you at the settlement house, if you will have me. I will do anything you assign. I can teach classes, watch children, organize the volunteers, or even help raise money for future funding. Would you think about it, Angie? Please consider my help. Let me know. It would ease my mind if I knew I had something constructive to do upon my return to New York.

On this subject, you asked if Harry financed the clinic venture. Although we should have thought of it, I am ashamed to say, we didn't. The funding did not come from the Steingolds. I have spoken to Harry about your settlement project. He believes it is a much needed endeavor and has promised to contribute toward the effort. We both would like to see Nativity House grow into a Henry Street Settlement House.

I am so glad you visited Henry Street. I knew Lillian would be a wonderful resource for you. I am delighted that she offered to write to Jane Adams about your clinic. Jane is a community organizer. She has not only organized the immigrants in her community, she has organized the settlement house leaders across the country to collaborate and share resources.

My Lillian is forever a nurse. Her focus is directed toward achieving and maintaining good health. That is why she started the Visiting Nurse Service. Lillian had recently graduated from nursing school, and was teaching a hygiene class at a local church. After class, a young girl approached Lillian. In tears, the girl reported that her mother was dying at home. Her mother had given birth two days earlier. The doctor, who had come to the house to deliver the baby, refused to return because he felt he was poorly paid for his services. The little girl carried her baby brother to an upstairs neighbor. The neighbor had recently learned that a nurse was teaching that afternoon in the neighborhood and instructed the little girl to fetch her.

Without question, Lillian snatched up the linens she was using for the classroom demonstration. She followed the girl across town, past littered streets, up dirty stairs, and through smelly tenement halls until they reached the postpartum woman. They found her in a bed of blood-crusted sheets. Lillian bathed her, and used the bedding she carried to make a clean bed. Tea and sugar were the only food she found in the house. She made a strong tea, and helped the woman drink it. Then, she went out and bought what was needed to start a vegetable soup for the family.

She left the apartment with a heavy heart. As she walked home, she decided that more help was needed for the immigrants. Lillian was spirited and energetic. Her family knew influential people. She raised enough funds to support a group of her nursing colleagues as they became the city's first visiting nurses. The settlement house grew and developed from there.

Angie Girl, I wish you the best of luck on your move to Brooklyn. Remember to not get too "settled" with the doctor when you arrive. No "settling" until there is a ring on your finger. I don't care how wonderful our dear Dr. Goodwin is!

Yours 'til butter flies,

Always,

Adeline

SUNDAY, OCTOBER 27, 1924
ELLIS ISLAND HOSPITAL,
PORT OF NEW YORK,
NEW YORK CITY

MRS. ADELINE FERMÉ STEINGOLD
TWO SUNSET LANE
PALM SPRINGS, CALIFORNIA

My Dear Adeline,

Great News! I am happy to report that I finally ordered my new shoes.

I went to Bartoli's Shoe Store last week. My sister, Celestina, accompanied me. As luck would have it, she had the afternoon off. I met her at Bellevue Hospital where she is a nursing student. Together, we took the Third Avenue El to Sixty-Seventh Street. We walked four blocks to Sixty-Third Street to Bartoli's Shoe Store on Third Avenue. It was easy to find because the name of the store is embedded in blue mosaic tiles on the entryway floor: "E. Bartoli Shoes, Est 1890".

We found Mr. Bartoli to be a bit stern at first, but he softened when we agreed with all his design suggestions. Instead of pure white, he suggested a light caramel-colored leather so that I can wear them outside the hospital setting. My new shoes will have a one-inch heel and a clever cross strap. I fell in love with the new style. I think you definitely would approve of my selection. The shoes will be ready in two weeks. I can't wait to see the finished product.

While we were there, Mr. Bartoli introduced us to his twenty-year-old daughter, Leonora. I mentioned that I wanted to show Celestina the fashionable Upper East Side. Leonora offered to give us a tour.

From Third Avenue, we walked up Sixty-Third Street toward Fifth Avenue. This is a very posh neighborhood lined with elegant brownstones and brick townhouses. Many are sheltered behind locked wrought-iron gates, hinged onto intricate iron work with shiny brass hardware. The houses stand three or four stories high. Each one is unique in color and design. Towering over the townhouses, stands the fifteen-story Barbizon Hotel for Women. After we peeked in the Lobby, the three of us talked about what it would be like to live at the Barbizon.

Leonora showed us an entrance to Central Park on Fifth Avenue and Sixty-Fourth Street. We descended the steps, and, within minutes, we found ourselves in the heart of the Central Park Zoo. We explored the park as far as the fountain sculpture of the Angel of the Waters, and rested by the lake.

Celestina told Leonora that she was attending Bellevue Nursing School, but had recently transferred from Teachers College. Leonora appeared to be somewhat in awe of us, and poured her heart out. She is bored at home with nothing to do except help the housemaid and do her embroidery. She yearns to become a teacher, but her father doesn't believe in women working. Her father won't allow her to work in his store, but the young woman appears determined. It is her intention to apply for a sales position at Bonwit-Teller's. After that, she plans to attend Hunter College, which is only four blocks from the shoe store.

After we rested, we exited the park on Seventy-Second Street. I noticed that the park is beginning to look a bit shabby with many overgrown trees and tall grasses that are in need of a good cutting.

We walked on Fifth Avenue until we reached Sixty-Fourth Street. Each block on that street is unique and lovelier than the last. Ornate lampposts and trees line the entire street. The houses are adorned with corbels and brass embellishments. Some have window boxes overflowing with ivy, and others have planters filled with autumn-color chrysanthemums posted at their entry doors. Windows are every shape and size: oval, arched, and bayed. Some are trimmed with white shutters. Others open up to romantic black iron balconies.

After we left Leonora at the shoe store, Celestina and I caught the Fifty-Ninth Street Uptown El to go to our brother's for supper. While we were on the elevated train, we could actually see through the train windows into people's apartments. We discussed how differently the rich and the poor live in the same city. I told her that I had visited two sharply different neighborhoods in two days. They are in striking contrast to each other. I imagine a neighborhood should be safe and clean, but doesn't have to be quite as elaborate as the Upper East Side.

I had an enjoyable day off, and it was good to get away from the hospital for a short time. As you know, we had a very hectic summer at Ellis Island Hospital. Activity at the hospital is finally slowing down, and the pace is gradually returning to normal. I will miss living on the island and looking out onto the harbor lights in the evening, but, for me, it's time to step off the island, out of Lady Liberty's protective shell. Yes, I am ready to proceed with a leap of faith, and go out into the real world.

Sending my best wishes for a speedy recovery,

Love and kisses,

Angie

XXX

Chapter Fourteen

❧

November 9, 1924
11:30 AM (11:30)

She'll buy brand new shoes for her feet,
And repair the old ones across the street.

Leonora examined herself in her mother's cheval mirror. Her dark black ringlets fell past her shoulders. She tied them back with a thick silk bow. She was four feet, eleven and a half inches tall. Always trying to reach five feet, she stretched up in an attempt to gain the elusive half-inch. Although she would have preferred to wear a more stylish chemise dress, the high-neck, long-sleeve dress she chose was perfect for her day's objective.

Before leaving the bedroom, she straightened the delicate pleats of her pink taffeta dress, and headed off to the dining room at the end of the hall. There, Millie, the family's maid, was setting the table for the midday meal.

Leonora politely asked, "May I help you set the table, Millie?"

"Sure, Missy, whatever you want. Here you go, now." Millie handed the sterling silver knives and forks to the young woman. "There's plenty more work for me in the kitchen before I put dinner on the table."

Leonora carefully placed the silverware at each place setting, folding the linen napkins with a twist and a turn. She wanted everything perfect in preparation for dinner with her parents.

Her father was a short, highly-excitable man who could easily get upset and was often prone to outbursts. Once irritated, Leonora and her mother prepared themselves for endless lectures on anything and everything that happened to annoy him at that particular moment. He would gesture wildly with his hands, and talk on and on. It was always the littlest things that set him off, like his rolls being a bit too crusty because Millie kept them in the oven a minute too long, or the smallest spot of lint on the luxurious Persian carpet. Sometimes, Leonora liked to guess what would be the catalyst of his daily theatrics. On that day, she needed things to be in order so that he would remain calm and quiet. She wanted to have a serious talk with him.

Eugenio Bartoli made custom-made shoes in his shoe store on the ground floor, and lived with his family on the fourth floor of the building he owned. As a young boy, he emigrated from Naples after completing his apprenticeship as a trade shoemaker. Upon his arrival in New York, he settled downtown among his friends, *paisans,* Napolitano countrymen. There, he made shoes in the evening in a small shared tenement. He sold the shoes from a pushcart during the day. Although rough on the exterior, Eugenio had a soft heart. He often accepted trades and barters for his quality shoes. As each year passed, he found it increasingly difficult to make ends meet. He discovered that the immigrants wore their shoes until holes appeared in the soles. They covered the holes with cardboard and newspaper. New shoes were the last thing they considered buying with their hard-earned money. Food and drink were the priority of the day.

After three years of struggling, Eugenio began to explore store locations throughout the city. During his search, he observed that wealthy people owned more than simply one pair of shoes. He decided, right there and then, that he would sell his top-quality shoes to the city's uptown elite. From that time on, he saved every cent he earned, eating only one meal of bread and soup a day. He often said, "When I sell-a downtown, I make-a no money!"

He used his meager savings to rent a small storefront on the outskirts of New York's fashionable Upper East Side. At night, he slept in a tiny, curtained-off corner of the rental space.

As word of mouth about his craftsmanship spread, his business grew. Soon, he was able to buy a four-story apartment building on Third Avenue. Reserving the ground floor and basement for his thriving enterprise, he added to his income by renting the second and third floor apartments. He saved the top floor of the building for the family he planned to have one day.

Thirty years later, Eugenio Bartoli was a prosperous businessman who advertised that he made the best shoes in the city. Each day, he closed his store at noon to lunch with his wife and daughter. Leonora could hear him slowly beginning to climb the three flights of stairs, stopping at each landing to catch his breath, until he reached the family's top-floor apartment.

To Leonora's relief, her father entered the apartment in a pleasant, jovial mood, boasting that he had written five orders for custom shoes that morning. He complimented Millie on the sausages and peppers that she prepared. He stuffed the sausages into her freshly-baked rolls, and smothered them with fried peppers and onions dripping in olive oil.

When Millie served Mr. Bartoli his demi-tasse of expresso with a thin twist of lemon peel, he took a sip and leaned back in his chair.

With a smile, Leonora offered him an almond biscotti. "Ah," he sighed. She decided this was her opportunity to speak.

"Papa, I would like a sales position in your store."

"How many times you talk about this?"

"But, Papa…"

"How many times, I say no! No daughter of mine is gonna-sell-a shoes!"

"Well, then, I should like to discuss plans for your store."

"Why you bother with my store? You be a good girl. Help your mama. She needs you to help her."

"I've thought of a plan to increase your business."

"Increase business? I have enough business."

"But Papa, every business must grow."

"Leonora, you talk-a-nonsense. I do all that. Women have no head for business."

"Papa, remember the nurse who came to order shoes. You know the one. She is coming to pick up her shoes this afternoon. She works all day on her feet. She needed a good pair of shoes. I was thinking that all nurses need good shoes for their feet."

"Yes, but only one thing, they can't afford to pay the price. So, you see, they no buy from me. I sell to rich people."

"Well, I was thinking. Perhaps, you could make a shoe specifically for nurses, not custom like you do, but a generic white nursing shoe of good quality. Perhaps, you can sell the shoe at a cheaper price."

"Cheaper shoes? Cheaper price? I make-a the best shoes. I go out of business if I make-a cheap shoes."

"Maybe you can sell your shoes to nurses at a discount."

"What? You want-a-me to sell my shoes for cheap? Next, you will be telling me to give away the shoes for free."

"No, Papa. Think about it. The nurses will talk to each other and tell other nurses. You will acquire more customers. Soon, your business will double."

"Only one thing, I already have a good business with customers coming and going. No need to change. Leonora, don't think so much. Help Mama more. Do your embroidery. Prepare your hope chest."

"I do not need a hope chest, Papa. That is an old-fashioned custom."

"You will need a hope chest when I find you a nice-a Napolitano boy to marry."

"No, Papa. I am not marrying a boy from Napoli!"

"I see you look at the boy across the street, the shoe repairman's son. What's-a-his name, Alonzo? He only fix shoes. He don't make-a shoes. I find you a good husband. You marry up-a, not down."

"His name is not Alonzo, Papa. His name is Alfonso. He is a very intelligent boy. He is going to night school. I am not going to marry. I want to be a career woman."

"It's-a good that you have no ideas about him. He's-a no good enough for you."

"Papa, may I come down to help you wait on the nurse when she comes into the store this afternoon?"

"How many times I have to tell you…NO!" He shouted, slapping the table with his fist.

"Please let me wait on her this one time. Please, Papa, please."

"How many times you ask me, over and over?"

Leonora persisted. "Just this one time, let me wait on her. P-l-e-a-s-e, Papa."

"Why is this so important? Fine, if it makes you happy, fine. You wrap up her shoes when she comes. They're already paid for…but only this one time.

"Really, Papa? I can? Oh, Papa, can I be excused?"

"Go, Leonora, I meet-a-you downstairs."

Leonora kissed him on the cheek and ran off. Eugenio shook his head. As his face reddened, his wife braced herself for a lecture. "Mama, you need-a-control that girl. How many times I tell-a-you that school put too many ideas in her head. All this trouble started when women got-a-the vote!"

Leonora was waiting at the front door of the Bartoli Shoe Store when Angie arrived. "Good Afternoon, Miss Bosco. How are you today?"

"Very well, Miss Bartoli, and how are you? It's nice to see you again."

"It looks a little overcast. It's good that you brought an umbrella with you."

"I did. It looks like it will rain any minute now. I'm glad I got here before it started."

"Your shoes are ready." Leonora said, proudly, as she opened the shoebox on the counter. "Here they are."

"Do let me see. They are beautiful."

Eugenio Bartoli stood behind the counter. "I'm glad you like them. I make-a-the best, you know."

"Papa! Miss Bosco, sit here. Try them on. I'll help you."

Angie sat down. Leonora knelt, and used a shoehorn to help Angie into the new shoe. Angie stood. She walked in a circle. "Oh my, they look very stylish, and they are so comfortable."

From behind the counter, Mr. Bartoli replied, "You have high arches. I raised the arches in the shoes for you to have good support. See my slogan." He showed Angie his business letterhead. His logo was a picture of a hand firmly supporting the arch of a foot.

"Yes, that's exactly how it feels, Mr. Bartoli."

"Why you no order the other pair of shoes like I tell-a-you last time? Your friend, the bride, paid for two pair."

"I don't know. I guess it seemed extravagant."

"Extravagant? You need-a-good shoes with all the work you do. Why, look at these!" He picked up the shoes Angie had been wearing and shook his head. "You need-a-new heels on these shoes, Miss."

"Can you fix them?"

"I no repair shoes. I make-a-shoes." Eugenio said, proudly. "You go across the street. The man there, he fix them, but that's all he can do. He only fix-a-shoes."

"Papa!"

"What you need is a good pair of shoes, not to fix the old ones. I tell-a-you what I do. You have nurse friends? You tell your friends to come to my store. I sell them shoes at a discount. You tell the nurses about my shoes. I make-a-them the best nursing shoes to work in. I give them a good price, too."

"Really, Mr. Bartoli? I will tell everyone I work with. They all need good shoes."

"You make-a-my business better that way. You tell the others."

"PAPA!"

"Sh! Sh! Leonora, be-a-good girl, wrap up the shoes for the nice-a-lady."

Mr. Bartoli shook hands with Angie. "Nice to see you, Miss. You come again. I have work to do now." He retreated into the shop room in the back of the store.

Leonora neatly wrapped up the new shoes in brown paper, tying the package with a white cord. She handed it to Angie and said, "Miss Bosco, I wanted to tell you that I've applied to Hunter College for admission next year."

"Really? That's wonderful. Does your father approve?"

"I haven't told him. I'm waiting for the right moment."

"Teaching is a noble career. I am certain he will approve."

"He doesn't believe in women working."

"Miss Bartoli, I have an idea."

"Call me *Leonora*."

"Well, then, you must call me *Angie*. I know that your father doesn't want you to work. Do you think he would approve of you volunteering? Would you be interested in volunteer work before you start college?"

"Oh, yes, I would. Papa might allow me to volunteer for the right cause."

"We will be opening a neighborhood clinic next year. We are in need of volunteers to watch children during the day. It would give you some teaching experience. Would you be interested?"

"I am interested, Angie. I would love that."

"The clinic is opening in January. However, it's across the bridge in Brooklyn. Would that be too far to travel?"

"No, I can take the train. It's a wonderful idea. When can I start?"

"I'll write you with the details."

Leonora laughed. "The timing is perfect. I may need until January to convince my father."

"I am so pleased, Leonora."

"Do you still want to fix your shoes today? The shoemaker across the street will make new heels for you while you wait. Ask for Alfonso. He will do a good job for you, and give you a good price, too. Here, I'll show you where the store is located."

Leonora walked Angie to the door, and opened it. She pointed to the repair shop across the street. "See, the store is right there...next to the drugstore."

A handsome young man was standing in front of the door of the repair shop. He looked up and waved. Leonora blushed the color of her pink dress. After a moment, she returned his wave and said, "On second thought, where are my manners? I should accompany you across the street and introduce you to Alfonso. Come, Angie, follow me."

Chapter Fifteen

November 27, 1924

Thanksgiving

Cherish the gifts that come in life,
Accept the blessings that are poured.
Go and happily live your life,
With a heart that is adored.

"Hi, Miss Angie, are you House Supervisor today?"

"Yes, Myrtle, Miss Elsie has the holiday off. Sister decided to rotate the chief nurses so that we each get the experience of house supervision."

"Yes, I know, I haven't had a turn yet. How's it going?"

"Only one small crisis this morning, and I was able to handle it without involving Sister Gwendolyn. How is everything on your unit today?"

"The children are all washed and ready for lunch, but the meal trays haven't arrived. Dietary is a little late." Miss Myrtle reported.

The children were seated at a long table, impatiently waiting for their food. Angie greeted them, "Hello, Children, Happy Thanksgiving to all of you."

"Hello, Miss Angie. Tell us the story of Thanksgiving again, please. Tell us the story you told us yesterday, Miss Angie."

"Okay, I haven't much time, but, let's see, where shall I begin? Three hundred years ago, the Pilgrims sailed from England across the Atlantic Ocean."

"Like us, Miss Angie?"

"Yes, but their ship was not as big as your steamships. It was much smaller. It was a sailing ship, called the Mayflower."

"Did it carry a thousand people?"

"No, the ship could only carry a hundred people."

"When they came to New York, did the Pilgrims see the Statue of Liberty?"

"No, Lady Liberty was not here at that time. In fact, the city wasn't even here. When the Pilgrims landed in Plymouth, they found only beaches and forests."

"If nothing was here, why did they come?"

"The Pilgrims came for the freedom to practice their religious beliefs. Soon, they met the Indians who lived in the woods."

"Were they wild Indians?"

"No, luckily, the Indians were friendly Indians. They were the Wampanoag Indians from Massachusetts."

"Where is that?"

Miss Angie answered them. "It is a state north of New York." She continued, "The winter they landed was a very, very cold one. Everyone was hungry. Many people got sick. In the spring, the Indians showed the Pilgrims how to fish, and how to hunt for deer, duck, and wild turkeys. They taught them how to plant seeds to grow vegetables. The Pilgrims did what the Indians taught them. When their crops grew, the Pilgrims were so grateful for their bountiful harvest that they invited the Indians to celebrate with them. They cooked the fish they had caught, and roasted the fowl they had hunted. They prepared a feast using all the vegetables they had grown: potatoes, squash, and corn. On Thanksgiving Day in America, we share a meal of turkey, mashed potatoes and vegetables with our friends and family. Like the Pilgrims, we give thanks for our blessings. We celebrate the holiday of Thanksgiving in honor of that first Thanksgiving Day."

Miss Angie's story was interrupted by a clatter in the corridor. "Listen, children, I do believe your Thanksgiving meal is on its way to you right now."

On cue, the dietary aide came into the Children's Ward, rolling in the lunch trays. While lunch was being served, the volunteer choir from the Immigrant Aid Society arrived to entertain the children.

Angie slipped out into the corridor to complete her rounds. As she turned the corner, she ran straight into Dr. Goodwin. "Hi, Angie, Happy Thanksgiving, how's your day going?"

"Nothing unusual, everything has been routine. How's yours?"

"Quiet. We are all set for this evening, Angie."

"I'm looking forward to it. Are you sure we will be back in time to catch the last ferry?"

"Positive, don't worry about a thing. All you have to do is meet me right here at twenty minutes past seven."

"As long as there are no emergencies, I'll be here, on time, and ready to go."

"Right, let's hope everything stays as quiet as it is. Do you have time for lunch?"

"No, I'm on my way to the CD hospital. I'm still on rounds."

"Until this evening, then..."

"Yes, until then."

Angie looked out the window. The day appeared gray and overcast. She took the enclosed pathway to the Contagious Disease Hospital which was located on the outskirts of the island. The corridor proved to be drafty and cold. She wished she had worn her wool cape. Her first stop was to the Men's Isolation Wards. She gowned up and found Miss Sarah.

"Happy Thanksgiving, Sarah, how are you today?"

"Not too busy, but Mr. Stewart has taken a turn for the worse."

"I'm not familiar with his case."

"He's the young man from Australia who was detained at the Registry last week. He has Scarlet Fever."

"Oh, yes, I remember. He forgot his passport on the ship."

"Apparently, he was coming to America to teach in Minnesota for a year. His family arranged for his internship. They bought him a first-class ticket. Deciding to save money, he cashed in his first-class ticket and purchased a cheaper one in steerage. On the day his ship landed, he was so excited to disembark that he forgot his passport and introduction papers. He left them on the ship, and wasn't allowed to return to retrieve them. He was detained at the Registry for three days, waiting for his story to be verified. However, while in detention, he came down with a fever."

"How is he now?"

"Still spiking a high fever, it goes up and down. The doctors ordered aspirin and alcohol rubs. I'm doing my best. He is dehydrated, and having difficulty swallowing. I'm giving him ice chips. I'm expecting the physicians to come here on their rounds any minute now."

"Sarah, I'll find them, and ask them to come, stat."

"Thanks, Angie."

Angie located the attending physicians on the next ward, and escorted them to Miss Sarah. When Angie was confident Miss Sarah had the assistance she needed, she continued with her Hospital Rounds.

Throughout the day, she met with family members who were visiting patients. She assisted with patient discharges, and acted as the liaison for the volunteers who were entertaining on the wards. Her only challenging task of the day was to assist an undertaker in locating a deceased body in the morgue. Because the morgue attendants had been given the holiday off, Miss Angie was called upon to open the morgue with her house keys. She needed to correctly identify the body. In order to do this, she was required to check the toe-tags of the corpses until she found the appropriate one. She felt uncomfortable doing this, but she braced herself and did what was expected of her.

Except for the news that Mr. Stewart was growing increasingly uncomfortable and becoming delirious, evening report to Miss Elizabeth was relatively uneventful. After reporting off, Angie had only minutes to change out of her nursing uniform before meeting Abe at their designated meeting spot.

Hand-in-hand, Angie and Abe hurried down to the quay. When they arrived, a small group of men were already assembled. They were waiting for Rudwick, the Assistant Harbor Deputy. When he pulled up to the dock in the motorboat, everyone hopped aboard.

During the boat ride, Angie asked Abe to review the names of his family whom she would be meeting that evening. Abe began, "My younger brother, Sam, will be picking us up in his Hudson. He's the bachelor-undertaker I told you about."

"Yes, I remember."

"My sisters are Flora, Etta, and Giselle. The oldest is Flora. Mama calls her by her real name which is Florentina. She's married to Dominick. They have three boys: Dom Junior, Danny and Paulie. My middle sister, Concetta, is called Etta, for short. She's married to Aldo. They have twin girls, Linda and Laura. Gisella, or Giselle as I call her, married Sergio two years ago. They have a baby girl, named Ellie."

Twenty minutes later, the boat landed. The small group disembarked at a deserted dock in the Red Hook section of Brooklyn. As planned, Abe's brother, Sam, was waiting for them. Sam was a handsome man who bore a strong resemblance to his older brother. He called out to Angie and Abe when he spotted them, "Here I am, Abe. Your coach is ready and waiting to whisk you away."

The two brothers hugged and kissed each other twice, once on each cheek.

"Thanks for coming, Sam. I want to introduce you to Angie. Angie, this is my brother, Sam."

"It's a pleasure, Angie. Abe's told us so much about you."

"Thank you, Sam. He's told me about you, too. It's nice to finally meet you."

"Well, off we go, Folks! The family has been eyeing the Thanksgiving desserts all afternoon, but Mama wouldn't let us touch a crumb until after you arrived."

When they reached Williamsburg, Abe looked disappointed. "I was hoping I could show you some of the sights, Angie, but it's far too dark to see anything noteworthy tonight. Sam, how about we take Angie on a motor tour of Brooklyn on our next day off?"

"Sure thing, I'll come into the city and pick you up."

Sam continued to drive east where the rows of attached town-houses and apartment buildings of Williamsburg turned into a wide boulevard of mini-mansions. Abe announced, proudly, "This is Bushwick Avenue."

"Oh, I've heard about this area. It's very fashionable, isn't it? I've always wanted to come here."

Sam explained, "Many of these houses were built by German brewers who came to Brooklyn to make beer."

"Now, doctors, lawyers, and even undertakers live here," Sam added.

"Does that mean you live here, too?"

"Yes, Walter and Mama live only minutes from here. They bought the house from a brewer who moved his entire enterprise to Canada when he realized prohibition was here to stay."

The enormous homes on Bushwick Avenue were aglow with electric lights, both inside and out. Sturdy brick Colonials, adorned with fat, white columns and circular entryways, were surrounded by beautiful gardens. Colorful Victorian-style homes with intricate turrets and gables were tucked behind wrought-iron fences.

"Here we are," Sam announced as he slowed down. Abe jumped out of the car to open the double wrought-iron gates. They followed a brightly-lit driveway, lined with autumn-colored mums. The house stood three stories high and had a steeple-topped turret on its southwest corner. Sam drove right up to the front of the house.

Abe's family came out onto the porch to greet them. The porch wrapped around the circumference of the house. Tagging along behind Mama and Walter, were Abe's three sisters, their husbands, and their children. Angie was greeted by dozens of double kisses and hugs. She felt instantly welcome and comfortable with the family as they introduced themselves to her.

Angie and Abe were ushered into the Dining Room. "Come. Sit. Sit. We have dinner ready for you." Mama said, "After you eat, we will all sit down and have dessert together. Did you eat anything at all today? Here, I kept everything warm for you." She served Angie and Abe huge plates of turkey, mashed potatoes, string beans, cranberry sauce and stuffing, all dripping in home-made gravy.

"Your home is beautiful, Mrs. Myers."

"Angelina, everyone calls me *Mama Myers*. You call me that, too."

"Thank-you, I always wondered what those turret rooms were like on the inside."

"After you eat, I'll show you. The one on the first floor is a reading room."

"Mama's sewing room is in the turret on the second floor," Abe added.

"I converted the third one into a playroom for the children." Turning to Abe, Mama asked, "Abe, did you show Angelina our Church?"

"No, we didn't have time, Mama."

"When you leave, you pass it, show her St. Barbara's."

Angie looked at Abe. Abe explained. "We have a beautiful church three blocks away. The breweries donated large sums of money. The one that donated the land insisted that they name the church after Saint Barbara. Coincidentally, his wife and daughter were both named Barbara. The church was completed a little over a decade ago. It's made of yellow brick and trimmed in white limestone. Stained glass windows and frescos of angels, blue skies, and pink clouds are painted on the walls and ceiling. Some call it a cathedral. We won't have time to go inside tonight, but we will try to pass by on our way back to the city. I promise, Mama."

"Were there many breweries in Brooklyn?"

"Yes, there were forty-eight before the eighteenth amendment put them out of business."

After Angie and Abe ate, the family gathered around the dining room table for dessert of pumpkin pie, apple pie, berry pie, pignoli cookies, and cannoli pastries.

Dominick Junior was excited. "Uncle Abe, we went to the parade today."

"Where was that?"

Flora explained, "We took the boys into the city this morning. Macy's Department Store sponsored a big parade today, like the Gimbel's Parade in Philadelphia."

Danny added, "It was terrific. We dressed up like hobos and saw Santa Claus."

"Was Santa in the parade, too?"

"No, Uncle Abe, he was in Macy's store window. He waved to us at the end of the parade."

"There were marching bands, and floats...," Flora said.

"...and animals from the zoo!" Paulie added, "I dressed up as a sailor."

"I'm sorry I missed your costumes."

"The parade was such a success that there's talk they will repeat it next year."

"Did you get many treats this morning?"

"Oh, yes, Uncle Abe. We took Laura and Linda with us. They were gypsies."

Suddenly, Sam looked up at the clock on the mantle, "Look at the time. It's after eleven. We're late. It's past the usual time we leave. We'll have to hurry."

"So soon? There's never enough time with you, Abraham, always coming and going, rushing in and out. Next time, Angelina, you come and stay awhile. You come and go to church with us, too."

"Yes, I will. Thank you for having me."

Sam hurried back to Manhattan as fast as he could drive. The ferry boat was just about to raise its ramp when Angie and Abe hopped aboard. As they were finding a seat, the ferry Captain made an announcement on his loudspeaker. "The King and Queen have finally arrived. We are now ready to leave." Everyone onboard cheered.

Abe walked Angie to the Nurses' Residence Cottage. As Angie approached the Cottage, she noticed the Living Room lights were on. "Good Night, Abe. I had a wonderful time. I loved meeting your family."

Abe leaned down and kissed Angie once, then again, passionately. They embraced.

"I don't want to let go," Abe whispered.

"Me too, Abe, but I think Sister may be waiting up for me. I must go."

"Until tomorrow then, reluctantly I leave you and say good-night, Angie."

"Night, Abe. See you tomorrow."

Angie opened the front door to the Cottage. She found Sarah sitting by the Living Room fireplace, staring into the fire. Her eyes were red and puffy. She looked like she had been crying.

"What's wrong, Sarah? Are you okay?"

"No, Angie. Mr. Stewart died three hours ago."

"Oh, no, how awful."

"The irony is that he would have never caught Scarlet Fever, if he hadn't been detained at the Registry. He would have never been detained, if he hadn't forgotten his passport on the ship."

"He could have avoided the Ellis Island screening procedure altogether, if he hadn't traded in his first-class ticket for one in steerage."

"I stayed late, after my shift ended, to try to lower his fever."

"How tragic for him, and his family, and here I was…out…having fun."

"You deserve to have fun, Angie. The doctors said that there was nothing more that we could do for him."

"I know, but I always feel a little guilty having fun when I know someone is suffering."

"Sometimes, I feel like that, too."

"Did you eat? Can I get you a cup of tea or anything?"

"No, Angie, just your being here helps. I think I'd better try to go to sleep soon. I have to work tomorrow."

"Me, too, Sarah, but let me make you a little tea and toast. Then, I'll go up with you and help you into bed. We've both had a very long day."

Chapter Sixteen

❧

December 24, 1924

Christmas Eve

Now it's your turn for contentment and pure bliss.
Get ready to experience the happiness you missed.

When Dr. Abraham Goodwin rushed through the doors of Ward 213 at 15:00 hours, Angie prepared herself for an emergency. She took a deep breath to steady herself.

Dr. Goodwin ran straight to Miss Angie. "Angie, Angie, I've been looking all over the hospital for you."

"I can imagine. I was supposed to be working on the South Wing, but I was floated here today."

"I have news! Father Benedetto has found the perfect location for the clinic."

"Where?"

"It's across the street from the Catholic school on Johnson Avenue, directly in back of the church."

"How wonderful! When can we see it?"

"Tonight."

"Tonight? It's Christmas Eve."

"The landlord is going out of town for Christmas weekend. He won't be back until Monday. That's five days from now. If the place is as good as Father says, we could firm up the deal before Christmas. The landlord left the key with Father. We could see it after work. If we approve, Father will contact the landlord before he leaves."

"I planned to go to my brother's house tonight after work. It's my very first Christmas off since I started working at Ellis. I thought I would leave right after work and sleep over. I want to be there when the children open their presents on Christmas morning."

"Can't we do both?" Abe asked.

"What do you mean?"

"Come with me to Williamsburg after work. Sam will pick us up. After we see the rental space, Sam and I will drive you uptown to your brother's house."

"You mean that?"

"Yes, of course, we'll deliver you to your brother's before Santa comes down the chimney. I promise."

"That might work, but there's so many holiday activities scheduled for today. I usually have to work late. I might not be able to leave at seven."

"Well, then, let's plan on catching the eight o'clock ferry. Sam will be waiting for us at the ferry building at 8:20. We'll be in Williamsburg before nine."

"Isn't that too late?"

"It's never too late when electricity is running."

"I'll do my best to be as early as I can. If something comes up, promise me you'll go without me."

"Not a chance. We're in this together. We both have to approve. It's all or nothing."

"You could go yourself to see it tonight. I could go on Monday."

"Nope, it's either both of us together tonight or both of us on Monday."

"Really? Okay, you got yourself a deal."

"I'll meet you at the quay at eight. If you can't make it, we'll skip it. We'll wait until Monday evening. Let's shake on it."

"Okay, Doc," Angie said, shaking his hand. "I'll try my best to be on time. I'm gathering the patients now to take them down to the Christmas Eve pageant. After that, there's Twilight Christmas Caroling. I'll organize my nursing notes during the shows."

"Great! See you later." Dr. Goodwin hurried out of the ward. When he reached the doorway, he turned and said, "Oh, I almost forgot..."

"What's that, Doctor?"

"Merry Christmas Eve, Angie!"

Angie smiled. "Merry Christmas Eve, Abe!"

"Until eight," Abe called out, before he disappeared down the hall.

Angie began to plan the remainder of her twelve-hour shift immediately after he left. She made a list of the things she had to do. In order to be on the eight pm ferry, she had five hours to do her charting, give report, run to the Nurses' Residence Cottage, change out of her uniform, and pack up her satchel with the Christmas presents for all her nieces and nephews.

A familiar voice inside her head said, "Impossible, Miss Angie, you won't make it on time. There's too much to do today."

Then, Angie asked herself: *What would Adeline do? Let me see...she'd say...shake a leg, Angie Girl, rise up fearlessly to this challenge. If need be, work a little harder, work a little faster, get the job done, and get going.*

Angie chose to listen to Adeline's voice instead of her own. She called for assistance to help escort the ambulatory patients to the auditorium for the Christmas pageant. She asked Miss Martha to keep a watchful eye on her patients during the show. She returned to the unit, organized the medication and treatment cards, and prepared another to-do list. There were still a number of bedridden patients on the unit. She would start their dressing changes. When Santa came to entertain them, she would begin her charting. Then, at the end of her shift, she would simply close her charts by adding the events of the last hour and signing off.

To her surprise, everything fell seamlessly into place. According to plan, Angie and Abe met at the dock. They caught the eight pm ferry with time to spare. Sam was waiting at Battery Park with the Hudson running.

"I'm glad to see you. Quite frankly, I expected you to be a little late tonight." Sam said, when they jumped into the car.

"Merry Christmas, Sam," said Angie. "Thanks for coming."

"Merry Christmas, Angie, my pleasure. It's good to see you again."

"Thanks again, Sam," Abe said.

In only ten minutes, they were crossing The Williamsburg Bridge. Suddenly, Sam hit his forehead with the palm of his hand. "Whoops, I almost forgot, I'm short one present. After I drop the two of you off, mind if I drive over to William's Rexall Pharmacy to buy a gift? I'll be back at nine-thirty. After that, we'll all go to Mama's. Let's synchronize our watches."

"Sam, I promised Angie we would take her straight to her brother's house."

"Okay with me, but don't you want to come over, Angie? Mama is looking forward to seeing you."

105

"Yes, of course, I do. When I rang up my brother at his store this afternoon, he said they were going to leave at eleven for Midnight Mass. I told him I wanted to see the rental and visit with your Mother. My brother said that he would expect us for the Seven-Fishes Buffet after Midnight Mass. Would that be too late to drive me?"

"Not for me. It's a perfect excuse to miss Midnight Mass."

"Well then, it looks like we have a plan."

When Sam's car pulled up to the brick building on Johnson Avenue at a quarter to nine, Father Benedetto was waiting for them with the keys. "You're right on time, Doctor. Here are the keys. Drop them off at the Rectory when you're finished."

"Aren't you coming with us?"

"Son, hasn't anyone told you that it's Christmas Eve? Many a priest is busier than Santa on a night like this." Father said, as he scampered away.

Sam laughed, "Folks, I'm off, too. I'll be back in forty-five. Merry Christmas to all, and to all a good night! Ho! Ho! Ho!"

Angie and Abe were left standing on the sidewalk.

"Let's go in. The suspense is killing me."

Abe opened the door. Angie found the electric light switch, and pushed the button. When she turned on the lights, they found them-selves in the Living Room of a ground-floor apartment. Abe studied the room. Three bay windows faced Johnson Avenue. The kitchen and bathroom were on their left. Behind the living room were three large bedrooms in a row. A small corner room was tucked away on the side of the last bedroom."

"Perfect, isn't it?"

"Yes, I agree. Let's see what's in here?"

They entered a spacious kitchen. "This will certainly double as our Utility Room. It looks as though there's ample cabinet space for storage, too."

"Do you envision the Living Room as our Reception Room, Angie?"

"I do, and the three back bedrooms will make excellent examination rooms, won't they? Perhaps, I can find someone with a sewing machine. I can make privacy drapes."

"I agree. Mama and Flora offered to sew draperies for our clinic."

"I was thinking that the last room could be used for classes or childcare." Angie said.

"Father said that there are two small one-bedroom apartments upstairs, as well."

"Are they vacant?"

"They're occupied now, but they will be available in September. Let's go up and explore. I have the keys."

They went out into the hallway, and climbed up one flight of stairs. The first door they faced was the door to the rear apartment. They opened the door and entered. It was a small three-room apartment with a large kitchen, a living room and a bedroom. Each room was filled with boxed crates. From the window, they looked down to see a cement driveway leading to a horse stable in the back of the building.

"No one seems to be living here. This is a business of some kind."

"Father said that they are a group of volunteers who ship supplies to the missions in South America."

An identical apartment in the front of the building faced Johnson Avenue. The single bedroom was filled with boxes and crates. Six bentwood chairs formed a circle in the living room. Two chairs were set aside by the window facing the street. Moonlight shone on a bouquet of red roses that had been carefully placed on a crate.

"Someone was just here. Perhaps, there was a meeting. Oh, look, roses, how beautiful. Imagine roses in the middle of the winter. Someone special will be receiving them tonight for Christmas Eve. What a lovely present!"

"You are, Angie. They are for you."

"Me? How? Why?"

"Sam came this afternoon before he left for the City. He bought them from the florist. I asked him to."

Angie picked up the bouquet and held it close to her heart. "How thoughtful, Abe. They're exquisite."

"I wanted this moment to be memorable."

"It is. It's the first time we stepped foot in the clinic." Angie said.

"Yes, but I wanted this moment to be memorable for another reason. You see, I was thinking...when Father said the apartments would be available in September. I was thinking..."

"Yes, I was thinking, too, Abe. We might be ready to open a child-care center in September."

"No, I mean, yes, of course, we can use one of the apartments for the clinic but the other...this one...we could. Sit here, Angie, right here in the moonlight, you look beautiful tonight."

"Thank you, Abe."

"Well, there's no way to do this but to do this." When Angie sat down, Abe knelt on one knee. He pulled a black velvet box from his pocket. "Angie would you consider marrying me in September?"

Angie found herself unable to speak. "I..." Tears began to roll down her cheeks. "I..."

"No, Angie, don't cry. I didn't mean to upset you."

Suddenly, a whisper, "Yes, Abe, of course...of course, I will marry you."

Instinctively, Abe stood, hugged Angie and kissed her in the moonlight. They were locked in an embrace when, from the hallway below, they heard, "I'm back, folks! Is anyone home? Does someone need a ride?"

Sam bounced up the stairs, two at a time. Through the open door, he saw Angie and Abe smiling, arm-in-arm.

"Well, I see you popped the question."

"I did, Sam."

"What was the answer?"

Angie grinned. "Sam, you know the answer was 'yes'. I heard you were in on this, too."

"I was following orders from my big brother. He planned it last night after Father called him. I only delivered the flowers."

Abe explained, "Yesterday afternoon, Father called about the rental. When the landlord told him that the apartment upstairs would be available, I started to think. I sent Sam to the florist. I was going to propose on Christmas morning, but tonight seemed like the right night."

"Yes, it is a very special night...full of surprises."

"Come on, let's spread the news! Shout it from the rooftops!"

"I'll have to tell my brothers. Can we still go to see them tonight?" Angie asked.

"Yes, of course, and they already know."

"What?"

"I met Giacomo and Santino at Katz's Delicatessen last month. I asked them for their permission to marry you."

"You did…and you didn't bring me a pastrami sandwich?"

"Okay, Lovebirds, we have quite a bit of celebrating to do tonight. Let's get on with it." Sam offered each of them one of his arms. "Shall we? This is going to be a Merry Christmas, a very Merry Christmas, indeed."

∾

Chapter Seventeen

January 1, 1925
1 AM (01:00)

Good Night, Dear Hearts, may you sleep well.
Stay safe and secure where ever you dwell.

Journal of Sister Gwendolyn Hanover
Superintendent of Nursing
Date: Wednesday, January 1, 1925
Entry Time: 01:00
Journal Notation:

Another year has come and gone. 1924 was filled with changes and challenges. It is one hour past midnight. 1925 is already presenting us with the first problem of the year. Tonight, as I look out my bedroom window from the Nurses' Residence Cottage, there is trouble brewing in the waters. I see the lights of seven ships lined up in New York harbor. There may be more behind them, but I can see only as far as the seven ships. It turns out that this unanticipated development is a direct result of the 1924 Quota Law. Let me explain.

The SS Regalia was first spotted a mile from shore the day before yesterday. It stood frozen, motionless in the water. There were no distress calls or signal lights dispatched from the steamship. This puzzled the Harbormaster who received no response to his radio messages. Suspecting a significant communication malfunction, he ordered a tugboat crew to the ship to investigate. The crew was granted permission to board. They were directed to the Captain's chambers. During their interview, the Captain explained that the steamship made the journey across the Atlantic from the Baltic in the record time of twelve days. It was scheduled to dock on New Year's Day. However, it arrived thirty-six hours early. The winds that blow from the west at this time of year had unexpectedly ceased. With no external resistance, the ship progressed faster than usual. Under different circumstances, both the Captain and crew would have celebrated this feat, which usually translates into a substantial monetary savings for the shipping line and extra shore leave for her crew. The Captain had not planned to arrive early because the immigrants onboard were all from Eastern Europe. The 1924 admission numbers for the Baltic countries had expired at the end of September. Immigrants from there had been denied admission to the United States since the beginning of October.

If the ship were to dock and register with the Harbormaster, most people on the ship would be denied admission and turned away. The ship would be forced to immediately return to Europe. The Captain's remedy was a simple one. He dropped anchor, waiting until tomorrow when the Ellis Island Registry Center officially opens with new admission numbers for 1925.

The Captain's solution is perfectly logical. It wouldn't be a problem if it were not for another ship that anchored behind the Regalia two hours later. Then, another came, and then, another. The ships dropped anchor and stood waiting, knowing that admission quota numbers would be refreshed at the beginning of each year.

No doubt, it will take all week to register the people onboard the seven ships. There isn't a thing we can do, except to prepare for an onslaught of two to three thousand immigrants registering every day this coming week. So, once again, we are facing an increase in the number of immigrants to be processed.

This time, however, after making a proper assessment, I followed my instinct. Yesterday, I directed the matrons to prepare all the hospital beds on both the North and the South Wings. As added insurance, I requested an extra laundry supply of sheets and towels. I added additional nurses on tomorrow's schedule. I believe I am prepared and ready to meet 1925 head on.

Contrary to earlier rumors, the hospital won't be closing anytime soon. There are still many immigrants arriving daily as quota numbers from Northern Europe remain high. The plan to open inspection stations at countries around the world will be a slow process. Facilities have yet to be built, policies yet to be written, and staff yet to be trained. The Commissioner is now projecting that it could take up to a decade for that to happen.

In the nursing department, changes are in the air. Miss Elsie and Miss Angie will be leaving us soon. Since Miss Elsie's arthritis has gotten the best of her, she reluctantly tendered her resignation in November. What will I ever do without her? We've worked together so well these past years. Miss Angie has accepted a leadership position at a new clinic. She is smart and capable. I know she will do well in her new post. I'll miss seeing both her serious determination and her smiling face.

As 1925 begins, I pray that the Lord will protect my *ladies-in white* from disease and injury. Like a blank slate, the year ahead is filled with possibilities.

Signed:

Sister Gwendolyn Hanover

Superintendent of Nursing, I

Ellis Island Hospital

Part Two

Williamsburg

Williamsburg, Brooklyn was settled by Dutch settlers after they bought a parcel of land from the Indians. Years later, a man named Williams was hired to plot out the land in this area. He named his project, *Williamsburg*.

Many Germans moved to this section of Brooklyn, establishing breweries in, what was then, vast farmland. During that time, a ferry carried people to and from New York City.

When the Williamsburg Bridge was built in 1903, connecting Manhattan and Brooklyn, upwardly mobile immigrants walked over the bridge and settled in Williamsburg. During the early part of the twentieth century, this section of Brooklyn was home to Irish, German, Jewish and Italian immigrants.

Chapter Eighteen

January 13, 1925
2 PM (14:00)

A house filled with laughter, music and good cheer,
Used for helping and healing, year after year.

Maureen O'Shaughnessy was a petite young lady. Thin as a rail and four-feet, ten-inches tall, she had a dainty appearance, but she was hardly delicate. Her wiry figure was lean and strong. She was a dedicated and determined nurse who always got where she was going, arriving with plenty of time to spare. That was the reason Miss Lillian Wald, Director of the Visiting Nurses at Henry Street, assigned Miss O'Shaughnessy to travel to the Williamsburg section of Brooklyn twice a week.

On Tuesdays and Thursdays, Maureen O'Shaughnessy traveled by train to Williamsburg. She persevered through the heat of summer and trudged through the cold of winter to visit her patients in the privacy of their homes. Wearing the navy-blue, double-breasted overcoat of a Visiting Nurse, Maureen's flaming copper curls bounced around her matching blue cap. The black medicine bag she carried, and the black shoes and stockings she wore, were uniform issue. The only articles of clothing not part of the official visiting nurse uniform were her galoshes. She needed to wear them that morning. It had snowed earlier. By noon, the sun melted the glistening snow. A

117

soft rain followed, turning the snow into a soupy slush. Maureen's rubber galoshes offered some protection, but moisture always managed to seep through the seams of her boots, wetting her shoes. She walked gingerly as she crossed the street, desperately trying to avoid the splashes of the passing horse-drawn carriages and automobiles. Her teeth chattered as she shivered from the cold. Her wool coat wasn't warm enough. She wished she had worn a sweater and brought a scarf along.

The Visiting Nurse Service was slowly acquiring Ford automobiles for the nurses who worked outside the city. It wouldn't be too long before she would be assigned one to use for patient visits. Maureen daydreamed of the required driving lessons she would soon be taking. Until all the Henry Street Visiting Nurses with assignments beyond the city limits were driving, Miss Wald found places for them to rest within their designated districts. Miss Wald had recently located a new clinic in Williamsburg where Maureen could write her nursing notes before returning to Henry Street.

With the thought of actually driving to her home visits in the not too distant future, Maureen suddenly got the burst of energy she needed to hop over a giant puddle. She had already completed most of her day's assignments, and was working her way to Seigel Street for her last home visit. When Maureen reached Montrose Avenue, the light misty rain turned into a downpour. The address of Nativity Settlement House and Health Clinic which Miss Wald had given her was two blocks away. Maureen revised her plan, and turned onto Johnson Avenue.

When Maureen reached the clinic and rang the doorbell, no one answered. Maureen was not one to be deterred. She looked through the window of the front door. Seeing some activity inside, she knocked loudly. An attractive woman in her late thirties came to the door.

"Good Afternoon, I'm here to see Miss Angie Bosco," Maureen said.

"Well, goodness, do get out of the rain and come in. No one should be out on a day like today. You must dry off. Here, let me help you with your coat. I'll put it near the fire to dry."

"I thought the clinic would be open."

"Not yet, the clinic opens in two weeks. Come, sit down near the fireplace."

"Are you Miss Bosco?" Maureen asked.

"No, I'll find her. Who shall I say is calling?"

"I'm Miss O'Shaughnessy from the Visiting Nurse Service."

"A visiting nurse...now, that explains why you're out roaming around town in the rain."

Dr. Goodwin's sister, Flora, ushered Maureen to a chair. As she was hanging up the wet coat, Angie entered the Living Room.

"Did I hear that we have a visitor, Flora?"

"Yes, we do, Angie. This is Miss O'Shaughnessy, a Visiting Nurse."

"How do you do, Miss O'Shaughnessy? I'm so glad to meet you. I wasn't expecting you today."

"I apologize for coming unannounced, but when the rain came down so hard, I thought I'd stop in and introduce myself. I didn't realize the clinic wasn't open. I can come back another day if today isn't convenient."

"Quite the contrary, Miss O'Shaughnessy, I'm delighted you're here. I have time today to show you around with no patients interrupting us."

"Miss Wald said that you might have a desk for me to finish my charts before heading back to Henry Street."

"Yes, I have a little desk set up in the back. Come, I'll give you a tour. Can I offer you a cup of tea first?"

The tour started in the kitchen where Angie made Maureen a cup of hot tea. "Here you go, Miss O'Shaughnessy."

"Thank you, this warm cup feels good in my hands. Please call me *Maureen*."

"Of course, and I insist that you call me *Angie*."

Angie led the way into the Reception Room where two dozen chairs were arranged in a horseshoe shape around a central desk.

"The next rooms are going to be our examination rooms. Dr. Goodwin's mother and sister are making draperies."

Two yellow drapes were already hung, separating half the room into three sections. Flora looked up. "Hello, Miss O'Shaughnessy. What do you think of the drapes?"

"They look bright and cheerful."

"Angie selected the fabric. She wants the clinic to be a warm and sunny place."

"Well done. They look very professional."

The next room was a large room with a fireplace, a room identical to the Reception Room. "We'll use this room for classes and childcare."

"That's good to hear. There are so many children left unsupervised during the day."

The last room was a small corner room, a backroom with an exit into the hallway. Dr. Goodwin had removed the door of the closet so that three desks could fit into the tiny space. Angie announced, "I know it looks a little tight, but we wanted to fit in three desks so that each of us had a place to work. We won't all be working here at the same time."

"It's perfect. It's more than I ever expected."

"Have a seat, and finish your tea. Miss Wald mentioned that you might be open to taking me on a few home visits."

"Oh, yes, anytime. I would love the company."

Angie asked, "Can you tell me about some of the cases you are following? What type of patients did you call on today?"

"There are many elderly patients who sit at home with nothing to do. There is a toddler who can't walk. His mother tied him to a bedpost to keep him safe while she went to work, and crippled him. Another family has three children with polio. Their mother stays home with them, but they won't have anything to eat if she doesn't return to work soon. A seven-year-old boy is recovering from rheumatic fever. His mother died some time ago. Poor guy is home alone during the day while his father works. I was on my way to see him when it started to pour. He is my last case of the day. There's a family with…"

Before Maureen could finish, she was interrupted by Flora. "Excuse me, Angie, Sam's here to pick us up. It's four o'clock. I don't know where the time goes."

"Thank you for coming, Flora, the drapes look beautiful…even Maureen noticed."

With the mention of her name, Maureen jumped up. "Four o'clock? I have another home visit today. I must go. Thank you for the tea."

"It was a delight to meet you. I'll look forward to having you stop in…"

"...On Tuesdays and Thursdays," Maureen added.

Flora had an idea. "Why don't you come along with us? It's still raining. My brother has the car. He will take you where you need to go."

"No, I'm only going four blocks. I don't want to impose."

"It's no imposition at all. You'll be soaked, through and through, if you don't come with us. Let my brother drop you off at your next home visit."

Angie interrupted, "Maureen, you might as well do as she says and go with them. Flora doesn't take *no* for an answer."

Flora laughed. "I don't, young lady. I insist that you come with us. Bundle up now. I'll get your coat."

The three women were putting on their coats, hats, and gloves when Sam appeared, looking dapper and carrying a giant umbrella. He looked around as if inspecting the clinic. "You're making great progress. I do believe this will be the best looking clinic on the planet earth."

"Sam, you are a flatterer, but thank you. I would like to introduce you to Maureen O'Shaughnessy, a visiting nurse. She needs a ride to Seigel and Bushwick. I told her you'd take her." Flora explained.

Sam took his hat off, and bowed. "A Visiting Nurse...how I wish I were sick so that I could be on your list of patients to visit."

Mama Myers scolded him. "Sam, behave yourself."

"Yes, of course, where are my manners? I couldn't resist. Please accept my apology. I hope I haven't offended you, Miss Shaughnessy."

Maureen laughed, "No, not at all. In fact, I hear that comment quite often."

Flora corrected Sam, "OH Shaughnessy, Sam, Miss OH Shaughnessy."

Sam graciously assisted the ladies into his Hudson. He drove four blocks and delivered Maureen to the apartment building of her next patient.

"This is it. Thank you for the ride." Maureen said.

"My pleasure, Miss Oh-Shaughnessy," Sam answered.

"Now, you will be careful when you walk to the train station." Mama Myers said, looking up at the sky. "Hopefully, it will stop raining by then."

Flora called out from the car window as Sam drove off. "Bye, I look forward to seeing you at the clinic."

When Maureen completed her visit and stepped out of the building, it was still raining heavily. Sam was waiting outside under his giant umbrella. He opened the car door for her, "Visiting Nurse Maureen Oh-Shaughnessy, the Hudson awaits!"

"How did you know I would still be here?" Maureen asked.

"I took a chance. After I dropped Mama and Flora off at home, I hurried back for you."

"You didn't have to. I could have walked to the train station."

"It's pouring out here. I didn't come to drive you to the train station. I'm driving you to Henry Street."

"No, it's out of your way."

"I insist, Miss Oh-Shaughnessy, and like my sister, Flora, I will not take *no* for an answer."

Chapter Nineteen

~

February 13, 1925
3PM (15:00)

His journey started years before,
He wanted to accomplish more.

Father Salvatore Benedetto sat in the rectory behind his massive mahogany desk sorting the afternoon mail. In the mountain of mail, piled high in his incoming mailbox, were three letters and one small package addressed to Miss Angelina Bosco. For a brief moment, he considered sending Miss Bosco's mail to Sister Mary Michael at the convent where Miss Angie was boarding. However, delivering it in person would give him another opportunity to visit Nativity House without appearing intrusive. Mail delivery was an ideal excuse. He looked out of his office window to check the weather. The day was cold and overcast. Fat dark clouds hung poised, ready to release afternoon showers. If he hurried, he would be able to reach Nativity House before the rain started.

Since The Nativity Settlement House and Health Clinic had opened its doors to the public two weeks before, Father Benedetto had taken every opportunity to visit on a daily basis. He took pride in reviewing the patient census, and was pleased with the community turnout which exceeded his expectations.

Of course, he thought, *that would be largely due to my efforts of cleverly weaving clinic announcements into my Sunday sermons.*

He took credit for encouraging his congregation to use the services of the free clinic. He wanted the Jewish and Protestants in the neighborhood to take advantage of the clinic, also. Because of this, he had met with one rabbi and two pastors, and had arranged to speak at two of their functions the following week.

He was proud of his accomplishment. A clinic for the immigrants was something he had envisioned since he was appointed pastor of Nativity Church. As a young boy, he witnessed his baby brother die of measles because his mother couldn't afford the doctor's fee.

Since becoming pastor of Nativity Church, his dream had taken five years to implement. In the beginning, the money dribbled in, small donations and broken promises, until an opportunity presented itself last summer. A business arrangement provided him with a huge windfall that was more than enough to get the clinic up and running. It could potentially finance the endeavor for three years. He had hand-picked the medical director, Abraham Goodwin, who proved to be the perfect candidate. Father had his eye on the young man since he graduated from medical school. Having spent his early years in the heart of the community, Abe Goodwin knew the neighborhood, and was sensitive to the needs of its people. He was a smart and talented physician who had successfully worked at Ellis Island Hospital for many years. Once hired, he made an excellent choice in selecting the clinic's nursing director. In Father's opinion, Nurse Angie was worth her weight in gold. Although at times, she asked far too many questions of him. Her friendly smile and easy-going manner had already won the trust of the Sisters at the convent.

Together, the doctor and nurse knew how to stretch a dollar, too. In a few short weeks, they had transformed a drab apartment into a vibrant clinic, decorating the clinic with used furniture and hand-me-downs, painting and repairing, and attracting people who eagerly volunteered their time and talent. The clinic was a happy, welcoming place. Its yellow walls were framed in wood molding painted pastel pink and baby blue. Angie herself had hand-painted a rainbow of soft pastel colors on a wall in the room she intended to use for community education classes.

The clinic was open four days during the week: Monday, Wednesday, Friday and Saturday. On Tuesday and Thursday, the doctor and nurse were available for home visits when necessary. The clinic opened from ten in the morning until two in the afternoon, and re-opened from four to eight in the evening. After assessing the needs of the community, they had decided to extend the clinic hours into the evening so that people who worked would have an opportunity to come after their workday. Mothers who were too fearful to bring their children to the clinic during the day would often come with their husbands during evening hours.

When Father entered the clinic, all was quiet. Miss Angie Bosco was industriously working at her desk during her afternoon break.

"Good Afternoon, Miss Angie, how are you? What are you working on so attentively?"

"Hello, Father, I'm making treatment cards for our patients."

"What are treatment cards?"

"When Doctor Goodwin orders a treatment for one of our patients, I will already have it written, and will be able to quickly give written instructions to our patients. For instance, here's one for impetigo rash…

For Impetigo
During the day, wash infected area every four hours.
First, wash with absorbent cotton dipped in alcohol.
Allow to air dry.
Next, wash with absorbent cotton dipped in hydrogen peroxide.
Allow to air dry. Leave uncovered.

"This one's for a headache…"

For Severe Headache
Take two Aspirin tablets every four hours.
Follow with a cup of strong coffee.
At bedtime, take two Aspirin tablets.
Coffee is not recommended before bedtime.

"Miss Angie, will you have them available in different languages for your patients who don't speak English?"

"Yes, I'm writing them in English and Italian. My former Nursing Superintendent at Ellis Island offered to help with the translations. I sent her the treatment cards in English. She is going to have them translated into Hebrew, Russian, German, and Polish."

"That's very clever of you, Miss Angie."

"I wrote up a census report for you today. We were able to treat twenty-six patients this morning: eleven upper respiratory infections, nine sore throats, three upset stomachs, one overgrown bunion, one case of the catarrh and one giant splinter wedged under a big toenail. To my surprise, I was able to successfully remove it after soaking the patient's foot in hot water."

"Good work, but it's not necessary to write up a daily report for me."

"You stop in everyday at this time and ask. So, I thought I'd have something ready for you today."

"Well, I have been very excited about the clinic, but today I came to bring you your mail. You received quite a lot of it this morning." Father said, placing the mail on Angie's desk.

"Thank you. Father, I have a question for you. I thought there would be people working upstairs, but there doesn't seem to be much activity at all. In fact, I haven't seen anyone this month."

"The agency is run by volunteers who collect clothes to ship to South America. They meet in the evening. Of course, all's quiet now, but they tell me that they're waiting for warmer weather when it's safe for their boats to maneuver the harbor. It's much too dangerous for small vessels to pass through the harbor during the winter months."

Angie looked puzzled.

Father cleared his throat, and quickly changed the subject. "Is Doctor Goodwin here?"

"Yes, he's in the bathroom, trying to fix a running toilet."

"How many times have I told him to call Luigi, the custodian at the church?"

"He said he wanted to take a look at it. He thought he could fix it with a minor adjustment."

"I think I'll see if I can offer the Doctor my assistance."

When Father left the room, Angie studied her mail. There were three letters and a package for her. It made the day feel like a holiday. She was excited to see a letter from Miss Jane Adams in Chicago. She opened it first.

February 2, 1925

Dear Miss Angelina Bosco,

I hope this letter finds you in good health. Miss Lillian Wald of Henry Street wrote me about your clinic project in Williamsburg. The beginning of a new endeavor is always a satisfying and exciting time. Miss Wald mentioned that your intention is to gradually expand the neighborhood clinic into a settlement house. I am writing to you to invite you to use me as a resource. During my thirty years at Hull House, I have come up against every conceivable hurdle and roadblock. I can help you plan or problem-solve, whatever the case may be. Throughout the years, I've been in contact with hundreds of settlement house directors. We stay connected through our newsletter. May I add your name to my list of recipients? Again, congratulations on your project. Please write with any questions or concerns you may have. Remember my three R's: Residence, Research and Reform!

Miss Jane Adams

Hull House,

Chicago, Illinois

Angie couldn't resist opening the package from Sister Hanover next. It contained a letter and the translated treatment cards that she had requested.

February 7, 1925

Dear Miss Angie,

How are you, my dear? Everyone here on Ellis Island misses you and the good doctor, too. They send their regards, along with best wishes for your continued success with the clinic. Enclosed you will find the translations of the treatment cards that you requested. I was delighted to be of assistance. The effort was coordinated by Miss Dorothy. It was a big job, but the nurses all pitched in. They each patiently worked with the appropriate translator. I know you will put them to good use.

Things are finally slowing down here on Ellis Island after an extremely busy six weeks. It seems the secret is out. Anyone coming to America will arrive at Ellis Island early in the year before their country's annual quota closes them out for the remainder of the year.

Miss Elsie sent us a short note. She is settling into retired life, and wrote it will take some time to get fully adjusted.

Do take care and best of luck with the clinic. Do not hesitate to call or write if I can be of any more assistance to you. We all are looking forward to your wedding in the fall. When you set the date, I will work with the schedule so that your friends at Ellis Island can attend. Hopefully, you will come and visit us before that time. Please give my warmest regards to dear Dr. Goodwin.

Sincerely yours,

Sister Gwendolyn Hanover

Ellis Island Hospital, Ellis Island,

Port of New York, New York City

Thinking of the nurses at Ellis Island Hospital made Angie smile. She opened the next letter.

February 8, 1925
Dear Angie,

I was so excited to receive your letter outlining the details of the sick-child center. Yes, yes, yes, count me in! I am available to watch the children two days a week on Tuesday and Thursday. I can't wait. You will be happy to hear that Papa has given his consent for me to work with the immigrants at Nativity House. He feels it is a most appropriate undertaking for a young woman of my station. Someday in the future, he will also approve of my teaching career, although I haven't told him about attending Hunter College in the fall. Well, one thing at a time. Thank you for sending the directions to Nativity House. I will be there, with bells on, bright and early, next Tuesday.
Yours truly,
Miss Leonora Bartoli
New York City, New York

Angie opened the last letter.

February 8, 1925

Dear Miss Bosco,

I am writing to thank you for working with Visiting Nurse O'Shaughnessy. She is thrilled with your plans for a sick-child center. I have never seen her spirits so high. She is delighted with her little desk at Nativity House, too. She selected six non-contagious children: three youngsters recovering from polio, a brother and sister recently recovered from rheumatic fever, and one little girl with a leg fracture. Visiting Nurse O'Shaughnessy will pick them up next Tuesday morning. By the way, I have written to Miss Jane Adams in Chicago about your clinic. You may be hearing from her shortly. Congratulations on a successful clinic opening.

Again, many thanks,

Miss Lillian Wald

Henry Street Settlement House,

New York City, New York

Chapter Twenty

February 13, 1925
9 PM (21:00)

Come with me to a place that only two can go,
A safe and sacred space where two can grow.

At the end of the day, Abe Goodwin followed Angie as she straightened the clinic, and collected the trash.

"Here, Angie, let me take that for you. I'll put out the garbage. It's cold out there." He took the trash cans from Angie, and hurried out the back door.

When he returned, he slammed the door shut. "Brrr, it's going to be a cold one tonight. I hope you wore your wool cape today."

"No, I brought my raincoat. It looked like rain this morning."

"Then, we'll have to cuddle close and keep each other warm when we walk back to the church tonight."

"You're so romantic."

Abe disagreed. "No, I must admit that I haven't been very romantic these past weeks."

"You haven't had time. You've been working nonstop all month."

"You, too, Angie, do you realize that we work together all day, and the only time we have alone is when I walk you back to the nunnery at night?"

"Stop, it's not a nunnery. You keep calling it that. It sounds worse than what it is."

"Well, this arrangement doesn't leave much time for us."

"I know. We've worked hard, but look at all we've accomplished."

"People say that the place is very welcoming."

"It turned out better than I imagined."

"Thanks to you, Angie, you're a talented woman. You even have the care center for sick children ready to begin next week."

Angie frowned. "Yes, but only two days a week."

"Two days a week is a start."

"We'll expand slowly. Maureen and Leonora are very enthusiastic about the project."

"Yes, they'll be a good team. Sam is smitten with Maureen, you know."

"Who doesn't know, Abe? It's adorable…the way he looks at her… and always hanging around when she comes in."

"Guess what?"

"What?"

"Tomorrow is Valentine's Day, and Sam's taking her out. All this doctor has planned for you is another full day of work at Nativity House. I'm ashamed that I haven't been very romantic."

"You've been a good doctor, Abe. This month was all about Nativity House. We painted, decorated, and stocked the clinic. Then, we hosted the opening. We did it, Abe. People are actually coming."

"I know, we have a lot to be proud of, but you must admit that we have been working hard. We need a break. How about I borrow Sam's Hudson on Sunday, and we drive out to Long Island?"

"It sounds wonderful. However, I haven't seen my brothers all month. I've been so busy. I haven't gone to a Sunday family dinner since New Year's Day."

"Well, that settles it. We'll go to Giacomo's this Sunday."

"This Sunday, dinner is at Santino's, but a ride in the country sounded so relaxing."

"We could go to Central Park instead. From there, we'll go uptown to Santino and Rosa's."

"Let's do it. It's a good idea. I hope the weather is nice."

On Sunday morning, Angie and Abe went to Mass together at Nativity Church. After church, Abe took the streetcar to pick up Sam's Hudson. When he returned for Angie, one hour later, snow flurries were beginning to swirl in the air.

Angie looked at Abe. Then, she looked up at the sky. "Should we change our plans and stay home?"

"Not on your life. There's nothing I would rather do than take a walk in the park with my best gal. A little snow isn't going to stop me. However, if it does begin to snow heavier, we can stop in the Metropolitan Museum of Art."

When they reached the city, tiny snow flurries turned into fat snow-flakes that clung together before reaching the ground. Abe looked out the window, and asked, "Museum or Park?"

"Central Park first!" Angie answered.

They parked the car on Eightieth Street, halfway between the Seventy-Ninth Street Entrance to Central Park and the Entrance to the Museum. It was snowing heavily as they walked through the pointed Greywacke Arch to Cleopatra's Obelisk. From there, they crossed the old iron bridge and walked toward the reservoir. Soft snow quickly blanketed the bushes, trees, and bridges of the park. They walked in silence, as if talking would disturb the snow from falling quietly in the winter snow globe they were walking in.

Angie broke the silence. "It's beautiful."

"Are you warm enough, Angie?"

"Perfect."

"Angie, when do you think we should start to plan our wedding?"

"Now, I suppose...now that the clinic is open."

"We should start with a date. What do you think about a wedding in the month of June?"

"Yes, I thought about a June wedding also, but I'm not certain that Adeline will be back and settled by June."

"July is your birthday month. We could plan for July."

"The apartment won't be vacant until September. I don't know. Let me think about this. I've had the clinic on my mind all month."

"Me, too, but no later than September, right, Angie?"

"Right."

"Do you think we should turn back now?"

"Not yet, it's much too beautiful."

They walked, hand in hand, until they came to the entrance of the museum, and slipped in. For the next two hours, they enjoyed the beauty of the art and ancient sculptures housed there. They arrived at Santino and Rosa's house with glowing smiles and rosy cheeks.

"Here are the lovebirds!" Rosa announced.

"Where have you been?" Santino asked.

"We went to Central Park and the Museum of Art."

Giacomo laughed, "In this foul weather?"

His wife, Isabella smiled, "When one is in love, Giacomo..."

The women crowded around the stove where Rosa was demon-strating how to prepare Manicotti shells.

"Come, Angie, you're just in time for the cooking show." Rosa continued. "Put a quarter cup of batter in the pan. You must tilt the pan. Twirl it around to cover the bottom…like this. Watch carefully, it will start to set quickly. When the crepe is set, turn it over immedi-ately. Don't let it brown."

Celestina asked, "How do you make the batter?"

"It's easy. Mix one cup milk, two cups flour and a pinch of salt. That's it."

"What's next?" Celestina asked.

"When the crepes are made, we fill them with ricotta," Rosa answered.

"Only ricotta?"

"No, the recipe calls for one pound each of ricotta and mozzarella, two eggs, and chopped parsley. Put two teaspoons of the mixture in each crepe and roll. Let's all do some. Come. We have twenty-four shells to fill."

The ladies gathered around Rosa, and began filling the crepes.

"Aunt Angie, when are you going to get married?"

"Yes," Isabella said, "I've been meaning to ask. Do you have a date for your wedding?"

Angie said, "Abe and I were talking about it this afternoon. We've been so busy with the clinic, we haven't have time to think about setting a date."

As he entered the kitchen, Giacomo overheard their conversation. "Don't wait too long, Sister. I want a little nephew…too many girls in this family. Seriously, when are you going to select a date for this wedding? I will pay for it."

"Giacomo, I couldn't let you do that. You've done so much already."

"Nonsense, you are my baby sister. I've been saving for this event. We'll have a nice church wedding."

"Which church...Nativity Church or St. Barbara's? What do you think?" Rosa asked.

"I will have to think about that." Angie said.

Giacomo added. "After, we'll invite everyone we know to a big football wedding."

"Daddy, you are joking. We are not allowed to play football in church."

"No, sweetheart, it is an expression." Isabella explained.

"What does it mean, Daddy?"

"A football wedding is lots of fun. There is singing and dancing. Everyone is having a good time and getting mighty hungry. When the food is served, they rush to the food table. 'Throw me a salami sandwich', Uncle Sal calls out as someone throws a fat salami sandwich to him. 'Pass a capicola, here', Uncle Guido shouts and prepares to catch a big capicola sandwich in his hands." Giacomo laughed.

"Daddy, you are pulling my leg."

"I'm not, little one. There are lots of sandwiches...and a little beer and vino...under the table, of course."

Isabella looked at her daughter. "Daddy is not joking. It's called a football wedding because they throw the sandwiches like a football."

"Really?"

"Really, sweetheart."

"Aunt Angie, who will you choose to be your maid-of-honor?"

"I don't have to give that a second thought. I choose my sister, Celestina." Angie turned to Celestina. "Darling, would you be my maid-of-honor?"

"Me? What about Adeline? I thought you would ask Adeline to be your maid-of-honor."

"She's a married lady now. I will ask Adeline to be my *matron-of-honor*. How would that be?"

"Perfect! Then, I accept."

"…And your bridesmaids, Aunt Angie?"

"I was thinking maybe Abe's two little nieces, Linda and Laura."

"Abe's nieces!"

"…and the three of you."

"Yeah," the girls abandoned the manicotti. They jumped up and down, clapping.

"We're going to be in the wedding."

"I'm so excited!"

"What shall we wear?"

Isabella said, "I'll make your dresses. Of course, that's if Angie wants me to."

"Thank you, Isabella. That would be perfect."

"You pick the fabric, Angie. I'll work with anything you chose. What colors do you like?"

"I don't know…"

"What's your favorite color, Aunt Angie? This is so exciting. Did you pick out your wedding gown yet?"

"Not yet…"

"When you go shopping for your bridal gown, can we come along with you?"

The girls were giggling. Santino and Abe entered the kitchen. "What's all this about?"

"We're planning Angie's wedding."

"So when is this wedding?" Santino asked.

"We don't know. Angie hasn't decided."

All eyes looked at Angie.

Angie laughed, "It looks like Abe and I will have to decide on a wedding date sooner than we thought, so that all of you can put your wedding plans into action."

Chapter Twenty-One

March 4, 1925
11:30 AM (11:30)

A fantasy to orchestrate,
A system to manipulate.

Frieda Kohl managed her boarding house with meticulous care. She ran a tight ship, and knew the comings and goings of all of her tenants. She was keeping a watchful eye on her newest tenants, the Fergusons, a young couple who had recently rented the third-floor-rear apartment for thirty days. Still a bit skeptical about the couple, she hadn't decided if she would allow them to stay past the end of the month. There was nothing particularly shady about them, just strange. One worked days, and the other worked nights. Frieda frowned upon that arrangement. She knew that was not a recipe for a happy marriage. Young Mrs. Ferguson looked nice enough, but Mr. Ferguson...well...she hadn't made up her mind. Her instinct told her that Mrs. Ferguson would do well to keep her husband home at night.

Frieda's thoughts were interrupted by the shrill of the doorbell. She hurried to open the front door to find Officer Murphy waiting outside. He asked for Mrs. Moretti. Maria Moretti lived with her son in the second-floor-front apartment. When Frieda was on watch, she never allowed strangers into the building, even a policeman. After she examined the officer from top to bottom, she sternly instructed him to, "Wait here!"

She called up to Maria Moretti from the vestibule. "Mrs. Moretti, a policeman is looking for you. Can you come down now?"

"Yes, Frieda, I'll be right down."

When Maria Moretti reached the ground floor landing, Officer Murphy introduced himself. "Morning, Mrs. Moretti, I am Truant Officer Murphy, employed by the New York City Department of Education. I'm here to inquire about the whereabouts of your son, Philip Moretti."

"What's he done?"

"Absent from public school for two days now. Do you know where your son is today?"

"I sent him to school this morning...like I always do. That's where he went. I packed him a good lunch, too."

"That's all I need to know, Mrs. Moretti. I know all the places the boys hang out. He's at the cinema, most likely. Don't you worry. I'll find the lad." Officer Murphy tipped his hat, "Good Day to you, Madame."

Frieda Kohl had remained in the hallway, listening to the conversation between Maria Moretti and Officer Murphy. When the truant officer was safely out of site, Frieda pounced. "Maria, why did you tell Officer Murphy that your boy is at school? He's been upstairs with you all day. I don't understand. Why didn't you tell him that Phillipi is home sick? You'll get into trouble with the school if the officer reports that Phillipi has been playing *hooky*."

"Oh, Frieda, I'm frightened. I don't know what to do."

"Maria, what's wrong? Tell me."

"Philippi has a problem with his eye. They don't like people with eye trouble in America. They'll send him straight back to Italy if they find out."

"Why do you say that?"

"That's what they said when the doctors examined us at Ellis Island. They checked our eyes. If they found a problem, they sent the people back. I saw them do that to a couple who traveled with us on the ship."

"Are you saying that Phillipi has an eye disease? Are you certain?"

"No, I don't know for sure, but his eye has been red and watery all week. I'm afraid to send him to school. People talk, you know. I kept him home yesterday and today."

"Maria, you need to have his eye checked by a doctor. He must return to school. You should take Philippi to the new clinic that opened on Johnson Avenue. Father Benedetto told us not to be afraid to go. He said to trust the doctor and nurse there. Everything is confidential. Take Phillipi to the clinic today. It won't cost you anything."

"No, Frieda, it might be dangerous. If he has a disease, they will report him. They will come to the house and take him away."

"Please, Maria, listen. You need to take your son to the doctor."

"I can't. Maybe, his eye will get better on its own."

"I have an idea. Use a different name. How about my name? I could tell the doctor that he is my son. Then, if they come looking for him, they'll never find him because I have no son."

"Frieda, will they believe you? He doesn't look like you...you with golden hair, and his hair as black as coal."

"That's all the more reason for the boy to have the *Kohl* name." Frieda laughed. "What shall we name him? Heinrich, *Heinrich Kohl*, I always wanted a son named Heinrich."

"Frieda, I don't know if this is a good idea."

"Nonsense, it's an excellent idea. There's no time to waste. Go, now, get him ready. We'll take him to the clinic straight away."

"No, Frieda. I can't."

"Then, let's take a walk down to the rectory. We'll ask Father Benedetto."

"Father's much too busy for such a trivial thing. Okay, you take him. Say he's your son. Tell them he is *Heinrich Kohl*. I will stay home, and pray to Mary that they believe you."

"Everything will be fine. You'll see, Maria. Tell Phillipi that he's coming with me to get his eye fixed."

Maria trusted Frieda Kohl. She had always looked out for her. After all, Frieda had been in America six years, and already owned an apartment building. Frieda was smart. She knew things about America that Maria didn't. She would listen to Frieda. Perhaps, it would be safe.

When Maria returned to her apartment, she carefully explained the plan to her son. Phillipi could never understand why his mother was always frightened. He wasn't scared of anyone or anything. He decided to go along with her plan because his eye was beginning to itch. He was bored. He wasn't about to stay home with his mother one more day. He wanted to go to school with his friends. If going to the clinic with Mrs. Kohl was the only way to get back to school, he would get dressed and pretend he was Mrs. Kohl's son.

Maria Moretti bundled up her son for the windy March day. She tied a wool scarf around his neck, and positioned his hat so that it covered his right eye. When she was satisfied with the way he looked, she delivered him downstairs to her friend, Frieda Kohl. When Maria returned to her apartment, she began the first of the ten rosaries she promised to say to the Mother Mary if she would allow her son's eye to heal.

Before Frieda and Phillipi entered Nativity House, Frieda took hold of Phillipi's hand. He looked up at her and winked. She winked back, "Now, don't say anything, Phillipi. Let me do the talking. Remember, your new name is Heinrich."

"Heinrich? What a dumb name! Do I look like a Heinrich? Couldn't you think of a better name for me? You should have named me *Hans*."

"Hans is not the same as Heinrich. Here we go. No more talking."

They entered a cheerful reception room, and were greeted by a young nurse who introduced herself as Nurse Angie. She asked what the problem was. Then, she asked for the boy's name, age, and address. Frieda did all the talking. When she explained that *her* son had an eye problem, Angie removed the boy's cap, and stared into his right eye. Phillipi stared back but, as instructed, he did not say a word.

Nurse Angie said, "I think the doctor will be able to fix your eye in no time. Looks like a case of pink eye."

Phillippi could not contain himself a moment longer. He firmly stated, "Pink eye, sounds like a girl's disease."

"Hush, Heinrich! What is this pink eye, Nurse?

"It is an infection. I'll have the doctor examine him. We have medicine for it. It will only be a short wait."

The woman and the boy sat together quietly. They waited until they heard the name *Heinrich Kohl* called. They were ushered into an examination room where the doctor greeted them. Dr. Goodwin introduced himself and spoke to the boy. He asked, "How do you feel?"

Silence. The boy did not answer.

Dr. Goodwin reworded his question. "Tell me. How are you feeling today, my boy?"

The boy looked at Frieda.

She nodded.

"Bad," the boy mumbled.

"When did the trouble start?"

"Last week."

"Would you say that your eye is getting better or worse?"

"Worse," he answered.

His terse answers made Dr. Goodwin smile. He examined the boy's eye in the light. Turning to the nurse, he said, "Conjunctivitis... Boric Acid Wash, four times a day."

To Phillipi, he said, "Son, you will be feeling better and should be back to school by next week. Let your mother rinse out your eye with the solution we give her. Nurse Angie will give you a doctor's note to give to the school authorities. If your eye doesn't clear up by Monday, come in again."

Frieda looked concerned. She had no intention of returning to the clinic next week. "Yah," she said, "I wouldn't know how to wash his eye, Miss."

"No problem, I will show you before you leave."

Angie demonstrated the eye-wash procedure to the newly appointed mother. Frieda was apprehensive, but listened to every word the nurse said. When she cautiously attempted to repeat the procedure, the boy looked alarmed.

"Stai Attento! Be careful!" He cried out, and reached for the nurse's hand.

Angie patted him on the shoulder. She spoke to him in Sicilian to help him relax. He appeared to understand. Her words calmed him.

When Frieda left the clinic, she had an envelope filled with six teaspoons of Boric Acid powder, written instructions for the eye treatments four times a day, and a blank doctor's note.

Frieda looked down at the Boric Acid instructions the nurse had given her. To her surprise, the instructions were written in English on one side and Italian on the other. Frieda took hold of Phillipi's hand and hurried home. She couldn't wait to return the boy to Maria, and relieve herself of the responsibility of motherhood. Being a mother wasn't as easy as she thought it would be. In the future, she would think twice before she considered being anyone's mother.

Directions for Boric Acid Wash
Boil 3 cups of water for five minutes.
After boiling, fill a clean cup with the boiled water.
Wait two minutes. Discard the water in the cup.
To the boiled water remaining in the pot, add one-fourth teaspoon Boric Acid.

Pour a small amount of the solution into the clean cup.
When cooled, rinse the eye three times using clean cotton each time.
Clean from inner eye (near the nose) to outer eye.
Discard cotton after each wipe. Discard used solution.
Repeat four times a day.
At the end of the day, discard the Boric Acid Solution.
Prepare a fresh solution of Boric Acid each morning.

Chapter Twenty-Two

❧

March 14, 1925
1:30 AM (1:30)

Beliefs are forgotten when you easily sway,
Your hopes and dreams are put on delay.

The pain started slowly at first, a tight cramping sensation that woke her in the middle of the night, and left so quickly she thought she had dreamt it. Falling back to sleep, she was soon awakened by a second spasm. She sat up in her bed, waiting for the pain to pass, wondering what she had eaten to make her feel sick. She had been careful not to eat too much, for gaining weight made the pregnancy harder to conceal. She retraced the day, straining to remember the meals she had eaten…a bowl of oatmeal in the morning…date-nut bread and cream cheese for lunch…the cup of leftover pea soup for supper. Was the milk in the oatmeal rotten? Was the cheese in the sandwich spoiled? Had the pea soup remained in the icebox too long?

The cramping sensation tugged deeper, making her squirm and change position. Hugging her stomach, she rocked back and forth until the cramp released. Relieved, she relaxed and allowed herself to drift off to sleep once more.

It wasn't until she was awakened a third time that she began to suspect that this might be something more. She counted the months. It was the end of July when she last saw him, the night before he sailed. Two months later, she boarded the ship with her parents, and set sail

149

for America. She was seasick on the trip, but then again, everyone was.

It was far too early.

"May," they had told her. The nurses at Henry Street told her the baby wouldn't come until the first week in May. She still had six… maybe seven…weeks left to find *him*.

Impossible, she thought, *the baby is not coming tonight. I am imagining this. After work tomorrow, I will go straight to the clinic to be certain everything is okay. It could be the corset. Perhaps, I've pulled it too tight.*

When her little bump began to bulge in January, she went to Macy's Department Store where she was certain no one knew her. She spent three-days-pay on the purchase of a heavy corset which squeezed in her tummy so tight that it took her breath away. As the months passed, she tightened the strings of the corset, concealing any suspicion of a pregnancy. She was determined to keep the pregnancy a secret until she found him. Once she located him, they would marry. The problem was, that after months of searching, her efforts had been unsuccessful.

She lied to her parents, telling them she was forced to work past closing to stock supplies. Instead, she went to the pool halls downtown. She inquired about the boy at the Immigrant Aid Society. She showed his picture at corner bars, and even visited churches. It was as if he had never arrived. Had his ship sunk? Perhaps, he had gotten ill. No one had seen him. No one knew him. He was nowhere to be found.

The pain gripped from within, interrupting her thoughts. It came slowly, at first. Then, pressed tighter, squeezing her insides, and ripping into her as if it were a knife. Fearing her parents would awaken, she muffled her groans by biting on her handkerchief. She didn't dare turn on the light. The pains evolved into a rhythm. They came softly...then stronger...pinching hard before releasing. She gripped her cotton nightgown, and buried her head in her pillow until the pain dissolved.

Then, without warning, came the urge to push.

She looked down upon a tiny thing...wrinkled...struggling to breathe...too small to cry. Falling back on her pillow, she thought.

This is not happening. It cannot be.

Thirty minutes passed. There was another push, another gush. Something...a clot of blood...was attached. The baby lay flaccid, gray and grunting with each small breath.

The alarm clock on her bedside table showed that it was five o'clock. She forced herself to stand. Could she leave the house and return before her mother's morning call? There wasn't a moment to waste.

The young woman dressed quickly, putting on a dark sweater and shawl. She wrapped her dying baby in the soiled and bloodied bed sheet. She tiptoed out of the apartment, and down the stairs. The new clinic was three blocks away. The people there would know what to do. As she walked in the dark, she felt as if she would faint. On Meserole Street, she passed the fruit and vegetable store. No one saw her steal a wooden fruit crate.

She turned on Johnson Avenue. The outside door of Nativity House was unlocked. The young woman entered the foyer, and opened the door to the hallway. She rang the bell. She knocked on the door. No one answered. It was too early in the morning for anyone to be there. No one was around. She left her baby at the foot of the door in the fruit crate, and hurried away.

151

Chapter Twenty-Three

~

March 14, 1925
7:30 AM (07:30)

It's not a chore or a duty,
To restore life and beauty.

After eating a hearty morning breakfast with Father Benedetto at the Rectory, Abe Goodwin went next door and called for Angie at the Nativity Church Convent. Together, they crossed the street, and walked one short block to Nativity House. The clinic was not scheduled to open until ten that morning, but they were eager to arrive early to prepare for a busy Saturday clinic.

Angie and Abe walked hand-in-hand. Abe squeezed Angie's hand, softly. "This walk is always too short, Angie. I wish we had a mile to walk before we arrived at our destination."

"Abe Goodwin, I do believe that is the sweetest thing anyone has ever said to me before eight o'clock in the morning."

Always a gentleman, Abe opened the front door of Nativity House for Angie. When Angie entered the hall, she heard a cry. Presuming it was a cat, Angie said, "A kitten must have wriggled his way into the hall last night and found a warm spot here." She was one step ahead of Abe when she spotted the baby and shouted, "It's a baby!"

"What?" Abe asked.

Angie pointed to the box on the tile floor. "Look...a baby!"

The baby was bundled in a wooden fruit crate. Stunned, they stared at the baby for a brief moment before they sprang into action. Abe lifted the crate off the floor as Angie fumbled with the key to the clinic. After opening the door, the doctor and nurse worked in silence. Abe placed the baby on the kitchen table and unwrapped the bedding to begin his examination. The tiny baby boy cried and shook with fury. He remained attached to his placenta. His umbilical cord had not been cut.

Angie rushed to the closet in the Exam Room for the one Delivery Pack she stocked at the clinic for an emergency. Returning to the kitchen, she grabbed a handful of towels. Once there, she placed the Delivery Pack on the kitchen table and opened it. She searched for what she needed…suction tubing, clamps, and scissors. She passed the clamps to Abe who swiftly clamped, then, cut the cord.

While Abe grabbed his stethoscope to listen to the baby's heartbeat, Angie filled a large pot of water and put it up to boil. She lit the oven, and threw the towels inside to warm them.

Abe broke the silence, "He looks to be about three or four pounds…maybe two months early. What do you think?"

"I agree. I'll weigh him after I wash him. He certainly has a hearty cry, doesn't he?"

"Yes, that's a good thing. Who could have left him?"

"I have no idea. Maureen is passing by this morning. She will know all the pregnant women in the neighborhood."

Angie shut the stove, tested the water, and moved the pot to the sink. The water in the pot was not hot, but warm enough to wash the baby. She wrapped the baby in a clean towel, and lifted him up with

153

one hand. Using only water and a dab of ivory soap, she cleaned him from head to toe. The baby cried with gusto as she dried him. Next, Angie carried him to the Exam Room to weigh him. Abe followed her. He watched as she put the baby on the scale.

"Three pounds, nine ounces…1650 grams," Angie announced, placing the baby on the examination table for the doctor to complete his exam.

Abe inspected the baby's fontanels for bulges and depressions. He looked for a broken collar bone, and checked his hips and legs. He tested the infant's reflexes. "Everything appears to be within normal limits, Angie. He wasn't born too long ago. He seems to be a strong little fellow, doesn't he? He's hungry, too. Do we have a baby bottle on the premises?"

"No. I thought ahead to anticipate every type of emergency, but I never imagined this one. I don't have any milk or canned evaporated milk here either."

There was a knock on the door. It was Maureen, the Visiting Nurse. "Good Morning, Everyone!" Maureen said, cheerfully. "I came by today to catch up on my…" Maureen stopped mid-sentence when she entered the Examination Room. "What's this?" She asked.

"We found a baby at our door this morning."

"A baby," said Maureen, "a real baby?"

Angie was gently rocking the infant, attempting to soothe him. Her efforts were unsuccessful. The baby continued to fervently cry.

"He's got a good set of lungs, doesn't he?" Maureen said.

"He's hungry. I don't have any milk for him, and no baby bottles. I'm afraid I'm not adequately prepared for this type of emergency."

"Wait here, I'll run to Mrs. Carbone. She produces so much breast milk that she sells it to the women in the neighborhood. She lives around the corner. I won't be long."

Maureen hurried to Mrs. Carbone's building. She rang the bell, and ran up the stairs without waiting for the bell to be answered. Luckily, Mrs. Carbone was home. She sold Maureen a pint of breast milk for three pennies. Maureen thanked her. She flew down the stairs and rushed out of the building, stopping only when she reached the Rexall Pharmacy. There, she purchased a baby bottle. Leaving the store, she bumped into Police Officer Gallagher. When Maureen reported the morning's events to him, the policeman accompanied her to Nativity House.

Maureen was gone less than fifteen minutes. When she returned, Angie was walking the baby, back and forth, across the room. The baby had quieted after finding a comfortable spot in Angie's arms. Maureen went into the kitchen to quickly prepare the bottle of breast milk.

Officer Gallagher began to ask routine questions for his report. The policeman wrote in his notebook as Abe answered his questions.

"Where did you find the baby, Doc?"

"...At our door."

"What time was that?"

"...Before eight this morning."

"What was he dressed in?"

"...A bed sheet."

"Anything else?"

"No."

"Do you have the bed sheet?"

"Yes, it's in the kitchen. Come, I'll show you."

Abe lead the way into the kitchen. Angie and the officer followed. Maureen had prepared the bottle and handed it to Angie, who started to feed the baby.

Officer Gallagher examined the bed sheet. "Mustn't disturb the evidence, you know," Gallagher instructed. "Would you have a pair of tweezers on hand?"

"Would a clamp be helpful?" Maureen asked, and handed him a clamp from the Delivery Pack on the table.

"The perfect tool," Gallagher answered. He poked the soiled linen with the end of the clamp. Then, he said, "I may have found something."

Slowly and carefully, he lifted up a white handkerchief. Placing it on the table, he spread out the handkerchief, exposing an initial. It was the letter, *M*.

"A clue," he whispered.

He turned to Maureen, and asked her if she knew all the expectant women in the neighborhood. Maureen thought for a moment, and answered. "I know three women who are pregnant. One is expecting her baby any day now, and in fact, is overdue. The other two are in the early stages of their pregnancies.

"Can you recall if any of these women have a first or last name that begins with the letter, *M*?"

"No, I don't know of anyone."

"Officer, where will you take the baby now?" Angie asked, holding the infant close to her chest.

"Don't know, Miss, there's nowhere to take him. Can't take him downtown. We wouldn't know what to do with him at the precinct. I don't believe the Foundling can handle a baby this small."

Suddenly, Angie smelled the towels in the oven. She passed the baby to Maureen. "The towels...I forgot the towels!" Angie opened the oven door. She was relieved to find the towels had not burned, but were nice and hot. She placed the hot towels on the table to cool off. "We can cover him with a warm towel when one cools down."

Abe continued. "Surely, the city has resources at a city hospital."

Officer Gallagher replied, "It may be best for the baby to stay with you until I investigate our next steps."

Abe offered a suggestion. "Perhaps we should consult with Dr. Martin at Coney Island. He might know what to do."

"Good idea, Doc," Officer Gallagher replied.

"It's much too early in the season, Abe. The Exhibit doesn't open until May..."

"Yes, but Doctor Martin may have run into a situation like this before. He might be able to tell us what to do."

Abe left the room, sat down at his office desk, and dialed the phone. He was surprised when Dr. Martin personally answered the telephone. After a brief conversation, Dr. Martin agreed to drive to Williamsburg to assess the infant.

Arriving at Nativity House within an hour, Dr. Martin went about carefully examining the baby. Everyone watched in silence. Minutes passed before he announced, "He appears to be a strong baby...perhaps 34 weeks gestation. He will require controlled feedings and a warm, sterile environment. I've spoken to my head nurse, Madame

Louise. We will monitor him at our Center. Madame Louise and my daughter are available to care for the baby."

Angie and Maureen breathed a sigh of relief. "Wonderful." They whispered.

After the consent and contact papers were signed by both Officer Gallagher and Dr. Goodwin, Dr. Martin drove off to his Luna Park nursery with *Baby M.*

Shortly afterward, the policeman left to file his report.

Angie looked at the clock. It was ten minutes to ten. She had ten minutes to prepare for the Saturday clinic. She quickly went to work. She scrubbed the kitchen and straightened the Exam Room.

On schedule, the doors of Nativity Settlement House and Health Clinic opened to the public at the usual Saturday Morning opening time of ten o'clock.

Chapter Twenty-Four

March 19, 1925
1:45 PM (13:45)

Curly hair and cheeks of rose,
A dimple, and a turned-up nose.

"Angie! Angie! Where are you? Luigi's come to fix the door."

"I'm in the playroom, Abe, with Maureen and Leonora."

Abe found Angie in the classroom sitting at a child's size table cutting circle shapes with the children. The custodian of the church, Luigi Paluzzo, accompanied him. Maureen and Leonora had planned a number of activities for the children in their Tuesday daycare class. Cutting paper dolls was on the afternoon agenda. Abe smiled, "Luigi, may I present you with the distinguished Director of Nursing of Nativity House."

"I couldn't resist. I came to check for head lice, and one thing led to another. The children begged me to play with them."

"Father Benedetto sent Luigi to fix a door. Do we have a door out of alignment?"

"Good Afternoon, Luigi. How are you today?"

"Fine, Nurse Angie. It's good to see you playing with the children. You are always working, night and day. You deserve a break, now and then. Which door is it that needs fixing?"

Angie stood up. "It's the kitchen door. Come, Luigi, I'll show you."

Luigi and Abe followed Angie into the kitchen. "It's this door," Angie said. The door groaned as Angie demonstrated the problem by opening and closing it.

"I see the trouble. I can fix it. I'm glad you called me." Luigi took out his tools in preparation for the repair. "The two of you work too hard. I see both of you working...always working. I never see you rest." He turned to Abe. "This summer, you take your pretty nurse out to my place by the beach to relax. I invite you. You'll have a nice day."

"It sounds wonderful. Where is your house?"

"It's only a bungalow, but I have a small farm, too. I'll show you all the vegetables I grow there...tomatoes, zucchini, and peppers. Everything I plant grows nice. My basilico is the biggest and the best in town. It's the soil. It's very good for plants."

"That sounds swell. Do you go there on weekends?"

"No, I live there all the time. It's not far, the first street of Rockaway Beach...still part of the city...right before the bridge to Long Beach... very close. It takes less than an hour to get there. You'll have no problem finding it." He laughed, "Just be sure you turn before you go up on the bridge or you will end up on Long Island."

Abe looked at Angie, and asked, "Angie, would you like to take a ride out this summer? I could borrow Sam's Hudson?"

"Just remember what I said," Luigi continued. "Don't go on the wooden toll bridge. Make a right turn before it. Follow the sign that says, *local streets*. My place is on First Street, down the driveway behind the tackle shop, only a block from the water. You can't miss it."

"We may take you up on your offer. We'll write down the directions before we go."

"We have a nice beach there. You can swim or fish off the jetty. You can even use my skiff. I cook for you while you relax." He stopped. "Looks like I need to oil these hinges. I left the oil can at the Church. I'll go fetch it. Don't wait for me," he called, as he was leaving. "I'll let myself in when I return."

When Luigi left, Angie and Abe returned to their office. Leonora followed them into the backroom. "Angie...Dr. Goodwin...may I have a moment of your time?"

"Yes, sit down."

"Well, I wanted to tell you that I love working here two days a week, and to let you know that my father said that I can spend more time here. I was wondering if you are still planning the afterschool program. I would like to be involved."

Angie sighed, "Oh. Leonora, that's a relief. I was certain you were going to tell me you were no longer available to work at the clinic."

"We hope to start the program in September." Abe said.

Angie added, "Weren't you planning on attending college then?"

"I'm thinking of postponing college for a year. You see, Papa said that if I am doing a good job here, I should consider becoming a teacher. He wants me to continue to volunteer for another year. If I am successful here, he will pay my college expenses."

"Well, that's what I call progress."

"Adeline will be back in New York by then. Angie, didn't you mention that she was interested in helping with the afterschool program, too?"

"Yes, she's planning to teach English and Hygiene this summer. She wants to organize an evening Parenting class in the fall, also.

Leonora, would you work with me to recruit volunteers for the program before Adeline arrives?"

"I'd love to. In the meantime, I had another idea. I'd like to come in on Wednesdays. I want to take the children to the Library. I've spoken to the Librarian. She will read stories to them. It will be good for them. They get bored at home. I'll pick them up and take them in the morning from ten to twelve. Then, help you in the clinic from twelve to two. I'll be back in the city by three in the afternoon. What do you think, Miss Angie?"

"I think it's a wonderful idea..."

Their conversation was interrupted by Luigi. "I'm sorry to disturb you, Miss Angie. I wanted to tell you about a little girl outside. She's been out there all morning."

Leonora said, "I saw her when I came in today. She's across the street, sitting on a pile of furniture. It looks as though her family may have been evicted from their apartment this morning."

"She's been there all day. It's going to rain soon," Luigi said. "I asked her if she wanted to go to the church to see the Sisters at the Convent. She wouldn't answer me...just shook her head. She looks frightened."

Leonora turned to Angie. "Would you like me to go outside to see if I can persuade her to come in? Maybe, she can play with the children here at the center this afternoon."

"Let's both go and see what we can do. Perhaps, we can talk to the neighbors to find out what's happened."

Angie and Leonora put on their wool sweaters before they stepped outside and crossed the street. They found the little girl, cold and shivering. She sat on a kitchen table, surrounded by an assortment of furniture. Wearing only a nightgown that was threadbare and worn, she wasn't properly dressed for the day. Her brunette hair was messy and untidy. Her face was dirty, smudged by tears that had been wiped away with grubby hands.

"Hello, little girl," Leonora said.

"Is your mother here?" Angie asked.

The little girl looked up, "No," she answered. "Mama's not here, but she's coming. She told me to wait for her. The men came. They put our stuff out here. Mama's going to be mad about that."

"Are you cold?"

"A little, Miss."

"Are you hungry? Did you eat anything today?"

"The O'Dwyer kids gave me bread and an apple. They like to feed me when Mama's not around."

"Where do they live?"

"They live right below us…on the second floor…over there." She pointed to the building behind her.

"Wait here, Leonora. I'll go in, and see if Mrs. O'Dwyer is home."

Angie went inside the apartment house. She walked up one flight of stairs, and knocked on the door. A woman answered. "Good Afternoon, are you Mrs. O'Dwyer?"

"Yes, I am, Miss. What can I do for you?"

"I'm Angie Bosco, the nurse from the clinic across the street."

"Oh, Miss, nice to meet you. The others were talking about the clinic just yesterday. They said you and the doctor are doing a fine job. I myself haven't had a need to go…knock on wood…but with seven little ones afoot, I'm sure I will find my way in there one of these days. Do come in. Would you like some tea and crackers? That's all I have to offer today."

"Mrs. O'Dwyer, I came to inquire about the little girl downstairs."

"Sure, Miss Angie, that's Sadie. She's four years old...almost five. Her mother went and left her again...always leaving the little girl...for days sometimes. She is a few months behind in her rent, too."

"It seems they were evicted this morning."

"I tried to get Sadie to come inside, but she wouldn't budge. My kids brought her a little something for lunch. I feed her when her mama's not around...that woman....a bit of a floozy, she is. Do you think you can convince Sadie to come in out of the cold? She's welcome to stay for supper, but my husband says she can't sleep overnight. We have too many kids of our own, you know."

"I can take her to the clinic, and then, to the convent, but I don't want her mother to worry about her when she returns. If you see her mother, will you tell her?"

"Sure, Miss Angie, but the girl probably won't go with you. She's stubborn."

Angie found Leonora talking to Sadie when she returned. Leonora asked her again if she would go with them.

"No, Miss, I can't!" Sadie said, sniffling.

"That's a problem, Sadie, because soon it will rain."

The little girl started to cry. "It's a secret." She said, "I can't tell."

"What is it, Sadie? Please tell us."

"Can I whisper it in your ear?"

"Yes." Leonora leaned over so that the little girl could reach her.

"I can't go with you. I pooped in my pants."

"You pooped?"

"Yes, oh boy, Mama is going to be mad about that, too."

"Come, Sadie, take my hand, and Angie's, too. Come with us. We have clean clothes across the street. We can wash you before your mother returns."

"Promise?"

"Yes, promise." Angie offered her hand.

Sadie reached up for Angie's hand, and then Leonora's. The three walked hand-in-hand until they reached the clinic.

When Abe saw the women with the child and learned what had happened, he smiled and asked, "Shall I call Officer Gallagher to file another missing mother report?"

Angie and Leonora nodded, and immediately went to work. Angie undressed the girl as Leonora prepared the bathwater. Sadie was bathed and dressed in clean, warm clothes when Officer Gallagher arrived at Nativity House.

"We all know Little Miss Sadie. Her mama will return. She always comes back for the kid. There are no other relatives around. I'd rather not file a report tonight. Last time, it took me an hour to prepare the paperwork. I had to tear the whole thing up when the woman showed up forty-five minutes later. You take my word, Miss, her mama will be back for her before dark sets in."

"Can we keep her here with us now?"

"You want too, Miss? I can take her down to the Precinct. She's waited there with us before."

"I told Mrs. O'Dwyer, the neighbor, that we would keep her here this afternoon."

"That's kind of you, Miss. I'll get the word out that Sadie's mother should come here for her daughter."

"If need be, I'll take her to the convent this evening to feed her and put her to bed."

"Sure, Miss, I'll be leaving her in your capable hands now."

"Thank you for stopping by, Officer Gallagher. We'll notify you if Sadie's mother shows."

As dusk approached, there was no sign of Sadie's mother. Before going to the church convent, they stopped by Mrs. O'Dwyer's to ask if she had heard any news. She hadn't, but she encouraged them to remain optimistic. She was certain Sadie's mother would appear before midnight.

Angie and Abe wondered how the good Sisters would react to a four-year-old sleeping at the Convent. For a brief moment, Angie was tempted to sneak the little girl into her room without telling them. Before reaching the Convent, Angie braced herself for a lecture from the nuns, but her worries faded within minutes of entering with Sadie. The Sisters were delighted to have the youngster as their overnight guest. They couldn't do enough for her. After they warmed supper for Sadie, they went about the Convent searching for nightclothes, flannels, and a pale-pink blanket. They prepared a small cot in Angie's room, and put Sadie to bed with a song.

When Angie entered her room to prepare for bed, Sadie was awake and whimpering in her pillow. Angie pushed the cot closer to her bed, and sat down.

"Sadie," she whispered. "Give me your hand." A tiny hand popped up through the flannel sheets and clenched Angie's hand. Sadie held on tight until she slowly drifted off to sleep. Angie sat beside her, thoughtful and quiet.

Sirina studied Angelina thoughtfully, watching her as she dusted the shelves of the study. Finally, she said, "Angelina, come and sit down next to me. Give me your hand."

"Why?"

"I want to study your palm."

"What will it tell you?"

"It may give me clues to point you in the right direction."

"It may give you clues, but it will give me worries."

"Nonsense, it will ease your worries."

Reluctantly, Angelina offered her hand to Sirina. Sirina held her hand in hers for what seemed like a very long time. Finally, she looked down and examined Angelina's palm."

"What does it tell you?"

"See here…this shows me there is a gossamer veil covering your heart."

"Why? What is it?"

"It is a delicate film."

"Make it go away."

"I cannot. It is barely a whisper of a coating, dear. For now, it is a good thing. It's protecting you from further heartbreak, but…"

"…But, what? Tell me, please."

"Love will never come to you unless you unveil your heart."

"How can I do that?"

"It will vanish the moment you decide to receive true love."

"How will I know true love?"

"Your heart will know."

"Will he be handsome and come to me riding on a large, white horse?"

"Where did you get such a foolish notion, child?"

"From stories, of course, the hero always comes to rescue his true love."

"Those are fairy tales. You won't need to be rescued, Angelina. In fact, it is more than likely that you will be the one to rescue your true love."

"How will I do that?"

"You will know when the time comes."

Chapter Twenty-Five

April 11, 1925
2:30PM (14:30)

Get used to the flutteries, there really is no cure,
Take advantage of their signals, and push yourself to soar.

MPA 191 R295CC IF FT

PALMS SPRINGS CA 842P MARCH 27 1925

MISS ANGIE BOSCO

NATIVITY CHURCH CONVENT STOP

WILLIAMSBURG STOP

BROOKLYN STOP

NEW YORK STOP

GREAT NEWS STOP

LEAVING CALIFORNIA WITH HARRY STOP

TRAIN SCHEDULED TO ARRIVE NY GRAND CENTRAL STOP

20:00 APRIL 10 1925 STOP

RESIDING AT WALDORF ASTORIA ON FIFTH AVENUE STOP

SIGNED MRS. HARRY STEINGOLD

ELLIS ANGELS ON THE MOVE

SATURDAY, MARCH 28, 1925
NATIVITY CHURCH CONVENT
BROOKLYN, NEW YORK

ADELINE STEINGOLD
TWO SUNSET LANE
PALM SPRINGS, CALIFORNIA

My Dear Adeline,

I received your telegram this morning and immediately said a prayer of thanks. Indeed, my prayers have been answered. I read your telegram a half dozen times before I truly believed it. I am overjoyed and excited that you will be coming home. I have so much to tell you.

In the past month, two children have found their way to Nativity House. Three weeks ago, a premature infant was left in a fruit crate at our door. Abe and I found the baby boy crying his eyes out in our hallway. We do not know who his mother is. Our only clue is a handkerchief that was found in his bedding. The handkerchief has the initial "M" embroidered on it. Because the baby was too delicate to bring to the Foundling, we called upon Dr. Martin. Although it is early in the season, Dr. Martin agreed to care for the baby at his Infant Incubator Exhibit until the baby stabilizes and reaches five and a half pounds. The latest report from the nursery is that he is growing and gaining weight. If his mother is not located, the baby will be sent to the Foundling next month. Without a mother's permission for adoption, the baby will stay at the Foundling until an investigation is complete.

Next to find her way to Nativity House is my new companion, Sadie. We found her last week patiently sitting in front of her apartment building, waiting for hours for her mother to return. The story we were able to piece together is that Sadie's mother left the apartment after she received an eviction notice. We are now certain she thought that the eviction would be delayed if Sadie was found alone in her apartment. Unfortunately, that was not the case. The following morning, Sadie was evicted and dumped outside, along with the contents of the apartment. There, she sat for hours until we found her, and persuaded her to come to Nativity House. It's been over a week. Her mother has not returned. The furniture was hauled away yesterday by the City's Sanitation Department.

Sadie has big blue eyes, the curliest hair, two dimples and the cutest little turned-up nose. Everyone falls in love with the little rag-a-muffin the moment they meet her. She has melted the heart of everyone at Nativity House, including the good sisters of Nativity Church Convent. Although she is only four years old, the Sisters have placed her in their Kindergarten class. After class, she comes to Nativity House. Maureen, Leonora and I have rotated taking her overnight this week. Officer Gallagher should have registered her with the city orphanage from the start, but he feels it is overcrowded and poorly run. We are all stalling the inevitable, hoping Sadie's mother will return.

The number of our clinic cases grows steadily each week. The word on the street is out. Nativity Settlement House and Health Clinic is slowly gaining the trust of the community. I wish that I could report the same for Father Benedetto…that we gained his trust, but we haven't. He comes to the clinic every day to investigate. I suppose he feels he is fiscally responsible, but he is beginning to make me feel uneasy. It feels like he is checking up on us. One afternoon, I found him sitting alone in the back office. Another time, he was coming down the stairs from the second floor. What was he doing in the second floor apartments when no one was around? Adeline, I must admit that gave me a strange feeling, deep down in the very pit of my stomach.

ELLIS ANGELS ON THE MOVE

I am certain we will need a nursing assistant in a few months' time, but I am reluctant to ask Father for the funds. Fannie and my sister, Celestina, offered to work at the clinic during their short summer recess. Fannie was the nursing assistant assigned to work with me at Ellis Island. She is now attending the Bellevue School of Nursing with my sister. Both are in the first year, and passed probation with flying colors.

Community outreach at Nativity House has begun. I had another opportunity to visit Lillian Wald at Henry House. I learn so much from her every time we meet. She advised me to meet with the people in the neighborhood to ask them to identify the community resources they feel they need. We hosted a number of afternoon and early evening sessions, inviting both men and women to come into the clinic for coffee, tea and cookies. Once assembled, discussions began. After a cold and snowy winter, they were concerned about the escalating price of coal. Many could not afford the high prices and suffered through the winter in the cold. Nativity House located a company that has offered a group rate at an extremely reasonable price. Nativity House now has created a buying cooperative.

The women of the neighborhood want to learn English and become citizens of the United States. Working mothers desire a safe place for their children to play after school. They expressed their frustration that they are not able to help their children with their homework. Leonora and I enlisted a handful of volunteers who are willing to assist with an afterschool and a tutor program. I can't wait until you get here so that you can be part of the planning, and start the English classes.

On the subject of planning, wedding plans are underway. I must admit that this is largely due to the efforts of my sisters-in-law. Both Rosa and Isabella, my brother's wives, as well as Abe's sisters, are bursting with excitement. They can't wait to begin. They already started their reducing diets. They met, and decided that Abe and I should be married in September at St. Barbara's Church. There is a large auditorium in the basement for church activities and parties. My sisters-in-law have made a list of the people they plan to invite. Between both sides and our friends at Ellis Island, there may be over two hundred people celebrating with us. When my brother, Giacomo, offered to pay for the sandwiches, pastries and cake, his wife, Isabella, appointed herself chief wedding planner. She often comes down to the clinic to discuss food, fabric colors and dress patterns. I'm struggling with making decisions. I desperately need your fashion advice about my wedding gown. As my matron-of-honor, I will beg you to help me after you are settled.

Adeline, I truly cannot wait to see you. I'll give you one day to rest after your journey. Abe and I will meet you at the Waldorf bright and early on Sunday morning.

Until then, dear friend,
Love and kisses,
Angie
XXX

Angie didn't have to look up from her desk to know that Adeline was in the room. She felt Adeline's presence moments before she entered the clinic on Saturday. Shocked and surprised, Angie dropped the medical chart she was working on. Angie and Abe had planned on visiting Adeline and Harry in the city the following day.

"Adeline!" Angie cried out, "You're here! I cannot believe it."

"Angie Girl, you are a site for sore eyes!" Adeline said, her arms opening wide. The women ran to each other and embraced. They hugged, gave each other kisses on both cheeks, jumped up and down, and hugged again. Little Sadie joined in on the excitement, laughing and clapping her hands.

"I'm flabbergasted!" Angie exclaimed, not wanting to let go of Adeline's hand, "Let me take a look at you. You look like the bee's knees... so tan and healthy. I think you might have even gained some weight."

"*Some* weight is putting it mildly. I've gained ten pounds."

"Well, it looks perfectly wonderful on you. I always said you were too thin. I thought we planned on meeting tomorrow. I wanted you to rest today after taking the long train trip."

"I couldn't stay at the hotel a minute longer. Harry had a business meeting. His driver drove him in the Packard. He told me to take his Studebaker."

"What? You drove here? When did you learn to drive?"

"During the war, but I've been practicing in Palm Springs."

"How is it that I've known you for five years, and I never knew you could drive?"

"I never had an automobile." Adeline felt Sadie petting the fox coat she was wearing. "...And who is this pretty little lady?" She asked, kneeing down to Sadie's height.

Sadie twirled around her. "My name is Sadie, Lady."

"I say, and you are a poet, too, Sadie, Sadie, cute young lady." Sadie laughed. "What a darling little girl you are." Turning to Angie, she said, "Angie, is this the young miss you've befriended?"

"Yes, this is my friend, Sadie. Sadie, this is my friend, Adeline."

"I am very pleased to meet you, Sadie." Adeline said, reaching down to pat Sadie's curls. "Where did you get your beautiful pink leather shoes?"

"Mr. Bartoli made them for me."

Angie explained. "Leonora Bartoli has taken Sadie home a number of times. Her parents are delighted with her. Her father made Sadie's shoes."

"I helped him," Sadie added.

"Sadie, they are pretty, and so are you."

"I like you, Lady."

"I like you, too, Sadie."

Adeline took a long look around the Reception Room. "Angie, this place…it's perfect…so bright and cheerful…exactly as you described it in your letters. I'm so proud of you, but where is everyone?"

"It's our afternoon break. Abe's at the post office. He'll be back soon. Clinic hours are from ten to two, then four to eight in the evening."

"Well, then, do you have time to show me around?"

"It would be my pleasure, Adeline. Come, Sadie, come with us."

Angie gave Adeline an in-depth tour of the facility with Sadie dancing along behind them.

"Angie, you did a wonderful job. I love this place, and I know your patients do, too. Can we see the apartments upstairs?"

"Not today, no one is around."

"Can't we simply take a peek?"

"I'm not fond of going up there. In fact, sometimes the place gives me the heebie-jeebies."

"Why is that? Aren't you planning on living there after the wedding?"

"That's the plan."

"What's wrong? Does this have something to do with why you are stalling your wedding?"

"I am not stalling my wedding."

"Well, you aren't planning it. Now you tell me that your honeymoon apartment gives you the jitters. What's eating you, Sweetie? You can level with me. Are you having second thoughts?"

"No, I'm afraid."

"Scared? Of what?"

"Abe is a wonderful guy, the real McCoy, but everyone has a dark side. I've been thinking that I've never really seen his. He's always generous with his time, thoughtful, and caring but..."

"Well, you know what you have to do about that, don't you?"

"Absolutely, Ad, I have to take a leap of faith. Find the courage to walk through my fear."

"Simply jump, and crash through it!"

"Right, Adeline."

Adeline looked down at the threshold of the reception room. "Well, let's do it, then. Sadie, take my hand. Angie, here, take the other."

"What are we doing?"

"Jumping, on the count of three, we jump. Ready...One...Two... Three...Jump!"

The three hopped over the threshold, giggling with laughter. When Angie caught her breathe, she hugged Adeline. "Oh, how I've missed you. You make everything fun. I feel better already."

"Everything will be absolutely fine. You can count on me to help. By the way, when do you want me to report for work?"

"Not so fast, Ad, you've just taken a cross-country train trip. You need time to rest a bit."

"I've been resting for over a year. I need a project. I want to start Monday morning."

"No, I won't hear of it. Take a week off to get settled, perhaps, the following Monday."

"Great Scott, Angie, one whole week…well…next Monday, it is then. I'll plan to come in Monday to Friday."

"Adeline…start slowly…two days a week."

"Three!"

"How can I argue with you? Okay, you can come in three days, but not full days…either mornings or afternoons."

"…Or evenings…remember that I wanted to teach an evening English class."

"Okay, it's a deal…three days but half days. How is that handsome husband of yours?"

"Wonderful…happy…starting a new store and looking for a town-house for us, Angie, we've been very happy together except…"

"…Except, what?"

"We want a baby."

"Patience, Adeline, all in due time, dear, everything will work out."

"It's so hard for me to be patient, Angie. You do that so well, but it's difficult for me."

"I know, Adeline, but you must believe it will happen."

"Yes, Angie. I know."

"I'm so happy you're here. We have so much to catch up on."

"I know…we should celebrate. Let's take Sadie for ice cream."

"Ice cream, ice cream, yum, ice-cream," Sadie jumped up and down.

"That's what I want to hear. Is there a soda fountain nearby?"

"Yes, Rexall's Pharmacy is down the street."

"Well, let's go ladies. I've been dying for an egg cream since the day I left New York a year ago."

Chapter Twenty-Six

∼

April 24, 1925
6:20 PM (18:20)

There was always work to do, dragons left to slay,
No time to enjoy the day, and little time for play.

Angie had moved the reception desk closer to the center of the clinic waiting room. From that spot, she was able to greet everyone who came through the front door, and register patients at the same time. Her welcoming smile and easygoing manner usually made people feel relaxed and comfortable, but Rosetta Tommaso, a new patient, was upset. Nothing Angie could do or say seemed to remedy the situation. In fact, the more Angie attempted to calm the woman, the more anxious she became.

Angie simply did not understand what Rosetta was saying. She tried her best to be patient and to listen attentively. However, she had no choice but to shake her head and repeat that she didn't understand. Rosetta began to cry.

Mrs. Kotlowski, who had come to the clinic to see the doctor for the swelling in her legs, stepped forward. "I think I can be of some help, Nurse. I speak Polish."

"Yes, please," Angie nodded in frustration.

Attempting to interpret, Mrs. Kotlowski spoke to Rosetta Tommaso in Polish, but her efforts were in vain. Rosetta continued to cry.

Mrs. Balasco, another patient waiting to see the doctor, could not contain herself. She offered her assistance. She spoke to Rosetta in her native language of Spanish.

The spirited conversation of the three women, standing in the middle of the room, made them the center of attention. Everyone in the reception room watched and waited, wondering what the problem was.

Finally, Mrs. Balasco turned to Angie and announced, "It appears that we have solved the mystery." She explained further, "It seems Rosetta has been earnestly practicing her *English* since coming to America. She garnered up her courage this evening to come to the clinic. She was excited to try out the new language she learned for the first time in a public place."

Mrs. Kotlowski interrupted, "...But she was speaking *Polish*, Mrs. Balasco, not *English!*"

"Exactly, Mrs. Kotlowski, that's why she's upset. I know the apartment building where she lives. Many immigrant families from Poland live there. Rosetta has been listening to their hallway conversations since she moved to Brooklyn. She believed they were speaking the language of America, *English*. She practiced the language that she heard the people in the apartment building speaking. You see, she thought she was speaking *English* this evening, but she was actually speaking *Polish*."

"Well, that explains things. Thank you, Mrs. Balasco, you are a lifesaver. Please tell her that I am sorry I upset her." Angie added, "...and let's not forget to ask her the reason she came in today to see the doctor."

"Yes, Nurse Angie," Mrs. Balasco turned to Rosetta, acting as her interpreter. She reported to Angie that Rosetta had a cough that was keeping her awake at night. Rosetta was having difficulty sleeping. Angie nodded that she understood. She told Mrs. Balasco that the doctor would see her shortly. She added, "Tell her that we are starting English lessons here at Nativity House. Please invite her to our classes."

"Rosetta is very interested in attending. She asks how much the lessons will cost."

"Tell her there in no charge. The classes are free to the people in the neighborhood. In fact, we can introduce her to Adeline, the English teacher, tonight." Angie wrote down the date of the first class. She handed the paper to Rosetta.

Doctor Abe entered the reception room, looking puzzled. He interrupted the conversation. "Ah, here are all my patients! The exam rooms are empty. I was wondering where everyone disappeared to this evening."

Angie laughed, "Yes, we are all here." She motioned to Rosetta to follow her to the examination room to see Dr. Goodwin. Mrs. Balasco offered her assistance as an interpreter, and accompanied them.

Angie called for Mrs. Kotlowsky next. She escorted her into the exam room. "One thing I can say, Nurse, is that these young girls come to this country not knowing much. Don't you agree?"

While Angie took her vital signs, Mrs. Kotlowsky continued to talk. "The poor thing, didn't know the difference between Polish and English. Can you imagine? I don't know how some of these girls are going to make it in America with no family and no relatives to guide them...which reminds me...there is a young girl living in my building.

She's no more than a child herself, with four babies to care for. The little tykes cry all day long, stinking and dirty with wet diapers. All she knows is to cook beans. Poor thing, what's going to become of those snot-nosed crying babies?"

"It sounds like she needs some assistance."

"I stop in from time to time to help her, but what I say goes in one ear and out the other. The others in the building try to teach her, too."

"Mrs. Kotlowsky, she would benefit from a home visit by a nurse. I could generate a referral. Do you think she would be open to that?"

"She'd let anyone in to help, Nurse. She's all balled up, meaning she needs all the help she can get."

"Miss O'Shaughnessy from the Visiting Nurse Service is making home visits in the neighborhood. I'll ask her to call on the woman. I might even go along with her. I'd like to persuade your young neighbor to attend the hygiene and baby-care classes that we teach here at Nativity House. Write down her name before you leave. I'll do the rest."

"Nurse, you know all the answers. Why, that's exactly the thing that young girl needs. She needs teaching lessons. I'm glad I talked to you about this today. Maybe, you nurses can help her."

Angie left Mrs. Kotlowsky to wait for the doctor in the exam room. She called for Mrs. O'Shea. Mrs. O'Shea and her two children followed Angie into the third exam room. "How are Nolah's warts, Mrs. O'Shea? Are they going away?"

"No, Miss Angie, that's why we are here again. We have been coming for weeks, but the doctor's recommendations aren't working."

"That is often the case with warts. They are a challenge to treat."

"I had the same problem when I was a little girl. My grandmother cured my warts."

"Really? How did she do that?"

"I remember her coming into my room, waking me up late at night. She squeezed the liquid from a plant on my fingers. The warts gradually disappeared. To this day, I wish I knew what plant she used to work her magic."

"I've heard of this treatment when I was a young girl in the old country. You must search for the fattest dandelion in the field, pick it at midnight, and apply the sap to the affected area."

"Does it work?"

"Some say it did."

"Well, I am going to give it a try."

"Yes, but be sure to discuss this with Doctor Goodwin." Angie took a deep breath. "Mrs. O'Shea, I'd like to talk to you about Nolah's brother. In the waiting room, I noticed that your little boy squints when he looks at his picture books. Have you had his eyes checked for eyeglasses?"

"No, but I noticed that too, Miss Angie. Do you think he may need spectacles?"

"We can check his vision."

"He doesn't know all his letters, Miss Angie."

"We will use a picture chart."

"We don't have extra money for eyeglasses."

"We made arrangements with Doctor Emerson. You can take him to his office. It's only two blocks from here. He will give you a fair price, and accepts small weekly payments."

At that moment, Dr. Goodwin entered the exam room and asked, "Now, what are you ladies discussing so secretly this evening."

When Angie reported her observations, Doctor Abe replied, "Let's test his eyesight today. If he needs corrective lenses, we'll send him to Doctor Emerson."

"Yes, Doctor."

"…And what did I overhear about a dandelion treatment for warts?"

Mrs. O'Shea blushed, "You were listening, Doctor."

"I couldn't help overhearing. Mrs. O'Shea. I suggest you to do this as an experiment, but you must promise to write down and document any changes you notice. I am always curious about these treatments from the old country. You must remember that many plants growing in America grow differently from those in Europe. It could be that the plants in Europe absorb certain chemical nutrients from the soil that are effective in wart removal."

Mrs. O'Shea was very impressed. "My, that is a very scientific explanation, Doctor."

As the evening passed, the reception room slowly emptied. By eight, all the patients, who had come for evening clinic, had been treated and were on their way home. Adeline's citizenship class was finishing up. After Adeline waved good-bye to her students, she joined Angie and Abe in the kitchen. "I have an idea. I want to ask you if I could take Sadie home with me tonight. May I have an over-night with her?"

"Really, Ad, are you sure? It's my night for her sleepover, but if she wants to go with you, I'd be delighted."

"Thank you, I'll go and ask her."

"I bet she will be overjoyed. Since you've arrived, I noticed Sadie is a happier girl. She follows you around everywhere. She loves you, Addie."

When Adeline left the kitchen, Abe turned to Angie. "If Sadie goes home with Adeline, you will be free tonight. How about we sneak away to Ricci's and have a late night supper at the restaurant?"

"It's a long walk to Ricci's."

"Yes, that's exactly why I'm suggesting Ricci's. It's a lovely evening."

Before Angie could answer, they heard a knock at the door. Abe asked, "Who can that be?"

Angie went to the door, and opened it. To her surprise, she recognized the woman at the door who was once her patient at Ellis Island Hospital. "Why Elsbeth, what brings you here tonight?"

"Oh, Nurse...it's you...Miss Angie from the hospital. You remembered me."

"Of course, Elsbeth, I still have the letter you sent me at Ellis Island. I was so moved. It was very thoughtful of you to take the time to write me. I always wanted to tell you how much I appreciated receiving your letter."

"Thank you, Miss, for sacrificing your shoes. I wasn't expecting to see you here tonight."

"You look quite well, but are you feeling ill?"

"No, Miss Angie, that's not why I came. I didn't even know a clinic for the sick was here. You see, my husband and I live six blocks away. Callum has been staying out until all hours of the night into the morning. I'm not always the suspicious kind, but last week I followed him to this house. It was late. It took me all this time to store up enough courage to return and investigate. I suspected there might be a pretty young girl living here. You know how boys are, Miss Angie. Do you live here?"

"No, Elsbeth, it's the Nativity Settlement House and Health Clinic."

"What was Callum doing here? Dear God, is my poor Callum ill? Did he come to see the doctor?"

"We're not at liberty to discuss our patients."

"That means…he is sick!"

"I didn't say that, Elsbeth. Please come in and sit down. Let's talk about this."

Elsbeth turned away, "No, I mustn't stay. I have to go."

Angie called after her as she left. "Elsbeth, please don't go. Come back."

"No, Miss Angie, he mustn't find me prying into his business." Elsbeth rushed out of the building, determined to return home quickly.

"Who was that, Angie?"

"Very strange…it was a patient from Ellis Island Hospital. She was looking for her husband. She thinks he may be a patient of ours."

"What's his name?

"Callum Ferguson…"

"Let's look at our records."

Angie and Abe went to their office to search through the clinic files.

"No one by the name of Callum Ferguson has come to see us."

"That's strange, Abe. She was certain he came here. Perhaps, he came and used another name…an alias."

"That is always a possibility. What does he look like?"

"I don't know. I never met him. I only met his wife."

Angie and Abe were interrupted by Adeline and Sadie. "Well, we are off. Sadie is excited about riding in the Studebaker, and spending the night at the Waldorf with Harry and me. We are going to have a great time. Right, Sadie?"

"Yes, Addie."

"We'll be back tomorrow," she said. Then, looking down on Sadie, she added, "Well, maybe tomorrow, if we're having a good time, it might be the next day."

"Now, don't get yourself too tired, Adeline. Don't do too much."

"A person can never have too much fun, Angie."

"Okay, ladies, have a good time. Let me know when you will be bringing Sadie back to Brooklyn."

Angie and Abe walked Adeline and Sadie to the Studebaker, and waved *goodbye* as they rode off.

"Miss Angie, may I interest you in a romantic supper for two this evening?" Abe asked, offering his arm.

"Yes, thank you," Angie said, taking his arm. "It would be my pleasure, Doctor."

Chapter Twenty-Seven

May 2, 1925
1:00 PM (13:00)

You can learn from happiness, as well as from the blues.
Try a new emotion. Go ahead, you'll get to choose.

Perhaps it was the colorful flapper dresses she wore, or her sparkly jewelry, or simply the way she grinned from ear to ear that made Sadie fall in love with Adeline. Adeline talked quickly with gusto and energy, using her hands. Sadie began to copy Adeline's movements and speech. When Sadie was in Adeline's company, there was always a smile on her face. In a matter of days, little Sadie slowly changed from a worried child to a carefree, happy girl.

For Adeline, the feeling was mutual. Adeline and Sadie became inseparable. Adeline planned exciting outings for Sadie. They shopped on Fifth Avenue, and went to see the animals at the Central Park Zoo. They watched silent movies, and went on boat rides. Sadie loved the boat rides best of all. When they weren't out and about town, they spent their time singing and dancing. Adeline played records on her Victrola, and taught Sadie to do the Charleston.

Beginning May 1st, Coney Island's Luna Park was opening on weekends. Adeline was excited to take Sadie on the rides. "Sadie, what do you think we are going to do today?"

"Maybe we will row in a rowboat in Central Park again."

"Do you like to go on rides?"

"Oh, yes, Addie!"

"Did you ever go to Coney island?"

"Mama took me there once." Suddenly, Sadie grew pensive, "I am worried about Mama, Addie. Where did she go?"

"I don't know, Sadie. Officer Gallagher is looking for her. As soon as he finds her, you can be certain that he will call you."

"That's a good thing because maybe Mama is lost, and trying to find her way home."

"I am sure she is, Sadie."

"I hope he finds her."

"I hope so too. I have an idea. Would you like to go to Coney Island today?"

Sadie clapped her hands. "Yes, oh, yes, Addie, that would be fun."

"Okay, it's settled then. Let's go this afternoon. On the way, we'll stop off to see Angie and Doctor Abe during their clinic break."

Adeline and Sadie dressed quickly. They were driving across the Williamsburg Bridge in Harry's red Studebaker in less than an hour. Adeline parked in front of The Nativity Settlement House and Health Clinic. She opened the car door for Sadie, and lifted her out of her seat. Sadie ran to the front door of Nativity House and rang the bell.

Angie answered, "Now, who is at my door, visiting me this afternoon? Let me see, who can it be? Could it be Miss Sadie?"

Sadie flew into Angie's arms. "I missed you, little one." Angie said. "Have you been having a good time with Addie?"

"Oh, yes, Angie. I love Addie."

Adeline chimed in, "…And Addie loves you."

"Are you going to stay over with me at the convent tonight?" Angie asked.

Adeline answered. "Yes, Angie, but first, Sadie and I have an afternoon outing planned."

"Where are you going?"

"We're on our way to Coney Island. I want to take Sadie on the Luna Park rides. Do you want to come along with us?"

"It sounds like fun. I would love to go, but I have another clinic starting in two hours. Why don't you stop in to see Dr. Martin, and check on our little baby while you're at Luna Park?"

"You mean the baby you found at Nativity House?"

"Yes, he's there for another two weeks. I think Sadie would enjoy seeing the baby."

"What a wonderful idea. We'll stop in. I'd like to see Madame Louise again. Okay, let's be on our way. Sadie, wave *goodbye* to Angie."

Angie walked the girls out to the car. She blew kisses to them as they drove off. Sadie started singing, "Rum-rummers-a-rumming. Rum-rummers-a-rumming."

"What are you singing, Sadie?"

"Rum-rummers-a-rumming. Rum-rummers-a-rumming."

"Where did you learn that song from?"

"From mama, she gets her hooch from the rum-rummers at Coney Island."

"I think you mean *rum-runners*, not rum-rummers."

"What are they?"

"They are boats that carry rum. It's like bootlegging."

"What is bootlegging?"

"Bootlegging came about during wartime when soldiers were not allowed to drink alcohol. They hid their bottles of alcohol in their boots."

"What's alcohol?"

"Hooch!"

"Why did they have to hide their hooch?"

"How do I explain this? Let's see. Alcohol makes people do silly things. Soldiers are like policemen. They must be alert at all times."

"Why?"

"Their job is to protect people. In America, there is a law that people cannot sell alcohol."

"Why?"

"Because when people drink alcohol, it sometimes makes them do foolish things. It can cause accidents and fights."

"People get mad too, like Mama."

"The government law says, 'no more selling alcohol'. It is called *prohibition*. The only problem is that the people still want to drink their hooch."

"Why?"

"It makes them happy for a short time. They forget their troubles. They relax. Now, the only way people can get their hooch is to make it themselves, or to smuggle it in from another country. Whiskey alcohol is made in Canada. It is smuggled or bootlegged into the United States. Rum alcohol is from the Caribbean Islands. In warm weather, small boats come up from the islands to smuggle in rum. They run the motors of their boats to get where they want to go to deliver the rum. So, they are called *rum-runners*."

"That sounds like a lot of trouble for a little hooch, Addie."

When Adeline and Sadie arrived at Luna Park, there weren't many people on the Midway. Some rides were still boarded up for the winter season, but the best ones were open. The first ride they rode was the *Loop-The-Loop*. Sadie was big enough to be allowed on, and wanted to ride a second time. Next, they rode on the roller-coaster. After that, they went in the haunted spook-house, the *Dragon's Gorge*. Sadie laughed during the entire ride. When they exited the *Dragon's Gorge*, they saw the *Infant Incubator Exhibit*. It was closed, but Adeline knew to ring the bell at the side door. Madame Louise answered. She was both surprised and overjoyed to see Adeline. The two began to talk in French. Sadie had never heard the French language before. She pretended to imitate them.

Madame Louise explained that the exhibit was due to open on Memorial Day weekend. She told them that she had one infant to show them, but he was no longer in an incubator. He was already in a bassinet. She offered them tea and cookies while they waited for the baby to wake up.

Soon, they heard grunting noises coming from the next room. Madame Louise said, "Come, follow me. It's time. The baby is stirring."

Adeline and Sadie followed Madame Louise into the nursery. The three of them looked down at the baby, sleeping on his stomach in the bassinet. They watched him squirm and stretch out his legs, getting himself ready to wake up. Madame Louise turned him on his back. He started to cry. She changed his wet diaper. Lifting and holding the baby in one hand, she changed the wet bassinet sheet with the other. "He is growing fast and gaining weight quickly. He's over five pounds already. In two weeks, we'll transfer him to the Foundling."

"What will happen to him?"

"The authorities will do an investigation. If the mother is not located, he will be detained. It may take up to six months for him to be cleared for adoption. Would you like to hold him, Adeline?"

"Yes, of course. Let me wash my hands first."

Madame Louise pointed to the sink in the corner of the room. "You can wash there."

"Come, Sadie, let's wash our hands before we touch the baby."

Adeline showed Sadie how to wash her hands thoroughly. After Adeline put on a face mask, Madame Louise passed the baby to Adeline. She left to prepare a baby bottle in the kitchen.

Adeline sat down so that Sadie could get a closer look. Sadie stared at the baby in Adeline's arms. She offered him her finger. The baby grabbed it, and held on tight. Sadie laughed. "He likes me," she said. Sadie touched his head and stroked his hair. "He's so soft and sweet."

"Do you like babies, Sadie?" Adeline asked.

"I love them, Addie. Can we take him home with us?"

"No, he's not our baby, Sadie. He doesn't belong to us."

"Who does he belong to?"

"He belongs to his mother, Sadie."

"Is Madame Louise his mother?"

"No, she's his nurse."

"Like Nurse Angie?"

"Yes, Sadie…"

"Where is his mother?"

"No one knows…"

"Is she lost like my mama?"

"Yes…"

"Oh, the baby must be sad about that. I hope his mama finds her way back to him."

"…And I hope your mama finds her way back to you, too, Sadie."

When Madame Louise returned with the baby bottle, Adeline handed the baby to her to feed him.

Sadie asked, "What is his name?"

"When he arrived, the doctor called him *Baby M*," Madame Louise answered, "however, I call him *Henri*."

Adeline and Sadie watched as Madame Louise fed and burped Baby Henri. When the feeding was finished, Madame Louise swaddled him tightly, and tucked him back in his bassinet.

Adeline looked at the clock on the wall. "It's time to go, Sadie. It's getting late. Angie will be waiting for us."

"I don't want to go, Addie. Can we come back and see Baby Henri again?"

"Perhaps, on another day, come, sweetheart." Adeline thanked Madame Louise for a delightful afternoon. Sadie kissed Baby Henri's head before they left.

As they walked to the car, Sadie said, "Baby Henri is like me, Addie. His mother is lost and is nowhere to be found."

They arrived at Nativity House as the evening clinic was finishing. Angie was straightening the exam rooms when Adeline and Sadie came running in. "Did you have fun, ladies?" Angie asked.

"Oh, yes, Miss Angie, it was fun, but it was a little sad, too."

"What was sad about it?"

"We met Baby Henri. His mama is lost, like my mama."

"How is our baby doing?"

"Angie, he's adorable. He's growing quickly, and is over five pounds. He is almost ready to be transferred to the Foundling. Madame Louise said that it may take up to six months for him to be ready to be adopted."

"Poor thing…"

"If Sadie had her way, she would have adopted him this afternoon."

"Adeline, have you considered adoption?"

"Yes, Harry has been encouraging it. He says that when people adopt, they are sometimes blessed with a pregnancy."

"Wouldn't that be wonderful?"

"Angie, I will admit I could have put that little baby boy right in my pocket and taken him home tonight."

"Why don't you?"

"Why don't I…what?"

"Take him home with you. Adopt him."

"It's much too soon."

"What are you waiting for?"

"I…I…I'm not ready."

"Scared?"

"Yes, suddenly I am terrified. I don't think I'm ready to take the plunge. I need more time."

"Take all the time you need. When the time is right, you'll jump into it, Ad. I know you."

"It's certainly something to think about. Heavens, look at the time. I better start heading back to the city. Harry will be waiting."

"I want to go with you, Addie." Sadie pleaded.

"It's Angie's turn to play with you tonight."

"Please, Miss Angie, can I go home with Addie again."

Angie looked at Adeline. "What do you think?"

"It's up to you, Angie. I love taking Sadie."

"Okay, if that's what makes the two of you happy, then it's off with the both of you. Have a good time."

Abe walked into the room, "Is that my friend, Sadie, I hear? How is Sadie this evening?"

"Good, Doctor Abe, I went to Coney Island. Guess what?"

"What?"

"I'm going home with Addie tonight."

Abe bent down and kissed Sadie on the forehead. Then, he kissed Adeline on her cheek. "Hi, Adeline, it's good to see you looking so well." He turned to Sadie, "Sadie, I thought you would stay with Angie tonight."

Angie explained, "Sadie has her heart set on being with Adeline. Therefore, I'm sending them on their way. Okay, you two, better get going. It's starting to get dark."

Abe looked at Angie, "Well, you know what that means, Miss Angie?"

"No, what does that mean, Doctor Abe?"

"It means that I get to take my favorite nurse out to Ricci's for dinner tonight. Hurry, Angie, let's straighten up, and eat out at Ricci's."

Chapter Twenty-Eight

May 9, 1925
2:30PM (14:30)

When a new path opens, straight and clear,
You shift your direction, ignoring all fear.

When the young woman rang the doorbell of the Nativity Settlement House and Health Clinic, Nurse Angie answered. "I have a bit of a scratchy throat, Nurse. My cousin told me that I might be able to see a doctor if I came by today. Is the clinic open?"

"We open this afternoon at four o'clock."

"Does the doctor charge very much?"

"There's no charge to see the doctor."

"I have to go to work at four."

"We're open until eight in the evening tonight."

"I work until nine. Can I come back tomorrow?"

"We're closed on Sunday. What's your name?"

"Greta, Nurse."

"May I ask your last name, too?"

"Yes, J-J-Jones, I'm Greta Jones."

"Please come in, Miss Jones. Have a seat. The doctor is on his break, but I'll ask him if he will see you now. Fill out this registration card with your name, address, and date of birth, and here is a list of the classes that we offer at Nativity House."

"Thank you, Nurse." Greta pretended to study the paper Angie gave her.

Angie said, "I must say you look familiar. Have we met before?"

"I don't believe so, Nurse."

"You remind me of someone. I meet many people. I..."

"I see here that you have infant care classes. Can anyone come?"

"Yes, everyone in the neighborhood is welcome to attend."

"Umm...speaking of infants, I heard that someone left a baby at your door."

"Yes, that was last month."

"What a shame that the baby died."

"No, Greta, the baby lived. He was a tiny little thing, but he was strong and blessed with a healthy pair of lungs."

"What happened to him?"

"We made arrangements for him to go to the Infant Incubator Exhibit at Coney Island."

"How is he doing?"

"He's doing quite well and growing."

"Really, Nurse?"

"Yes. Excuse me a minute. I'll ask the doctor if he will see you now. I'll be back in a moment."

Abe was working in the back office. When Angie asked Abe if he had time to examine a patient, he put his work down and followed her into the reception room. However, when Angie and Abe entered the room, they discovered that Greta Jones was gone.

Angie was puzzled. "That's strange. Where did she go?"

Abe looked around and asked, "Did she fill out a registration card?"

"Yes, here it is. She left it on the desk."

"Maybe she stepped out, and plans on returning. Call me when she returns." Abe was turning to leave, but stopped when he heard the doorbell. "That must be her now." He opened the door to find Officer Gallagher.

"Good Afternoon, Officer Gallagher, I haven't seen you in a while. How are you?"

"Not good, Doc, I don't have good news to report."

Angie and Abe both asked, "What happened?"

"Well, I am here to tell you that we found a Jane Doe floating in the East River early this morning. The fingerprints on the body match those we have on record for Sadie's mother."

"Oh dear, Sadie will be heartbroken."

"I know she will. Sadie's been a good little girl, always listening to her mother. In fact, I think it was little Sadie who took care of the woman. No other relatives around to speak of. You would think that Sadie was the mother of the two...the way Sadie worried. The child waited for her mother's return. Somehow, her mother always found a way of coming back to Sadie, but her luck ran out today."

"Would you like me to tell Sadie? I can explain the news about her mother when I put her to bed tonight."

"No, Nurse, I have to take Sadie in now."

"What do you mean?" Abe asked.

"After the identification was made, and we knew for certain Jane Doe was Sadie's mother, I sat down and submitted my police report. I turned it in two hours ago. The City Orphanage has been notified. They are on the alert, waiting for us to bring her in to be processed. They're expecting her at the orphanage tonight."

"No, Officer, not tonight, that will be confusing and much too difficult for her. Please let her stay the night with us. We can break the news to her gently."

"Orders are orders, Nurse. Is she here?"

"Yes, she's in the playroom with Maureen and Leonora."

Maureen and Leonora had come in on Saturday to decorate the playroom.

When Officer Gallagher entered the playroom and spotted Sadie, he kneeled down to be eye-to-eye with the little girl. "Sadie, how would you like to come down to the precinct with me to say hello to my fellow officers? The policemen downtown miss you. They would like you to come and visit them again."

"I would love to, Officer Gallagher, but I can't today. I am waiting for Addie to finish her work. Then, I am going home with her."

With the mention of her name, Adeline came into the room. "What's going on, Officer?"

"Routine, Nurse Adeline, I need to take Sadie down to the City Orphanage."

"Why?"

"Because her mother was located and identified."

"Is she here? Is Sadie going home with her mother?"

"Like I said, Nurse, I'm taking Sadie to the City Orphanage. Her mother's in the morgue."

The policeman reached for Sadie's hand.

Maureen gasped.

Adeline pleaded, "Please, Gallagher, can't she stay here with us? Sadie will be happier here."

Confused, Sadie started to cry. She ran to Adeline, and clung to her.

Leonora added, "We've all grown fond of Sadie. She's comfortable with us. Please let her stay."

"If it was up to me, you know I would, but the law is the law, Miss."

"What's the law?" Abe asked.

"When a minor is orphaned, the child is to be turned over immediately to the City Orphanage to be processed. You people are not making this easy for me."

Sadie was in tears. "Addie, Addie, I love you. I don't want to go... tell him."

"Gallagher, surely there must be something we can do? Would it be possible for us to take Sadie down to the orphanage tomorrow?"

"There's nothing you can do, unless one of you is thinking of adopting her. Then, I could name you in my report, and the orphanage officials will contact you to process the paperwork. Since, that's not happening, I have to..."

Adeline interrupted him. "If that were to happen, could Sadie stay with us?"

"Yes, Nurse."

Adeline stood up tall. She looked directly at the policeman and announced, "Officer Gallagher, I am going to adopt Sadie. Please submit your report with the names of Mr. and Mrs. Harry Steingold as her future guardians. We intend to adopt Sadie."

Officer Gallagher looked relieved. "Really, Nurse, you're going to give the child a respectable home?"

"Yes, I am."

Maureen jumped up and ran to Adeline. "You and Sadie…I can't believe it!"

Leonora was standing next to Adeline. She hugged Adeline. "Oh, Adeline, how wonderful."

Abe put his arm around Angie. Angie asked, "Are you certain, Adeline?"

"Oh, Angie, I've never been more certain of anything."

Sadie flew into Adeline's arms. Adeline lifted her up and hugged her.

Officer Gallagher took off his police cap, and scratched his head. "Well, if this isn't the happiest moment I could ever imagine, I'll eat my hat. Nurse, all I need is your address, and I'll be off. Wait until I tell the fellows down at the precinct. Ladies, Doctor, a very Good Afternoon to all of you."

The policeman repositioned his cap on his head. After Adeline wrote down her address, he turned to Sadie before leaving. "Sadie, you be a good girl now for Miss Adeline, and keep in touch with Officer Gallagher."

Sadie looked puzzled. "I don't understand. I don't know what you're talking about."

"Sadie, let's go back to the hotel. We'll sit down with Harry. The three of us will have a little talk tonight. Come, dear, let's go. Harry and I will explain everything to you."

Angie kissed Adeline. She whispered in her ear. "I'm happy for you, Ad. You're my hero. I'm so proud of the way you jumped in with no fear."

"At that moment, I had no fear…no fear, at all, Angie. It felt like the right thing to do."

Maureen and Leonora hugged Adeline. They kissed Sadie good-bye as Adeline and Sadie left Nativity House.

"Well, we couldn't have asked for a better outcome," Abe said.

"It was like a miracle, Doctor Goodwin." Maureen cried out, excitedly.

Leonora wiped away a tear. "I'm so happy for them."

"Now, ladies, dry your tears. There really is nothing to cry about."

"Doctor Goodwin, I noticed you were a little misty a minute ago." Maureen teased.

"I can't wait to tell Papa. He's grown attached to that little girl," Leonora said. "Oh, and I must remember to tell Adeline that Papa is going to make all of Sadie's shoes. He'll look forward to seeing her when she comes in for a new pair of shoes."

"The Sisters at the Convent are going to be disappointed, too."

"Angie, did you know Adeline was going to adopt Sadie?" Maureen asked.

"We had a discussion about adoption. I know Adeline was delighted with Sadie, but it was Harry who was considering adopting. Adeline wasn't ready to take the plunge."

It was Maureen's turn to cry. "It was all so sudden, and so beautiful."

"Adeline's always taught me to step up and face my fear. She often told me that if fear is holding you back, you must crash right through it. In fact, I think I'm going to follow her example."

Abe chuckled. "Are we going to adopt a baby when we get married?"

"No, Doctor, I have a better idea. We're going to get married. Let's do it! Let's select a date for our wedding day."

"Today, Angie?"

"Today, Abe. Flora and Isabella gave me three dates to choose in September: the thirteenth, the twentieth, and the twenty-seventh."

"Let's look at the calendar in my office and decide."

"Let's just select one now."

"Now?"

"Yes, what's it going to be?"

"I definitely think you should make this decision." Abe insisted.

"Okay, I'll decide…lucky thirteen…September thirteenth."

"Well, September thirteenth, it is then. Is Number Thirteen always lucky for you?"

"No, I chose it simply because it's the earliest date. You know, I've never really had a lucky number, but I think thirteen might be lucky for me from now on."

Chapter Twenty-Nine

May 10, 1925
7AM (07:00)

*After she takes time to weep, she may awaken from her sleep
To travel far and journey deep for secrets buried down so deep.*

Angie and Abe were crossing Johnson Avenue on their way to Nativity House when Angie suddenly stopped.

She shouted, "MERTA!"

"What, Angie?"

"Merta! Merta! It just came to me. Greta Jones is Merta. I knew I remembered her, but I couldn't place where I knew her from."

"Angie, I don't know what you're talking about. This humble physician may require a bit more of an explanation."

"Oh, I am sorry, Abe. It's been on my mind all night. Suddenly, it came to me."

"Okay, Angie, from the beginning..."

"Remember the woman who came into the clinic yesterday. I asked you if you had time to see her. When we returned to the Reception Room, she was gone. She said her name was Greta Jones."

"Yes, go on."

"When I met her yesterday, I was certain I recognized her from somewhere. She said she didn't know me."

Abe opened the front door of Nativity House. He held the door open for Angie to enter. He said, "Angie, this sounds important. Let's sit down and have a cup of coffee in the kitchen. You can tell me the whole story."

He offered Angie a chair while he prepared the coffee to brew. "Go on," he said.

"She was a patient at Ellis Island. Her name was Merta. Merta...I can't remember her last name. She was admitted for nausea and vomiting. We assumed that she was seasick from the long sea journey. She was at Ellis Island Hospital for three days. During that time, her physician ordered a number of routine blood tests, including a pregnancy test. I received the results of the pregnancy test after she was discharged. It was positive."

"Did they notify her?"

"I don't know. I returned the test reports to the laboratory with a stamped notation that the patient had been discharged."

"Sounds like you were following protocol."

"I was. Merta asked about the baby yesterday."

"What baby?"

"Baby M, Abe, the baby we found."

"How did that come about?"

"I had given her the list of classes that we are starting at Nativity House. She noticed the infant-care class. She said she heard that someone left a baby at the clinic who died."

"And..."

"...And I told her that the baby was alive and doing well at the Infant Incubator Exhibit at Coney Island. Abe, why did she think the baby had died?"

"Now, I'm starting to understand. When was the pregnancy test taken?"

"I can't remember. It was when I was preparing to leave Ellis Island Hospital. No, it was earlier...maybe August or September." Angie rested her head in her arms on the kitchen table. "Oh, Abe, I can't remember. I'll have to think a little more about this."

"I'm sure it will come to you."

"Merta was expecting her parents the night she was discharged. Her father and mother were delayed. We talked while she was waiting for them to pick her up. She told me about a friend of hers who was pregnant. She wanted to know where her friend could go to confirm the pregnancy."

"Is Merta married?"

"No, maybe my imagination is getting the best of me, but Merta may be the baby's mother."

"You may be right, Angie. Do you remember the handkerchief we found with the initial, 'M', embroidered on it? The pieces are beginning to fit. All that's missing are the dates. When was she discharged from the hospital?"

"It was a summer night. I think it was before we went to Luna Park. I could go back to the convent and look at last year's calendar to check when that was."

"No need for that. We went to Coney Island on August twelfth."

"How did you remember the date?"

"How could I ever forget it, Angie? It was our first date."

"You are a romantic man, and I am a lucky girl."

"Listen, I'm certain Sister Gwendolyn can search for the patient's last name if you know the week she was discharged."

"I'll give Sister a call. First, I want to ring up Adeline to see how it went with Sadie last night."

"We also have to call Isabella and Mama to tell them about our wedding date. They will be very excited."

When Angie called Adeline, Adeline reported that Sadie seemed to understand what had happened. After they told her the news about her mother, Sadie said that she was very sad. She cried herself to sleep. However, when she woke up in the morning, she said she was half-sad and half-happy. She was happy because she was going to be with Adeline and Harry.

Harry had already called both his attorney and the City Orphanage. He had scheduled an appointment for their interview on Monday. Adeline was planning on taking the ferry to show Sadie the Statue of Liberty. She felt a boat ride would cheer up Sadie. Afterward, they were going to meet Harry for dinner.

When Angie told Adeline the story of Merta, alias Greta Jones, Adeline said she would be delighted to stop off at Ellis Island. She wanted to show off Sadie to their nurse friends at the hospital, and promised to ask Sister Gwendolyn Hanover about a former patient named *Merta*.

"Look, Sadie, it's the Statue of Liberty!"

"Why is the statue green?"

"She is made of copper, like a penny. Copper turns green when it is oxidized by the air."

"Why isn't she shiny like a penny?

"The green covering is protecting her delicate copper. The statue was a gift from France."

"That's where you were born, right?"

"Right, Sadie. The French sculptor who made the statue is Frederic Bartholdi. He called her *Liberty Enlightening the World.*"

"Why does she have her arm up in the air?"

"The fire in her torch is a symbol of the United States of America, shining new light on old European ideas. Look, Sadie, the ferry is already approaching Ellis Island. This is where Angie and I worked for many years. It is the place where immigrants from other countries come to enter the United States. If they are ill when they arrive, the nurses and doctors take care of them at the hospital."

"That is kind of them. Do you like being a nurse, Addie?"

"I love it, Sadie, and I think I will love being your mother, as well."

"I'm glad about that, Addie."

Adeline pointed to a three-story cottage at the tip of the island. "Look, sweetie, see the little cottage there? That's where Angie and I lived when we worked at the hospital. Our rooms were on the third floor. We could see the Statue of Liberty from our windows. Harry and I were married there before we left for California. The house was filled to the brim with white flowers on our wedding day. It was beautiful."

"Will Angie be married there, too?"

"No, Angie and Doctor Abe are going to get married in a church in Brooklyn. When the ferry lands, I'll show you the hospital where Angie and I worked. After that, I want to introduce you to my nurse friends."

The ferry was filled with Sunday afternoon hospital visitors, carrying flowers and baskets of fruit. Adeline and Sadie patiently waited for their turn to disembark. "Easy, easy now...no running, no running allowed," shouted the Ferry Captain.

Sadie looked up at Adeline, and said, "They're allowed to run on the rum-rummers boats, right?"

"You mean the *rum-runners* boats. No, you can't run on a boat."

"But, you said they ran for the rum."

"It means the boats ran their engine motors to deliver the rum."

"Oh," said Sadie.

Their first stop was to the office of Sister Gwendolyn where they found the Nursing Superintendent behind her desk. She looked pale and drained, but color brightened her cheeks when she saw Adeline.

She stood up to greet her. "Adeline, this is a surprise. I'm delighted to see you. Angie told me you were coming back to New York this month. I'm so glad you stopped by to see us."

"I couldn't wait to come."

"Who is this little sweetheart?"

"This is Sadie. Harry and I are applying to adopt her."

"How very wonderful. I wish you the best."

"It's Sunday Visiting Day, I thought this would be a good day to show Sadie the Hospital and the Nurses' Cottage."

"Yes, everyone will be so glad to see you. I just noticed Ruth and Rose sitting out on the porch of the Nurses' Cottage. I have a suggestion. When you go to the Contagious Disease Hospital, I'll take Sadie to the Well-Children's Unit where she can color and play while she waits for you. By the way, how are Angie and Doctor Goodwin?"

"They send their regards. Last night, they decided on a date for their wedding in September."

"I've been waiting to hear from her."

"September thirteenth is the day."

"Wonderful. I'll start preparing the September schedule."

"Oh, before I forget, Angie has a question for you. A patient came into her clinic, using an alias. Angie remembers her as a former patient at Ellis Island Hospital. She knows her first name, but not her last. Can we look up her last name in her medical record?"

"No, unfortunately, all the medical records are filed by the patient's last name."

"Angie knows she had a positive pregnancy test when she was here, would we be able to search the laboratory files to look for women with positive pregnancy tests during that time?"

"That won't work either. The laboratory reports are also filed by the patient's last name."

"Well, there should be another system."

"Oh, Adeline, do you think we have a magic machine that spits out this information automatically?"

"Yes, we should be able to enter that information into an electronic machine, push a button, and out would pop the answers...like the names of all the women with positive pregnancy tests, or all people who were discharged on a certain day."

Sister Gwendolyn laughed. "Adeline, you always could make me laugh. How, in the world, do you think up such silly notions? Now, I do have another way to approach this problem. Do you know her date of discharge from the hospital?"

"Actually, Angie narrowed it down to sometime within a week."

"Well, the discharge office keeps a handwritten log. Why don't I go over and look at it? Give me all the information you have. Go ahead and show your face around town. Meet me back here in two hours. After my Hospital Rounds, I should have the answer to your question."

Before Adeline went to sleep that night, she called Angie.

"I have her name and a contact address. She is Merta Flanagan."

"Yes, of course, Flanagan. How did you get it?"

"I got the information from Sister…both her last name and the forwarding address of her aunt. When the ferry landed at Battery Park, Harry was waiting to take Sadie and me out to dinner. I asked him to drive me to Merta's aunt on Broome Street. I pretended to be a friend of hers. Although she looked at me a little strangely, she gave me Merta's Brooklyn address. It's on Humboldt Street. Angie, it's only three blocks from Nativity House."

"We should call Officer Gallagher in the morning, and give him her name and address."

"No, Angie. Let's not involve Gallagher. I have another idea."

Chapter Thirty

❧

May 12, 1925
7 AM (07:00)

Mistakes are made, you can be sure.
But she will learn from each detour.

After Adeline kissed her husband, Harry, *good-bye*, and wished him, *a very good day*, she hurried to the bathroom to scrub the morning makeup off her face. Next, she washed the neat little finger-waves out of her hair. She parted her hair down the middle, and made two Indian-style braids on each side of her face. Lifting the braids on top of her head, she pinned them into a circle crown. She opened the brown paper bag from Gimbel's Department Store, and pulled out a cotton housedress. Shopping at Herald Square the day before, she had bought a navy-blue dress with yellow daisies and a white peter-pan collar. She tried on the dress. Satisfied with how she looked, she went into Sadie's room to wake her up for breakfast, and to get her ready for school.

After dropping Sadie at the kindergarten class at Nativity Church, Adeline rushed across the street to Nativity House.

"How do I look, Angie Girl?"

"Do you really want to know?"

"Of course, I do, on the level now."

"Well, it's not your style...not exactly the cat's meow."

"Good! Do I look like a young immigrant lady?"

"Yes, you do. What do you have up your sleeve, Adeline?"

"We're going to find Merta today."

"We are?"

"Yes…you and me."

"…And I am going with you?"

"Yes, I need you so that she'll recognize you as the nurse from the hospital."

Adeline shared her plan with Angie. They were going to go to Merta's apartment to confront her.

"…and that's the reason you're dressed like this today?"

"Exactly, when I talked to her aunt on Sunday, she looked at me rather suspiciously. So, I thought it would be wiser to dress the part."

Adeline opened the paper bag from Gimbel's, and showed its contents to Angie. "Here, I bought a dress for you." Inside was a pink cotton print dress with a scalloped, yellow collar. "Try this on."

"It's sweet, Ad, the dress I never wanted. Okay, what's the plan? Are we to pretend we are immigrants?"

"We aren't pretending. We are immigrants."

"Yes, but we came to America when I was twelve, and you were four. We're citizens now, Adeline."

Angie slipped into the dress, and buttoned each one of the pearl buttons lining the dress from its collar to its hem. "When do we go?"

"The sooner the better…you don't have a clinic today. Let's go now."

It wasn't difficult to find the address of the apartment building that Merta's aunt had given Adeline. A moment before Adeline rang the bell, Angie said, "Adeline, I'm nervous."

"I know…so am I, a little."

"Why are we doing this? Can't we simply give all the information we have to Officer Gallagher? The police have special ways of investigating. They can find out if Merta is the mother of Baby M."

"I'm convinced that will scare her off. She will never admit she left the baby at Nativity House, but if she sees you…"

"I get it, but…what shall I say?"

"You don't have to say anything. Just be there. I'll do the talking for both of us."

"What are you going to say?"

Adeline laughed, "I don't exactly know yet, Angie. Okay now, stay calm, look like a happy-go-lucky kind of a gal."

Adeline rang the bell. Merta's mother answered. They walked up to the third-floor apartment, and knocked on the door. After introducing themselves as Merta's friends who met her at Ellis Island, Mrs. Flanagan invited them in.

Adeline explained, "When Merta left the hospital, she gave me the address of your sister. I was passing the other day, and stopped in. She gave me this address."

"How lovely of you, young ladies, to come by today. I am sure Merta will be happy to see you again. Although, what a shame, she's not here this morning. She's working."

"That's wonderful. I'm glad she found work."

"Yes, she's working at the five-and-ten-cent store down the street, you know…Woolie's."

"Yes, it's called *Woolworth's*. It was very nice meeting you. Please tell Merta we stopped by to say *hello*. We'll come back another time."

"Whom shall I say called for her?" Mrs. Flanagan asked as the two ladies were leaving her apartment.

"Sadie," Adeline said.

"…and Greta," Angie added.

After Angie and Adeline left the building, and walked down to the street, Angie asked, "So, mastermind, what's our next step in this caper?"

"We go to Woolworth's."

"Now?"

"Now!"

As the women stood outside F. W. Woolworth & Co. pretending to look at the merchandise displayed in the store window, they discussed their strategy.

"What next?" Angie asked.

"We go in. Act like we are shopping. Look around."

"For what?"

"For Merta, of course, when you recognize her, squeeze my hand."

Angie and Adeline entered the store. Angie spotted Merta immediately. She whispered, "There she is, Adeline, behind the cookie counter."

"You were supposed to squeeze my hand, Angie."

"I forgot."

"Are you sure it's her?"

"Of course, I'm sure. What do we do?"

Adeline shrugged her shoulders.

Angie looked at Adeline confidently. "I'll handle this, Ad."

Merta was behind the counter. There were no other customers around. "Hello, Merta," Angie said. "You came into Nativity House the other day."

"No, Miss, you must be mistaking."

"I'm sure it was you. Aren't you Merta Flanagan?"

"How do you know my name?"

"Don't you remember me from Ellis Island Hospital?"

"No, Miss, I never saw you before. Please, leave. I could get into trouble for talking to you during work hours."

"Is there someplace we can go to talk in private?"

"Go away. I don't want trouble. Please."

"We know you left your baby at Nativity House."

"Please go away. Please. No one knows about the baby...no one."

"Can we talk privately?"

"Shhh..." Merta put her finger to her lips. She turned, and called to a saleslady at the next counter. "Nellie, I need a bathroom break. Can you cover?"

"Sure, Merta, but don't be too long. You know how hard it is to cover two counters at one time."

"Follow me," Merta said. She ushered Angie and Adeline into a storeroom.

"Please, ladies, no one knows about the baby. I'm dating a college man now. I need a fresh start. The baby...I thought...he was dead."

"Is that why you left him at Nativity House?"

"I'm not married. My parents didn't even know that I was pregnant. No one knew. Please leave it at that. Someone will adopt the baby."

"You don't want the baby?"

"I can't. I am certain that the authorities will see to it that he finds a good home."

Adeline spoke, "I want to adopt him. I am a nurse. Angie and I worked together at Ellis Island Hospital. I'm married, and I can't have children right now. I visited your baby at Coney Island. I would love to adopt him."

"Really, Miss? I suppose you can do that."

"The process would be easier if you signed the adoption papers as his mother."

"What's in it for me?"

"What do you mean?"

"I was thinking you might have a little something for me for cooperating."

"You aren't considering selling your baby?"

"No, it's nothing like that, Lady. You see, I want to go to college and get educated."

"What do you want?"

"You see, Lady, I want to make something of myself in America. I can't be working at the five-and-dime forever. I'll sign the papers for you, but maybe you have a little something extra to share. That's all I'm asking."

"Listen, here's the deal. My attorney and I will meet you here at five o'clock tonight. Would you give us permission to enter your name on the baby's birth certificate?"

Merta hesitated for a moment. "Yes, it's the right thing to do... but you must keep this a secret. No others must know that I am the baby's mother."

"I promise, Merta. My attorney and I will bring the adoption papers tonight. I will also have him draw up a separate agreement stating that I will agree to pay for your tuition and college expenses for four years. All you would have to do is submit your bills to my attorney's office."

"That's kind of you, Lady. Yes, I'll be here. Right here, in this spot, at five o'clock tonight, after work."

One week later, Adeline, Harry, and Sadie drove to the Infant Incubator Exhibit at Luna Park to pick up Baby Henri and take him home.

Six weeks after that, Harry and Adeline submitted papers to New York State to become Sadie's legal guardians.

When Harry and Adeline returned to their suite at the Waldorf Astoria in New York City as a family of four, Harry announced, "Now, it's time to find this family a real home."

Chapter Thirty-One

∽

July 2, 1925
4 PM (16:00)

Sometimes in life the bad guys win.
They lure us down the path of sin

At noon, the temperature in Brooklyn reached 95 degrees. It grew warmer as the day wore on. At four o'clock, when the temperature should have started to dip, it felt just as hot as it did at noon. Leonora and Maureen gave each child in the playroom a cool drink of water. They instructed them to rest their heads on their worktables to cool off before they started to walk home. While the children were resting, the women darkened the room by shutting the lights and closing the blinds in an attempt to cool the room. Opening the windows of Nativity House didn't help. There wasn't a hint of a breeze blowing. The rooms seemed warmer with the windows open.

Nurse Angie tiptoed through the playroom to her office. Doctor Abe was sitting at his desk. "Abe, it's too hot to do anything today. Leonora and Maureen are resting the children before they walk them home. It's a good thing we didn't have a clinic scheduled for today. I hope it's not this hot tomorrow."

"Unfortunately, I think it will be. They are predicting high temperatures for the remainder of the week."

"Abe, do you think we should cancel the clinic?"

219

"I would hate to see that happen. We could use three or four fans circulating air through these railroad rooms. It gets especially stuffy in the exam area. Listen, why don't I go downtown to buy the clinic some fans? I'll ring up Sam and ask him if the Hudson is available this evening for an errand."

"That's a great idea. I don't think we can hold a clinic tomorrow without fans."

"Do you want to come with me?"

"No, I think I'll stay. I'll use the time to catch up on my filing. It will be nice and quiet when the children leave at five. I'll get a lot of work done."

"It's hot, though. Won't you be cooler at the convent?"

"No, it's hot there, too."

"How about I go, buy the fans, and take you to the cinema when I get back tonight."

"Okay, I'll wait for you here. We can set up the fans, and then leave."

Abe made arrangements to borrow Sam's car. Shortly afterward, Leonora and Maureen left to take the children home. Angie always treasured her alone-time at Nativity House. She enjoyed being organized and liked to file. As she worked, she wondered why she always procrastinated when it came to this type of job. Angie came to the conclusion that filing took a considerable amount of time. She was always busy, rushing around, with so much to do. It actually felt like a luxury to sit quietly and organize her work. The hours passed quickly. Angie stood to stretch her legs. She walked to the window, and opened it to test the heat of the night. An evening breeze blew in softly, fragrant and cool. Relieved by the sudden drop in temperature, Angie stood at the window, enjoying the refreshing night air. There wasn't a sound to be heard. Angie looked at the clock. It was almost nine. There was no sign of Abe.

Then, Angie heard quarreling coming from the second floor. She had never seen or heard the tenants upstairs, and was startled to hear angry voices. The argument turned into a row. Chairs fell. Angie stood stunned. She could hear every word of the fight.

"Where were you tonight, Callum? Where's the shipment you were supposed to meet."

"They didn't show!" Callum shouted.

"They never showed? They said they did. They waited for you. They said *you* never showed."

"Believe me, they never showed."

"What kind of a fool of a driver are you, Callum? Can you read a map? Did you even find the meeting place?"

Suddenly, the window upstairs slammed shut. Angie jumped. She stood up from her chair with the intention of checking if the front door was locked. When she reached the door, she could hear that the argument had escalated. She remembered her Zia Dona telling her that her curiosity would get the best of her, but nevertheless, she found herself climbing the flight of stairs to the second floor. She stood in the hallway, listening.

Where have I heard the name, Callum, before? Elsbeth's husband is named Callum. I wonder if this could be the same Callum. What am I doing up here, eavesdropping? I better go down, and leave immediately before some-one sees me.

A commotion downstairs startled her. A group of men were approaching, coming up the stairs toward her. Frightened, she slipped into the curtained alcove opposite the doorway. The alcove was a small space, only four feet by four feet with a ladder leading up to the roof. Angie could hardly move without making noise. She held her breath. Her hand rested on the wooden ladder.

Perhaps this ladder leads to the roof. I wonder if it's safe to go up.

Deciding to escape unnoticed, Angie began to slowly climb the ladder. She climbed up as quietly and deliberately as she could. When she reached the sixth rung of the ladder, it cracked. Angie tumbled down, landed with a crash, and passed out.

Angie woke up in the back seat of a moving car. Her hands were tied. In the front seat, she could see that a man was driving.

"Where are we going?" She asked.

"Quiet back there!"

"Are you Callum?"

"How do you know my name?"

"Callum Ferguson, isn't it?"

"Do I know you, Miss?"

"No, I know your wife. I cared for her at Ellis Island Hospital. You came to America in August. What have you gotten yourself into, Callum? If you're caught, you and Elsbeth will be deported, for sure. She's worked so hard for you."

"Ah, Miss, I never thought they were bootlegging. Back then, I didn't even know it was against the law. They hired me as a driver. That's what I thought I'd be doing. The dough was real good. One thing led to another. I started to figure things out. They're rum-runners, all right. They meet the boats at Red Hook. Then, they take the booze down to Rockaway to dilute it at Luigi's."

"Do you mean Luigi, the custodian at Nativity Church?"

"Yes, Miss, he has a place down by the beach. That's where they told me to take you tonight."

"Why?"

"They have their ways of making people disappear."

"What do you mean?"

"It's like this, Miss. Luigi is a janitor. Ever ask yourself how Luigi acquired a big piece of property down by the beach? The rum-runners bought it for him. Get it, Miss? They need the land around the house to bury the booze and to dispose of their mistakes, if you know what I mean?"

"Do you mean to tell me that they bury bodies there?"

"Miss, are you going to make me tell you everything? Soon, you'll be making me feel bad. I don't know how I got into this mess...me...taking you to Luigi's...and you...being a friend of Elsbeth. Hey, are you the nurse from Ellis Island who gave Elsbeth those shoes?"

"Yes, Callum, I am."

"Oh, Nurse, now we are both in for it, we are!"

"What do you mean?"

"If I let you go, they'll be hunting me down, for sure. No telling what they'll do to Elsbeth. Guess there's only one thing to do."

"What's that, Callum?"

Callum shouted, as he turned the steering wheel of his car up onto the sidewalk of Woodhaven Boulevard.

"HOLD ON TIGHT, NURSE!"

With his foot still on the accelerator, Callum drove right through a stone wall, and crashed the car into St. John's Cemetery.

Chapter Thirty-Two

July 3, 1925
2:30 AM (02:30)

They fool us with a great disguise.
Confuse us with outstanding lies.

When Angie awakened, she was in the hospital emergency room. For a brief moment, she felt calm and rested until the frightening memory of the previous night jolted her to consciousness. Forcing herself to open her eyes, she was relieved to see Adeline and Harry staring down at her.

Adeline was overjoyed. "Angie, Angie, you're awake!"

"Ad…where am I?"

"In the hospital, dear, you were in an auto accident."

"I remember…Callum."

"Yes, Callum caused the crash…on purpose, it seems…to save your life."

"Was he hurt?"

"Not a scratch, but the Buick did flip on its side. The window cracked. You hit your head, and lost consciousness. You've been out for more than four hours. I'm so glad you're awake and talking."

"What happened?"

"That's what everyone wants to know. The Police Detectives spent the night trying to piece the story together. After Callum spilled the beans, they raided one of the largest bootlegging rings in the city.

When the cops came, the mobsters were caught off guard, smoking cigars in one of the second-floor apartments at Nativity House."

"They were?"

"Yes. In exchange for immunity, Callum confessed everything. He ratted on the whole lot of them. They offered him the option of voluntary deportation. At this moment, he should be halfway to Canada with Elsbeth right now. It seems he couldn't get out of town fast enough."

"What did he tell them?"

"According to Callum, he knew nothing about the illegal bootlegging, at first that is. He was hired as an evening driver. It seems small boats sneak up from the Caribbean during the summer. The gang meets the boats. They sort the cargo and send it to different locations. Callum picked up the goods designated for Brooklyn. He then, drove the hooch to Nativity House to be stored for future distribution."

"No! Did Father Benedetto know what was going on?"

"Actually, he says he didn't know. As the months passed, he began to get suspicious. He started to snoop around, but he wasn't successful at finding anything. He's with the Bishop now. Angie, you won't believe this. Listen, dear, it was the bootleggers who financed Nativity House."

"How?"

"They approached Father last summer. Father didn't ask questions when they gave him their generous donation. Nativity House was an ideal cover. With immigrants, coming and going, in and out of the clinic, no one suspected a bootlegging operation."

"Oh, no! What will happen to Nativity House? Abe will be so disappointed."

"There's one more thing I have to tell you, Angie."

"What's that, Ad? Tell me."

Adeline took a deep breath. "Angie, we can't find Abe."

"He borrowed Sam's Hudson, and went downtown last night. He went to buy fans to cool off the clinic."

"Did he return?"

"No, I was waiting for him last night at Nativity House. I remember. He was late."

"Angie, do you think Abe knew about the illegal operation going on upstairs?"

"No, Adeline. He would have told me."

"He's missing. No one knows where he is. The police questioned Father Benedetto. They called Sam. Sam's car is missing. They want to talk to Abe. They're out looking for him."

"Abe doesn't have anything to do with it. Harry, tell them."

Harry looked at Angie. "Who knows for sure?"

"I know, Harry!"

"He wanted the clinic so desperately. Perhaps, he compromised his values to help the poor, you know, like Robin Hood."

"Harry, I don't believe that." Tears welled up in Angie's eyes. She started to cry. "It can't be. Adeline, tell him. Tell him about Abe."

"Now, now, dear, I'm certain Abe will show up any minute. He'll clear up this whole mess. First things first, let's get you checked out of this hospital. Harry and I are taking you to our suite at the Waldorf. After a good night's sleep, everything will look brighter in the morning."

Chapter Thirty-Three

$\curlyvee$

July 3, 1925
8 AM (08:00)

Seize your dream with all your might!
Never give up and hold on tight.

Perhaps it was the sedative that Angie received in the hospital, or the overall excitement of the day that caused Angie to sleep so restlessly that night. Angie was fidgety and uneasy in the hotel bed. Dozing on and off, she experienced multiple levels of sleep. The lightest sleep state allowed her to feel that she was awake and aware of her surroundings when she was actually sleeping. This was followed by a sleep so deep that she felt she reached down to the deepest depths of her consciousness to reveal the truths she was searching for. She dreamt complex dreams with such intensity she could not decipher what was fantasy, and what were real events, long hidden in her memory.

Visions of Abe penetrated her disturbed sleep with his strong arms always protecting her. There was Abe, walking curbside, shielding her from the spray of the streetcars. Again, Abe appeared, opening a door for her, allowing her to enter before him. Turning around, Abe disappeared. Luigi Paluzzo appeared. He spoke in Sirina's voice. "Angelina, it is more than likely that you will be the one to rescue your true love. Come," Luigi said, "my place is down the driveway behind the tackle shop, only a block from the beach. Turn off before you reach the bridge. You can't miss it!"

With a jolt, Angie woke up and sat up straight. She bolted out of bed, and run to the mirror. Studying her reflection, she whispered, "I think I know."

Angie took a deep breath. "Angie Girl, if you know, you must proceed with a leap of faith."

She quickly grabbed her bathrobe, and rushed out into the drawing room to knock on Adeline's bedroom door.

Adeline and Harry were abruptly awakened by loud banging. Half asleep and thinking Baby Henri was crying, Adeline hurried to open the door.

"What is it, Angie? What's wrong? Is the baby okay?"

"He's still sleeping. Adeline, I know. I know!"

"What do you know, Angelina?"

"I know, Adeline."

"What, Angie? Are you okay? Do you feel all right?"

"I know where Abe is."

"How?"

"It came to me in my dream. I dreamt it."

"Slow down, Angie Girl. Tell me everything."

"Okay, I remember that Callum said he was taking me to Luigi's farm."

"Luigi, the custodian?"

"Yes, Callum said the bootleggers gave Luigi the land. They needed an out-of-the-way place to dilute the liquor and hide evidence."

Harry called out from under his blanket. "Should we call the doctor, Adeline? Angie's not making much sense."

"They financed Luigi's farm so that they would be able to bury bodies there."

"Angie, sit down. Harry, let's listen to what Angie has to say. Okay, honey, tell us again, slowly. You see, maybe this all makes sense to you, but it doesn't to us."

"I'm talking about Luigi, the custodian. One afternoon, he invited Abe and me to his farm by the beach. He came to Nativity House to repair something...a door. He came to fix a door. He told us that we were working too hard, and suggested a day at the beach this summer. He invited us to his bungalow at the beginning of Rockaway Beach. He actually gave us directions. He said it was right before the entrance of the Long Beach Bridge. Instead of going straight ahead, you bear right. I remember. That's where Abe is, Harry. He's there. I'm certain."

Adeline asked, "Should we call the police?"

Harry jumped out of bed, and flew to his closet. "If Abe's there, let's get on the road. Adeline, check the baby. Wake up the nanny to watch the children. Angie, you can't go out looking like that. Get dressed! Hurry, ladies, you have ten minutes to get ready. There's no time to lose. I'll get the car from the garage. Meet me outside under the canopy."

Angie and Adeline dressed quickly. They had just entered the hotel lobby when Harry drove up in his Studebaker. They jumped in the car. Within minutes, they were crossing the Fifty-Ninth Street Bridge. Harry was thankful there was no traffic. "I'm glad it's early, and there's no beach traffic."

They exited the Bridge on Queens Boulevard. Once on the road, Angie gave Harry the directions, as she remembered them. She told him to go *straight* on Rockaway Boulevard until the end. Then, follow the signs to Long Beach.

When they approached the onramp of the entrance of the wooden bridge, instead of going straight ahead, they turned when they saw the sign for the local streets. First Street was lined with a number of sun-bleached beach bungalows. They quickly spotted the weathered sign of the tiny tackle shop. A winding driveway behind the store led directly to Luigi's bungalow.

When Harry stopped the car on the driveway, they stared at the house. All was quiet. The front door was closed. They got out of the car, and slowly made their way to the front window. They peeked in. The room was dark. No one was in sight. Staying together, they cautiously circled the house, checking each window. When they were certain the house was deserted, they tried the doorknob of the front door. It was unlocked.

Slowly and carefully, they thoroughly searched each room of the bungalow, looking for Abe. They opened closets, looked behind doors, and checked under the beds.

From one of the bedroom windows, Adeline spotted a small, one-car, wooden garage in back of the house.

"Angie, Harry, Come." She shouted. "Abe may be in there."

They exited the house through the back door, and followed the driveway to the garage. Finding the double door to the garage pad-locked, they circled the garage. There was a side window.

They peered in. There was Abe, sitting on a chair, with his hands and feet tied.

Harry broke the window with his shoe, and was about to climb in.

"Wait!" Angie and Adeline shouted in unison.

"What a relief! How did you ever find me?" Abe called out.

Angie used her sweater to break off the jagged pieces of glass in order to make a space big enough for Harry to unlock the window and open it.

Harry jumped through and quickly untied Abe. "There you go, old sport."

"Thanks, Harry. I felt like I couldn't stay in that position one more minute. My back was killing me."

Angie was next to follow Harry through the window. She flew into Abe's arms.

"Angie, Angie, you're safe. What happened?"

"Oh, Abe, I'm so glad you're alive. My head is still reeling. You won't believe what happened. I had visions of..."

"Me, too, Angie. Are you okay? They said they were taking you here."

"How did you get here?"

Harry interrupted, "Let's get out of here. Someone may come back any minute. Let's go while the going is still good."

"Yes," Abe agreed, but added, "They may be gone already. I heard them pack up and leave."

"Who?"

"Whoever it was who was here. I'm afraid I only recognized Luigi's voice. He left hours ago."

"Come on! Let's go!"

Once out of the garage, Abe asked, "Do you see the Hudson parked anywhere?"

"No, let's circle the property and search for it."

Harry walked left, and Abe walked right. They found Sam's car hidden between two large hedgerows lining the property.

Harry and Adeline drove their Studebaker to the city, while Abe and Angie followed in Sam's Hudson. Once on the road, Abe explained what had happened to him the night before. He had gone downtown and bought two fans, but decided he needed more. He went from store to store until he found a third one. The search for the fan delayed him. He returned to Nativity House at 9:30 pm to find the clinic empty. Abe was about to leave when he heard arguing upstairs. He listened. He heard a group of men talking about a nurse who was spying on them. They were fighting over what to do with her. The big boss had given instructions to Callum, their driver, to take her down to Luigi's beach bungalow. He said, "Luigi will know what to do with her."

"It didn't sound good, Angie. I listened for a minute more. That's when I realized they were involved in rum-running. After that, I didn't waste time. Without thinking, I jumped in the Hudson and drove to Luigi's." He continued, "While I was riding, I recalled the conversation we had with Luigi. I remembered everything he told us."

"I did, too, that's how I found you."

"I spotted the tackle shop with the driveway behind it. I drove down to the house and got out. I believe I must have been bumped off then because that's the last thing I remember. When I came to, I was being tied up. I watched them load up their trucks, and off they went. They cleaned out everything. What do you make of it, Angie? What happened?"

Angie told Abe everything she knew: how she waited at Nativity House...the open windows...hearing the mention of Callum's name...

the curiosity that got her caught…riding in the car with Callum…and finally, the car crash.

"What do we do now?"

"The first thing you are going to do is to get some sleep. We're going to Harry and Adeline's suite at the Waldorf."

"What about tomorrow's clinic?"

"The police closed all access to the building. They're confiscating the booze."

"What will become of Nativity House?"

"I don't know, Abe, because there's something you should know."

"What's that, Angie?"

"Our upstairs neighbors financed Nativity House. The bootleggers provided all the money we needed to start the clinic. No one has any idea if there will be enough funds for Nativity House to continue to operate."

Chapter Thirty-Four

July 3, 1925
5 PM (17:00)

The man and dream must come alive.
He needs his dream to grow and thrive.

Angie and Abe awakened to the cry of a baby.

Adeline knocked on their door. "May I come in? There's someone here who wants to say *hello*."

"Of course, bring in that little cutie."

Adeline opened the door, carrying Baby Henri in her arms. Sadie followed behind her. Angie and Abe were in bed.

"I'm sorry to wake you. Your little friends wanted to see you. How did you sleep?"

"Wonderful," Abe said. "The best sleep of my whole life. I guess Angie's been the missing piece in my life. I could get used to sleeping next to her for eternity."

"We needed to be together," Angie started to explain, but stopped. She jumped out of bed and held out her arms to hold the baby. "Let me have him."

"Our little guy is almost four months old. Can you believe it? He's getting so big."

"He's my baby brother, now." Sadie said, proudly.

Abe asked Sadie. "...And how is Sweet Sadie today?"

"I'm happy, Doctor Abe. I was worried when you got lost. I thought you might be lost like Mama. I prayed how the Sisters taught me."

"Thanks, Sadie. I believe your prayers worked."

"Sorry to disturb the both of you, but there's a few things on the docket this evening."

"What time is it now?"

"It's already five in the evening. Harry made a few calls. He reported your story to the police. They'll be here at six to take your statements."

"Good. I should call Sam to tell him that his car is here and in one piece."

"Harry already did that. Sam needs the Hudson tonight for a hospital pick-up. He's coming over with Maureen. We invited them for dinner at eight. They'll attend to the funeral business after they eat with us."

"Anything else?"

"Well, actually, there is. Angie, your brothers called. I told them what happened, and reassured them you were fine. Abe, Harry had your suit cleaned and pressed while you were sleeping so that you would have clean clothes after you shower."

"You've thought of everything, Adeline."

"I knew you wouldn't want to go out. When I ordered room-service, the hotel suggested eating downstairs in a private room. Would that be okay?"

"Perfect. Thank you, Adeline."

"One more thing, Leonora is going to dine with us. She was frantic about the both of you. When she called this afternoon, I invited her. She's bringing her friend, Alfonso."

"They've been secretly seeing each other."

"I know. She hasn't told her father that he is courting her. She plans to tell him after Alfonso graduates from law school. He's half-way through."

"I hope she doesn't get caught before that."

"She won't. Listen, there's something Harry and I have been considering. We want to share it with you tonight."

"Do you want to tell us now?"

"No, it can wait until tonight. For now, I ordered a tray of sandwiches because I thought you might be hungry when you woke up."

"Sounds great, Ad, I'm starved."

"Another thing…you're both staying over tonight. Harry has a boat ride planned for Sadie tomorrow. It's the Fourth of July. We want you to join us. Celestina said she'd come, too. She needs to see you, and can't get away tonight. Oh…and I've reserved a hotel room on this floor for you tonight, Abe."

"Adeline, isn't that extravagant? Why don't I just stay right here with Angie where I belong?"

In 1925, the Waldorf-Astoria Hotel was one of the grandest hotels in the city. Built on the footprint of the Astor's Fifth Avenue residence, the opulent mansion had been converted into a luxurious hotel before the turn of the century. Its timeless elegance set the standard for grandeur, attracting the most affluent of travelers who were greeted with fresh flowers in the Lobby. Modeling the stately castles of Europe, French Aubusson carpets, sumptuous couches, and crystal chandeliers completed the decor.

ELLIS ANGELS ON THE MOVE

The grand hotel's masterpiece was the Astor Dining Room. It was covered from floor to ceiling in dark walnut paneling which had been meticulously reassembled, piece-by-piece, from the original Astor mansion. Antique tapestries, brass lamps, oil paintings and thick velvet draperies set the stage for ambiance and elegant dining. A small room off the Main Dining Room was a miniature replica of the grand room fashioned to serve a party of two or twenty in the utmost of privacy.

The Steingold Party was greeted by the maitre d'hotel, and escorted to their private dining room. The table was set with Wedgewood China and Baccarat Crystal. A menu had been placed at each place setting.

Menu
Steingold Party
French Onion Soup
Chef's Waldorf Salad
Choice of:
Halibut with Hollandaise Sauce
Stuffed Chicken and Deviled Sauce
Medallions of Sea Bass a La Joinville
Cherry Sorbet, Blueberries, Strawberries
Whipped Cream, Lady Fingers, Macaroons

The head waiter allowed the guests to study the menu. He stood in the corner of the room, quietly available to answer any questions they might have.

Maureen was the first to ask, "I've heard of a Waldorf Salad, but I don't know exactly what it is. Could you tell me?"

"Yes, Madame, allow me. Your first course is soupe a l'oignon served in a ramekin topped with croutons and melted gruyeré cheese. Next is our world-famous Waldorf Salad. Chopped apples, grapes, celery, and walnuts are delicately mixed in a light lemon-mayonnaise dressing. You must try it. You won't be disappointed. The Fresh Halibut is grilled, covered with a rich lemon-butter hollandaise sauce. The Chicken Breast is stuffed with mushrooms, onions and secret spices accompanied by a flavorful onion gravy. Fresh Sea Bass a La Joinville is pan-seared fresh bass in a white wine sauce, topped with lobster, shrimp, and mushrooms. All entrées are accompanied by scalloped potatoes and Carrots a La Vichy, slowly simmered in sweetened butter. Dessert is a red, white and blue Fourth of July Special."

After orders had been taken and the French Onion Soup had been served, Adeline stood up to make an announcement. "Thank you for coming this evening. I'm overjoyed that we are all together tonight in this beautiful dining room. I want to express how thankful I am that Angie and Abe are safe and sound. I know everyone at this table shares these sentiments. Harry and I invited you this evening for a reason. Harry was busy investigating Nativity House finances today. He had a number of conversations with both the Bishop and The Williamsburg Bank concerning the financial future of Nativity House. Harry will tell you the details. Harry..."

Harry stood up. "It seems Father Benedetto slightly exaggerated the amount of funds that were deposited in the Williamsburg Bank for Nativity House. According to the Bank, the Nativity House account would cover six months of expenses. That would keep Nativity House in the black until the beginning of next year.

"The Bishop is impressed with the number of people you served in the short time since opening in January. He feels the program of community classes is desperately needed, and should continue. The Bishop is proposing that Nativity House remain under the umbrella of the Church. The Dioceses is offering their guarantee to cover thirty percent of your annual expenses.

"In addition, the Steingold Family will contribute the remaining seventy percent of next year's operating expenses. During 1926, Steingold Jewelers will host a series of fundraisers to ensure the continued viability of Nativity House. With this financial plan in place, we are confident that Nativity House will be around for many, many years."

"Well done!"

"I'm so relieved!"

"Hip, Hip, Hooray, Harry!"

"That is so generous of you!"

"Our prayers have been answered."

"We are all so thankful that we can resume our programs."

Harry continued, "You are most welcome. With that aside, I want to add how happy Adeline and I are to be sharing this meal with all of you tonight. Oh, yes, one thing more..."

"What's that, Harry?"

"Bon Appetit! Let's eat!"

Chapter Thirty-Five

∾

August 10, 1925
9:30 AM (09:30)

We hope your feet fall off from dancing all day,
And you get dizzy from having your way.

"Cooties, Adeline?"

"Yes, Cooties, the baby has Cooties. Angie, you must come quickly. Now!"

"Adeline, you've cleaned favus and fungus at Ellis Island, and you're afraid of lice?"

"…But he's only a baby. I refuse to use that pesticide shampoo on him."

"His hair is so fine. I am certain with a few repeated washings you can clean up his head in no time."

"You must come over and help me."

"How did he get lice?"

"I took Sadie to the park. She found a friend. The little girl asked to see the baby. She said, 'Oh, what a pretty baby', and shook her head over the baby carriage. Who knew her head was full of lice? What are you doing? You don't have a clinic scheduled today."

"I was going to finish my filing, but I suppose it can wait. Let me check with Abe."

"Okay, but Seymour is on his way in the Packard as we speak. I sent him to pick you up. He will be there in thirty minutes. Hurry, Angie."

Seymour arrived at Nativity House within a half hour. He escorted Angie to Adeline's Packard, and held open the rear door for Angie to enter. She stepped into the car to find Adeline, dressed in a silk summer suit, sitting in the back seat.

"Adeline! I thought Seymour was picking me up to come to you. Why are you here?"

"We have an appointment."

"What about the baby?"

"I took care of the lice."

"I knew you didn't need me to help you."

"I need you today to select a wedding gown. Your wedding is only a month away. We're running out of time."

"Isabella said she would sew it. We picked the pattern. All we have to do is buy the fabric. She's working on the girls' gowns now."

"I've spoken to Isabella. She's going to meet us at Madame Renee's. We have an appointment in an hour. I'm buying your bridal gown as a present. I want you to have a gorgeous wedding dress. We're picking up Abe's mother, now. I hope that's okay with you."

Seymour drove to Bushwick Avenue to call for Abe's mother. Angie greeted her future mother-in-law with a kiss. "Good Morning, Mama Myers. How are you this morning?"

"Very fine, my dear, I am delighted that Adeline invited me today."

"It's my pleasure, Mama Myers. We are happy you could come with us." Adeline added. "I asked Rosa and Isabella to meet us there, also. They may take the girls with them."

"Angie, do we have time to stop and show Adeline St. Barbara's Church?"

"Yes, I believe we do. Our appointment isn't until eleven. I would love to take a peek at the Church where Angie and Abe will be married." Adeline said, instructing Seymour to stop three blocks away at Central Avenue, between Menahan and Bleecker Streets.

St. Barbara's Church was easy to find. Seymour spotted the dome and the two tall bell towers soaring over the neighborhood, and followed them to Central Avenue and Bleecker Street. Sister Maria Vincenzia was standing on the church steps and greeted them. She offered to take them on a tour of the church.

Once inside, Sister pointed out twenty-five intricate stained glass windows, glistening statues, and radiant frescos. A magnificent blue center ceiling dome was the focal point of the interior. The glistening white alabaster altar rail, the elaborately-carved wooden pulpit and the over-sized pipe organ added to the splendor of the cathedral-like church.

Adeline was impressed. "Oh, Mama Myers, now I understand why you wanted Angie and Abe to be married here."

"Isn't it a lovely church?" Angie asked.

"It is absolutely beautiful, and I can see the most beautiful bride walking down the aisle in her most beautiful wedding gown." Adeline said.

"Yes, I agree, and I believe it's time to select that wedding gown." Mama Myers added.

"Okay, let's be on our way."

The ladies thanked Sister Maria Vincenzia, and hurried back into the Packard to keep their eleven o'clock appointment with Madame Renee.

When they arrived at Madame Renee's, Angie's sisters-in-law and nieces were already there, waiting on sumptuous couches in Madame Renee's luxurious studio. She had served them tea and biscuits while they waited. She greeted Angie dramatically, and clapped her hands for the selection process to begin. Her salesladies quickly paraded around the women, carefully displaying the details of each dress. After Madame Renee instructed Angie to select six possible gowns, she took Angie into her opulent dressing room to try them on.

Angie slowly modeled each dress to the *ooh's* and *aah's* of her family. Her three nieces were so excited, they could not contain themselves. They jumped, up and down, as each gown was presented.

"That's the one, Aunt Angie. Pick that one." They shouted.

Rosa and Isabella attempted to hush their daughters. "Settle down, girls."

When Angie appeared wearing the fourth dress she had chosen, the decision was unanimous. Everyone was in agreement. Rosa and Isabella sighed. Mama and Adeline had tears in their eyes. Angie stared at herself in the three-paneled mirror.

The wedding gown that Angie selected had a simple scoop neck and an empire-waist. The delicate white fabric was covered with intricate beading, sewn in flowers and swirls that weighted the skirt of the gown so that it twirled and flowed around her. Madame Renee assisted Angie into an Alisson lace jacket which covered her arms and shoulders, and formed a six-foot long circle train of lace in the back of the gown.

Madame Renee went into a closet, and emerged with a beaded headdress. She carefully positioned it on Angie. "May I suggest this headdress? It perfectly complements this gown."

In her excitement, Rosa stood up. "Yes," she cried.

"Oh my." Isabella said.

"It's exquisite." Mama Myers sighed.

"There's no doubt about it." Adeline added.

Angie was silent. She stared into the mirror. A bright smile appeared on her face, revealing the dimples on each side of her cheeks. Her eyes sparkled.

"Yes, this is the one." Angie whispered.

Chapter Thirty-Six

September 1, 1925
2 PM (14:00)

Your life will change forever as new beginnings start.
You'll share your life together connected in your heart.

Mr. and Mrs. Giacomo Bosco

Cordially Invite You to the Wedding of

Angelina Bosco

To

Dr. Abraham Goodwin

Son of Mr. and Mrs. Walter Myers

On Sunday, the Thirteenth of September

Nineteen Hundred and Twenty-Five

At Two in the Afternoon

St. Barbara's Church

Brooklyn, New York

Reception to Follow

Tucked in the turret room on the second floor of her Victorian home, Mama Myers sat on her cushioned window seat, reading her son's wedding invitation. She wondered what it would be like to be the mother-of-the-groom. Perhaps, her sole duty of the day would be to pin the stephanotis boutonnières on her sons, Abe and Sam. What a shame that would be.

Having wed three daughters, Mama felt there was nothing more memorable than a wedding. She cherished the memory of her daughters' wedding days. Closing her eyes, she remembered her daughters in their lovely bridal dresses. Even when money was scarce, her two oldest daughters, Florentina and Concetta, had worn beautifully designed gowns, hand sewn by both the girls and herself. Gisella, her youngest, was the one daughter who prepared for her wedding from the house on Bushwick Avenue. The large Victorian suited a bride, and Gisella was an exquisite one. Gisella stood right in that exact spot, looking into the cheval mirror, while her mother adjusted her veil and gown. Mama recalled the fragrance of flowers floating through the house after the florist delivered the five cascading bouquets of roses and cream-colored stephanotis for the bride and her four bridesmaids.

Mama could still hear the giggles of the girls as they dressed, the click-clacking of their shoes on the hardwood floor, and the swish-swashing of their organza dresses as they moved through the room. Laura and Linda, her twin granddaughters had scampered about, chasing young Paulie, the ring-bearer. When it was time to leave for church, everyone frantically searched for her grandson until they finally found Paulie hiding under the dining room table.

Mama Myers sighed. It definitely would not be as exciting to spend the morning with her two sons on the day of the wedding. She imagined how lovely Angie would look as a bride. The gown she had chosen was perfect for her. She was grateful that Angie and Adeline had included her when they shopped for the wedding gown last month. Mama found herself wondering who would assist Angie. Angie's mother had passed when she was a little girl. The aunt, who raised her, lived in Sicily and would not be attending the wedding.

Careful not to overstep boundaries, Mama Myers picked up the phone and called Isabella, Angie's sister-in-law, who was in-charge of the wedding. When Isabella came to the phone, she bombarded Abe's mother with dozens of questions, giving her little opportunity to answer.

"Oh, I am so awfully glad you called, Mrs. Myers. How are you today? What do you think of the wedding invitations? Do you like them? I am undecided about the menu and want to ask your opinion. I've estimated that two hundred people will be at the reception. Do you think that estimate is accurate? We are inviting two hundred and twenty-five. I am wondering how many will actually come. Will five hundred sandwiches be enough? I'm thinking half should be hot sandwiches, pastrami and corned beef. Perhaps, the other half should be assorted cold sandwiches: mortadella, capicola, salami, ham and provolone. I ordered potato-salad, coleslaw and pickles. Have I forgotten anything? I think Katz's catering will do a wonderful job, don't you, Mrs. Myers? I will order cookies and pastries, in addition to the wedding cake. Is that too much? Do you think everything will be eaten? People always like to take home left-over goodies, don't they? I'm so happy that your daughters offered to make the candy-covered almonds as favors. I never dreamed that there would be so much to do...not that I mind. It's been a pleasure."

"Everything will be perfect, Mrs. Bosco. You've planned a wonderful menu. The food from Katz's is always delicious. Everyone will be pleased. I called concerning your plans for the morning before the wedding. Will you be inviting the bridesmaids to your house?"

"*Before* the wedding…should I plan for that, too? I have all to do to plan for the reception *after* the wedding. I suppose I'll have to ask Angie what she would like. If that's what she wants, I'll do it. Oh my, yet another thing to worry about…"

"Well, Mrs. Bosco, I would like to offer my house as a gathering place that morning. I can make a light buffet, perhaps an antipasto and a few frittatas. Although, when Gisella married, the bridesmaids were too excited to eat a thing. All they did was nibble, like little birdies. I want to help in any way I can. We can all meet here at my house…you, Rosa, Adeline and the girls. Perhaps, we can arrange to arrive at the church at the same time. Would that be convenient for you?"

"I think that's a perfectly splendid idea, Mrs. Myers. Your house is lovely, and so close to the church…only three blocks away. However, you must be sure that the groom doesn't see the bride before the wedding. It's bad luck, you know."

"I'm thinking of sending Abe and Walter off to Sam's. Of course, I must ask Angie what her plans are, but I did want to check with you first. I thought Angie might like the extra room, as well as company, while she prepares for her wedding."

"Oh, do ask Angie! I think she will adore the idea. With so much to do, it certainly is one less thing for me to worry about. It helps me out tremendously."

While the others planned the food, flowers, and the music, Mama Myers made a list of things to do.

MAMA MYERS' MEMO

1. Discuss with Angie. Invite Angie to sleep over the night before the wedding. Perhaps, she would like to invite her sister, Celestina.

2. Banish Walter and Abe to Sam's apartment above the funeral parlor. Make a lasagna for the boys to take to Sam's so that they have plenty of food.

3. Dust the library reading-room. Wax the hardwood floors. Bleach and blue the white lace summer curtains. Polish the silver. Wash and starch the white linen napkins.

4. Prepare the morning's buffet menu.

5. Assign Florentina to be *in-charge* of transportation.

6. Assign Concetta to be *in-charge* of keeping all the nieces occupied.

7. Ask Gisella's mother-in-law to watch Baby Ella.

When Mama Myers invited Angie and her sister to sleep at her house the night before the wedding, Angie cried. Thinking she upset Angie, Mama apologized.

"No, Mama, it's just that..." Angie paused to wipe away a tear. "There's nothing I would want more. You see, I was beginning to feel a bit sorry for myself. I have so much to be thankful for, yet I found myself wishing my own mother was still alive to see me in my wedding gown. What would I do, all alone in my tiny cell at the convent? No, I'd much rather share the morning with you and Celestina, but are you certain, Mama Myers? Where will Abe go?"

"I plan to send Walter and Abe off to Sam's apartment. It's close to the church. They will meet us there."

"Thank you, Mama. It is so thoughtful of you to invite my sister, also."

"Angelina, it's my pleasure. You see, darling, as a young married woman, I missed my mother terribly. Although I planned to return to Italy to see her, I never had the opportunity. The last time I saw my mother was the day I left the old country."

"You've made me feel special…like I have a mother, again."

"You do, Angelina, and from now on, I have a fourth daughter." Mama Myers laughed. "Maybe…even a fifth…if Celestina is your sister, I will have to adopt her, too."

When Angie opened her eyes on the morning of her wedding day, she found her sister, Celestina, staring at her. Mama Myers had bedded the sisters together in her old double bed the night before, tucking them in with a goodnight kiss.

"I was thinking…" Celestina whispered.

"About what, dear?"

"We've never slept together in the same bed like this. It's nice."

"Let's do it again. We will start a tradition of a sisters' night once a year."

"Where will your husband go?"

"Maybe we will banish him to his brother's, like Mama Myers did last night."

Celestina laughed. "I am certain your new husband won't appreciate that idea. Angie, Abe's mother has been so kind to us. Sometimes, I find myself wondering what our mother was like. Do you remember her?"

"I have only a handful of memories left. In my mind, I can still picture her bathing and dressing me. One afternoon, we were walking outside. I remember holding her hand and feeling safe."

"That's a nice memory."

"Whenever I'm frightened, I try to recall that image."

"Angie, what does it feel like to be getting married? Are you nervous?"

"I thought I would be, but I'm not. I feel happy. This is the happiness part of life."

"The happiness part...what do you mean?"

"Last night, Mama Myers said that she hoped I enjoyed my wedding day because it is one of the happiest times in a woman's life. She said life offers us sad times and happy times. Happy times are to be enjoyed and savored."

"Sometimes, it's easy to forget that, especially when I'm surrounded by sickness and sadness in the hospital."

"She said that was why she wanted to mention it. When we come face-to-face with heartache, it's comforting to believe in the cycles of life. There are times of great happiness in store for us, and we must treasure them."

"I'll try to remember that when I am working at the hospital."

Mama Myers knocked on the bedroom door. "May we come in?" She asked.

"Oh, yes!" Angie answered.

Mama and Myrtle, the housemaid, each carried a breakfast tray. "We've brought breakfast."

"You shouldn't have. We were getting ready to go downstairs."

"Nonsense, ladies, a bride should have breakfast in bed on her wedding day."

"Thank you, you've been so kind to us."

"It's my pleasure. How are you feeling this morning? Are you nervous?" Mama asked.

"Not at all, I feel happy."

"A good sign, darling, a happy bride means a happy marriage. Now, eat. We brought you a little something. Myrtle and I set a beautiful buffet downstairs, if you want more. We made artichoke frittatas, peppers and eggs, a cheese tray and a fruit salad. It's nine o'clock now. The others are coming at ten. You have exactly an hour to eat and wash before they arrive."

When they heard the doorbell ring, Mama and Myrtle left the bedroom to see who was at the front door downstairs.

They returned ten minutes later. "The bouquets arrived from the florist. They are beautiful."

Celestina hopped out of bed and said, "I can't wait to see them."

"First, finish eating. Then, come. I asked the florist to arrange the bouquets around the table. They look gorgeous. Angie's bridal bouquet is over three feet long. Sadie's flower-girl basket of rose petals turned out to be a precious thing."

During the next hours, all the women arrived at the house: Abe's sisters, Angie's sister-in-laws, the little nieces, the big nieces, Adeline and Sadie. Once again, the old Victorian house was filled with people and perfume, corsets and corsages, and lipstick and laughter.

As Mama was helping Angie arrange her bridal veil around her jeweled headdress, the bells of St. Barbara's Church began to ring.

"What's that?" Angie asked.

"That's our thirty minute notice. I asked Sister Maria Vincenzia to ring the church bells at one-thirty. It's time for us to go to church."

Mama Myers turned to her daughter, Flora. "Florentina, please tell the ladies who they will be riding with." Mama clapped her hands as she announced, "Everyone, we must start to get ready to leave. Our drivers are waiting outside for us."

"Listen for your car assignments," Flora began. "Aldo is driving Isabella, Rosa and their girls. Sergio is taking Mama, Myrtle, Adeline and Sadie. Angie and Celestina are going with Seymour in Adeline's Packard. Etta, Giselle and I are riding with Linda and Laura in our car."

Soon, everyone was assembled in the wood-paneled vestibule of St. Barbara's Church. Adeline squeezed Angie's gloved hand. She said she was a ball of nerves because she didn't think that Sadie would remember everything they practiced.

When the music started, five-year-old Sadie, the flower-girl, was the first to go down the aisle. Sadie took slow, tiny steps, and remembered to carefully drop the pink rose petals from her basket, one at a time. Next, came the twins, Linda and Laura, walking together, looking adorable. Angie's three nieces followed, walking slowly, leading the way for Adeline, the matron-of-honor. After her, Celestina, Angie's maid-of-honor, followed.

When it was her turn, Angie took hold of Giacomo's arm and confidently walked down the aisle. She saw a sea of friends and family in the church pews. She recognized the smiles on the faces of her friends from Ellis Island. She saw their neighbors from Johnson Avenue, the nurses from Henry House, and the Sisters from Nativity Convent. As she turned, she noticed all of Abe's family and friends.

Just then, Angie felt her knees begin to buckle. She told herself: *Almost there, Angie Girl. Keep going a bit more.*

Angie looked up to see Abe staring at her. Their eyes met. Her brother, Giacomo, lifted her veil and kissed her. When Abe took her hand, Angie felt herself relax. Father began Mass. During the Mass, Father announced that the wedding vows would be exchanged. There wasn't a sound to be heard in the church as everyone listened attentively.

"We are gathered here today to witness the marriage of Angelina Bosco and Abraham Goodwin. Angelina, do you take this man to be your lawful wedded husband?"

"I do." Angie said, softly.

"Abraham, do you take this woman to be your lawful wedded wife?"

"I do!" Abe shouted.

"I now pronounce you, man and wife. Abraham, you may kiss your bride."

Abe could not wait to kiss his bride, but paused for a moment. He whispered something, very softly, into Angie's ear.

"I love you, Angie, with all my heart." Abe said, just before their lips met.

The End

Author's Notes

*Tell your story with truth and tact, or Fact
Becomes Fiction and Fiction becomes Fact.*

Ellis Angels On The Move: Making A Difference In Brooklyn is a work of fiction presented in a historical setting. By weaving fiction into fact, historical fiction can be a fascinating teaching tool. However, it carries the potential of compromising real-life events, sometimes enhancing history and sometimes distorting it.

Some people, places and events in this novel occurred in the past, and are not a product of my imagination. Because much of the historical data and medical records from Ellis Island Hospital were lost or destroyed, I relied on the documentation of oral histories and thousands of photographs to fit this history puzzle together. The following historical facts were incorporated into the fiction of *Ellis Angels On The Move: Making A Difference in Brooklyn.*

Aviation:

Although many believe Charles Lindberg was the first pilot to fly across the Atlantic Ocean, it was actually John Alcock and Arthur Brown who flew from Newfoundland to England nonstop. However, when Raymond Orteig offered a prize of $25,000.00 to anyone who could fly from Paris to New York or New York to Paris, Lindberg won the prize in 1927 in his airplane, *The Spirit of St. Louis.*

ELLIS ANGELS ON THE MOVE

Bellevue Hospital School of Nursing and Hunter College:

Bellevue Hospital Center can trace its origins to a six-bed infirmary in New York beginning in 1736. Bellevue Hospital was the largest city hospital in the 1920s. Currently, it is an 828-bed member of the New York City (NYC) hospital system affiliated with New York University (NYU) School of Medicine.

The *Bellevue Hospital School of Nursing* was established in 1875 as a three-year diploma school. In 1969, the school merged with Hunter College at Park Avenue and 67th Street to offer its graduates a four-year Bachelor's of Science in Nursing.

Hunter College was founded as a women's teaching college in 1870. Men were admitted in 1964. Today, as part of the City University of New York, it is a prestigious coed university offering many diverse fields of study.

(www.nyc.gov)

(www.hunter.cuny.edu)

Bridges of Lower Manhattan:

There are three bridges that connect lower Manhattan to Brooklyn. *The Williamsburg Bridge* was built in 1903. It connects Delancey Street to the Williamsburg section of Brooklyn. Slightly south, you'll find *The Brooklyn Bridge* built in 1883. It is the oldest suspension bridge in the United States. At the southernmost tip of Manhattan is *The Manhattan Bridge*, built in 1909, connecting lower Manhattan to Brooklyn.

Also mentioned in this novel is *The 59th Street Bridge* or *The Ed Koch Bridge* (formally, *The Queensborough Bridge*), connecting Manhattan at 59th and 60th Streets to Long Island City, Queens, New York. In Chapter Thirty-three, Harry takes this bridge to Queens because the

Mid-Town Tunnel wasn't built until 1934. Additionally, the wooden toll bridge to Long Beach was torn down in 1952 and replaced by the *Atlantic Beach Bridge*, a drawbridge, connecting Far Rockaway in Queens to Long Beach, Long Island.

Businesses in the 1920s:

Katz's Delicatessen: Take the **F** train to Second Avenue and treat yourself to a pastrami sandwich at Katz's Deli at 205 East Houston Street in New York City. They have been making their thick, hot pastrami and corned beef sandwiches for the residents of the Lower East Side and NYC tourists since 1888.

(www.katzsdelicatessen.com)

Luna Park opened as an amusement park at Coney Island in 1903. With the biggest rides and best attractions of the 1920s, it was labeled *The Heart of Coney Island*. Coney Island was nicknamed *The Nickel Paradise* because the NYC subway system charged only five cents to ride the trains from Manhattan to Coney Island in Brooklyn.

(www.history.com)

(www.smithsonianmag.com)

Nathan's Famous Frankfurters: Nathan Handwerker, a polish immigrant, opened his hotdog stand at Surf Avenue and Stillwell Avenue in Coney Island in 1916. You can still enjoy a Nathan's hotdog today in that very spot, or buy one at hotdog carts or supermarkets across the country.

(www.nathansfamous.com)

Rexall Pharmacies: In 1902, Louis Liggett united 40 privately owned pharmacies into a Rexall Cooperative. Each business kept its original name, but added *Rexall* to their name. (Example: The signage of *Smith's Pharmacy* was changed to *Smith's Rexall Pharmacy*.)

(www.rexall.com)

R. H. Macy's & Co and Gimbel's Department Stores: Located at Broadway and 34th Street on Herald Square, Macy's and Gimbel's were department store rivals for decades. Rowland H. Macy opened a dry-goods store on 14th Street in 1858. Forty-four years later, he expanded his store, moving it to Herald Square in 1902. The first Macy's Thanksgiving Day Parade was held on November 27, 1924. However, this wasn't the first parade of its kind. Gimbel Brothers hosted the first parade in 1920, which is credited as being the oldest Thanksgiving Day Parade. In 1897, Adam Gimbel started his chain of department stores in Indiana.   He quickly expanded his stores to Illinois, Pennsylvania, and New York. Although Gimbel's closed its doors in 1997, Macy's continues as the world-famous Macy's on Herald Square.

Did you notice that Dr. Goodwin's nieces and nephews went *trick-or-treating* on Thanksgiving Day? In the 1920's, it was common practice for NYC kids to dress up and go *trick-or-treating* on Thanksgiving morning.

(www.macysinc.com)

(www.philadelphiaencyclopedia.org)

The Bartoli Shoe Store was established in 1890 by Eugenio Bartoli, my husband's maternal grandfather. He sold high-quality, hand-crafted shoes on Manhattan's Upper East Side. Eugenio would not allow his daughter, Eleanor, to work in his shoe store. She didn't attend Hunter College to become a teacher, but she did marry Albert, a shoe repairman's son, after he graduated from law school.

The Sanger Clinic was founded by a nurse, Margaret Sanger (1879-1966). She was an activist who founded the Birth Control League in 1921. This was to become Planned Parenthood.

(www.plannedparenthood.org)

F. W. Woolworth and Company: In 2011, F. W. Woolworth's closed its doors, after 118 years as a *five-and-ten-cent store*. Selling a variety of household goods from women's jewelry to pie plates, the store was named a *five-and-ten-cent store* because, until 1930, nothing was priced over a nickel or a dime. (11)

Waldorf-Astoria Hotel: Did you notice that the Waldorf-Astoria Hotel in this story was located on Fifth Avenue? The original Waldorf Hotel was located in a Fifth Avenue mansion on 33rd Street. Built by William Waldorf Astor in 1893, the hotel became the grandest hotel in the world after William collaborated with his cousin, John Astor, to open The Waldorf-Astoria Hotel. These hotel buildings were torn down in 1929. The present-day Waldorf-Astoria Hotel was built on Park Avenue between 49th and 50th Streets. What became of the Fifth Avenue and 33rd Street location? It's the site of the Empire State Building in New York.

(www.waldorfnewyork.com)

Ellis Island Hospital:

Ellis Island Hospital closed their doors over sixty years ago, but the buildings still stand on Ellis Island. The General Hospital opened in 1902 and the Contagious Disease Hospital, in 1911. In the 1920s, it was one of the largest hospitals in New York, second only to Bellevue Hospital. When you come to New York or New Jersey, don't miss a visit to the Statue of Liberty and Ellis Island Monument operated by the

National Park Service. For the cost of the ferryboat ride, you can visit both Ellis Island and Liberty Island. Before landing at the Ellis Island Immigrant Museum, the ferry will pass the southernmost part of the island. Look for the buildings that were once the 450-bed Contagious Disease Hospital and the magnificent 275-bed General Hospital where my fictional character, *Miss Angie,* worked. You won't find the *Cottage* at the tip of the island. The residence cottage, where the nurses lived in 1924, deteriorated many years ago. It was demolished in 1934.

The non-profit *Save Ellis Island Foundation* was established to increase public awareness and funding to preserve the hospital complex as a future educational conference center. Visit their website for maps, pictures and more information on plans for the site. (www.saveellisisland.org)

Ellis Island Immigrant Processing Center:

Ellis Island served as one of the immigrant registration centers in the United States (U.S.) from 1892 to 1954. Screening guidelines were determined by a multitude of U.S. immigration laws that were passed between the years 1875 to 1946. (18,19,20) The Statue of Liberty and the Ellis Island Museum are operated by the National Park Service. They are accessible by ferry from New York and New Jersey. When you visit, arrive early and spend the entire day. There are three floors of exhibits and displays. Sign up for the presentations given by the knowledgeable National Park Rangers, watch the movies, listen to the oral histories, and learn more about the screening procedures and requirements for admission into the United States, including the minimum amount of money the immigrants were required to have in order to be admitted. The nurturing kindness of the *ladies-in-white* is frequently mentioned in the recordings of the Ellis Island Oral History Project. (15)

(www.nps.gov)

(www.ellisisland.com)

(www.ancestry.com)

(www.ellisislandimmigrants.org)

Henry House:

Lillian Wald wrote, *A House on Henry Street* (17) in 1915, recording the history of The Henry Street Settlement House, and the beginning of The Visiting Nurse Service. Her story is retold by Adeline in Chapter Thirteen of *Ellis Angels On The Move.* Today, the Henry Street Settlement House remains a vital community resource, reaching more that 50,000 people annually. For information on its current activities, visit the Henry Street website which states: "Henry Street settlement opens doors of opportunity to enrich lives and enhance human progress for Lower East Side residents and other New Yorkers through social services, arts, and healthcare programs."

(www.henrystreet.org)

Hull House:

Jane Adams and Ellen Starr founded Hull House in 1889 to help the immigrants in Chicago, Illinois. Their venture was so successful that settlement houses across the country consulted with them. Adams philosophy is outlined in her book, *Twenty Years at Hull House* (1), in which she refers to the three "R's: Residence, Research, and Reform" (residing in the community, researching community needs, and initiating social reform).

ELLIS ANGELS ON THE MOVE

Immigrant Stories:

Immigrant stories in this novel were inspired by Ellis Island photographs and oral histories, as well as the documentation of authors. (3,4,5,13) A single photograph of a barefoot girl arriving at Ellis Island evolved into the story of Elsbeth Ferguson.

Through interviews with immigrants, Peter Coan's work, *Ellis Island Interviews: Immigrants Tell Their Stories In Their Own Words*, documented 1) the story of the boys who frequently escaped the hospital to play by the dock in the evening, 2) the Ellis Island guard who made extra money by lending out his twenty-dollar bill, and 3) the betting and gambling that occurred during detention. (4)

The story of the young man from Australia is a fictionalized version of the fate of Ormond Joseph McDermott who arrived at Ellis Island in February of 1921. He had traded in his first-class ticket to work as a member of the crew. He contracted scarlet fever while being detained, and died at Ellis Island Hospital. His medical records were sent to his family in Australia. Years later, Lorie Conway contacted them. They allowed her to publish pages from his medical chart in *Forgotten Ellis Island: The Extraordinary Story of America's Immigrant Hospital*. (5)

American Passage: The History of Ellis Island by Vincent Cannato describes the many ships waiting in the harbor until quota numbers would be refreshed on January 1, 1925. (3)

Infant Incubator Exhibit:

The fictional characters, *Dr. Martin and Madame Louise*, honor Dr. Martin Couney and his head-nurse, Madame Louise Recht. The original incubator design was the idea of Dr. Tarnier. However, Dr. Couney used an adaptation of Dr. Lion's incubators from France. In 1903,

Couney opened the *Infant Incubator Exhibit* at Coney Island's Luna Park following the strict guidelines he learned in France from his mentor, Dr. Pierre Budin. Labeled by some, *The Father of Neonatology*, his life-saving techniques were highly efficacious. The money he earned from the exhibits financed the care of the infants. After forty years of service, he closed the exhibit. He felt that he had completed his mission when New York Presbyterian Weill Cornell Medical Center opened the first hospital center for babies born prematurely in the NYC tri-state area. (8,12,14)

(www.neonatology.org)

(www.pediatrics.aappublications.org)

(www.prematurity.com).

Prohibition (The 18th Amendment)

Prohibition is the era of prohibition of alcohol in the United States from 1919 to 1933. Making, selling, or transporting alcohol was *prohibited* by the 18th Amendment to the U.S. Constitution.

(www.history1900s.about.com)

(www.lawcornell.edu)

(www.constitutioncenter.org)

St. Barbara's Roman Catholic Church:

Built in 1909, the two tall bell towers of this Spanish Baroque style church still soar over the community in the Bushwick section of Brooklyn. The land for the church on Central Avenue, between Menahan and Bleecker Streets, was donated by the Eppig Brewery family. Intricate stained glass windows, colorful frescos and beautiful statues from the original design have been preserved and restored for the current congregation to enjoy.

(www.stbarbarascatholicchurch.com)

The Statue of Liberty:

The Statue of Liberty has been standing in New York harbor on Liberty Island (formally Bedloe Island) since it was dedicated in October, 1886. The structure was designed by French sculptor, Frederic Bartholdi (1834-1904), and engineered by Gustave Eiffel (1832-1923). Called *Liberty Enlightening the World*, it was offered as a gift from France to the United States, and remains a symbol of democracy.

(www.statueofliberty.org)

(www.nps.gov)

Acknowledgments

I want to thank my readers for spreading the word about *Ellis Angels: The Nurses of Ellis Island Hospital*, my first novel. Without your encouragement and reviews, this sequel would never have been written.

Readers asked for more immigrant stories and more romance. The stories were easy to research. Romance was a challenge. My generation of nurse did not fall in love with the doctor. We practiced in the shadow of the Women's Liberation Movement. The original outline of *Ellis Angels* featured Angie as an independent career woman, a feminist, ahead of her time.

My daughters, Caroline and Michelle, insisted that *Angie and Abe*, as well as, *Adeline and Harry,* fall in love. Try as I might to break up the romances early on, they developed a life of their own. As in real life, love has a way of burning no matter how many times you intentionally try to smother the flames. In the end, Angie and Adeline chose their career *and* marriage. In that way, they were women of the 1920s who were ahead of their time.

The cover of this novel should read: "By Carole Limata with lots of help and encouragement from her two Alberts". My husband, Al, critiques and edits my work. My son helps me with rewrites and encourages me. He is a writer in every sense of the word. His work has not yet been published, but when it is, we are all in for a treat. One night, he called and said, "One way you can thank your readers is to keep writing." His words lit a fire under me. I started research on this novel that night.

"Feedback makes it better," were the words of Dr. Edgar Schoen, the former Medical Director of Screening at the Kaiser-Permanente Department of Genetics. I am grateful to him for teaching me the importance of not being afraid to put your work out for feedback. Thank you to my sisters, Dr. Patricia Marcellino and Madeline Dittus, for your feedback, editing, and proofing. Thank you to my daughters, Caroline and Michelle, for your proofing and feedback. Another thank-you to my dear friends, Theresa Campisi, Elaine Eastman and Jennifer O'Keefe, nurses and early readers, who struggled over the errors and mistakes of my first drafts to an attempt to give me feedback.

A big thank-you to Frank and Marilyn Marcellino. Frank designed the cover of both *Ellis Angels* and *Ellis Angels On The Move*. He didn't think he could top the cover of *Ellis Angels*, but he did. He is an artist and architect who shares generously of his time and talent. Marilyn Marcellino, Frank's wife, is the beautiful woman on the cover of the Ellis Angels novels. Both are friends and family to me. They are my sister's brother-in-law and sister-in-law, and therefore, I decided, mine also.

Special thanks to those of you who shared your family stories with me. My sisters, Patty and Madeline, remember walking with me to the settlement house in Williamsburg when we were little girls in Brooklyn. We went to story-time while Mom took an art class. We love the story Mom tells about six-month-old, *Baby Patty*. She got the *cooties* after a little girl came up to the baby carriage, put her head in, and shook head lice over the baby, saying, "Oh, what a pretty baby!"

Thank you to my longtime friend, Terry Campisi, who shared the stories of her father, Nick Campanelli. Nick lived in the Lower East Side, and had polio as a child. The New York Visiting Nurses brought him to the Henry Street Settlement House for daycare while his mother worked. They gave him nutritious food to eat and kept him busy during his long recuperation.

As a young girl, I remember walking home after school on Bushwick Avenue. I would often try to imagine the interior of the stately mansions that I passed. I wondered what it would be like to sit on a window seat in a circular turret room, looking out onto the Avenue. Many of the Bushwick Avenue mansions are still there, standing proudly. Three blocks away is St. Barbara's Church, which remains a vital church for its congregation in the Bushwick section of Brooklyn.

A special thank-you goes out to my St Barbara Grammar School classmates, Class of 1962, who meet annually to keep the spirit of St Barbara's Grammar School alive.

Heart Connection

Sometimes in your
  wandering,
you'll recognize a friend.
You'll look into their eyes to
think the union has no end.
No end and no beginning,
just a long enduring trend
As two hearts come together,
and two mighty spirits
  blend.

Often you will wonder:
How can this really be?
That she can look at you,
but into your soul she'll see.
Giving and receiving
with ease and mutuality,
Two people, two hearts,
one shared philosophy.

You each agree to love
and to protect each other,
A pact of care between a
daughter and a mother.
An oath of loyalty pledged
by sister and brother.
The faith entrusted
to a special lover.

Somewhere along the
  journey,
you know you'll never part.
For when you love each other,
love lives within your heart.
Your life will change forever
as new beginnings start.
You'll share your life
  together
connected in your heart.

By Carole Lee Limata

Resources

(1) Adams, Jane, *Twenty Years at Hull House*, New York: Dover Publications, 2008. (Originally Published by The Macmillan Company, New York, 1910)

(2) Brick, Michael, *And Next to the Bearded Ladies and Premature Babies*, The New York Times, New York Region, June 12, 2005.

(3) Cannato, Vincent, J., *American Passage: The History of Ellis Island*, New York: Harper, 2009.

(4) Coan, Peter M., *Ellis Island Interviews: Immigrants Tell Their Stories In Their Own Words*, New York: Barnes and Noble Books, 1997.

(5) Conway, Lorie, *Forgotten Ellis Island: The Extraordinary Story of America's Immigrant Hospital*, New York: HarperCollins Publishers, 2007.

(6) Feld, Marjorie, *Lillian Wald: A Biography*, North Carolina: The University of North Carolina Press, Chapel Hill, 2008.

(7) Friedman, Michael and Friedman, Brett, *Settlement Houses: Improving the Social Welfare of America's Immigrants*, New York: The Rosen Publishing Group, Inc, 2006.

(8) Liebling, A. J., *Profiles: A Patron of the Premies*, The New Yorker, June 3, 1929, pp. 20-24.

(9) Moreno, Barry, Ellis Island, *Images of America*, California: Arcadia Publishing, 2003.

(10) Moreno, Barry, *Children of Ellis Island, Images of America*, California: Arcadia Publishing, 2005.

(11) Nilsson, Jeff, *Woolworth: A Five and Dime Story*, New York: The Saturday Evening Post, Feb 21, 2011.

(12) Silverman, William A, M.D., *Incubator-Baby Side Shows*, Pediatrics 64 (2): 127-141, August, 1979.

(13) Werner, Emmy E., *Passages to America: Oral Histories of Child Immigrants from Ellis Island and Angel Island*, Washington D.C.: Potomac Books Inc., 2009.

(14) *The Coney Island Baby Laboratory: Incubators for Newborn Infants Were Developed Not in a Medical Research Facility but Amid Barkers, Sideshows, and Gawking Crowds*, Innovation and Technology Magazine, Fall 1992, Vol 10, Issue 2.

(15) Oral History Project: 1892 to 1973. A collection of two thousand oral histories by the Ellis Island Oral History Program of the Ellis Island Immigration Museum

(16) Smith, Betty, *A Tree Grows in Brooklyn*, New York: Harper Collins Publishers Inc, 1943.

(17) Wald, Lillian D., *The House on Henry Street*, New York: Forgotten Books, 2012. (Originally published by Henry Holt and Company, 1915).

(18) 1891 Immigration Law: Session II Chapter 551, 26 STAT. 1084, 51st Congress, March 3, 1891.

(19) 1921 Emergency Quota law: An act to limit the immigration of aliens into the United States H.R. 4075; Pub. L. 67-5, 42 Stat. 5, 67th Congress May 19, 1921.

(20) 1924 Immigration Act: An act to limit the immigration of aliens into the Unites States. H.R. 7995; Pub. L. 68-139, 43 Stat. 153, 68th Congress May 26, 1924.

About The Author

Carole Lee Limata graduated with an Associate Degree (AAS) in Nursing from Queens College, New York in 1968. After taking her Nursing Boards that summer, she worked as a Registered Nurse at New York City's Metropolitan Hospital, and then, at the City's Premature Nursery Center located at Elmhurst Hospital before moving to Northern California. She received a Bachelor's Degree (BSN) from Sacramento State University and earned a Master's Degree (MSN) from the University of California at San Francisco (UCSF) in 1980. She is a member of the National Nurses Honor Society.

Throughout her forty-year nursing career, Carole worked as a staff nurse, supervisor, maternity faculty member, and prenatal educator before becoming a Director of a Maternity Department. In the early 1980's, she expanded the prenatal education curriculum into the Oakland community, offering more than twenty different classes to expectant mothers and their families.

In 2008, she retired from her final position as Supervisor of the Screening Programs at the Kaiser Permanente Genetics Department in Oakland, California.

Carole has three wonderful grown children, two terrific son-in-laws, and three beautiful grandchildren. With her husband, Al, she divides her time equally between both coasts.

Carole can be reached at EllisAngelsNovel@aol.com

Discussion Guide One

1. Sister Gwendolyn, Miss Elsie and Miss Angie discuss the qualities of a good nurse. If you were a patient in a hospital or healthcare setting, what characteristics would you hope and expect from the nurse who was caring for you? (Chapter 3)

2. There are many stories about the immense generosity of the immigrants, sharing the little they had with each other. Do you personally know of any? (Chapter 4)

3. Have you ever experienced having the jitters before you were expected to do something important? How did you calm yourself? How did you feel afterward? (Chapter 5)

4. There is a recurring message to *take a leap of faith and crash through your fear* throughout the book. Have you ever experienced this before you did something you were meant to do? What was the outcome? (Chapter 5)

5. Sister Gwendolyn writes in her journal that she *had a hunch. Something told me…wait. Did I follow my instincts? No!* Do you always follow your instincts? How do you know to do this? Has there ever been a time when something hampered you from following your instincts? (Chapter 7)

6. In the same journal entry, Sister Gwendolyn states: *the old boys had a club meeting without me.* Have you observed or experienced a division between the men and the women in management? (Chapter 7)

7. Today, it is almost inconceivable to work overtime without getting paid appropriately for your extra work unless you are in a salaried position. When did an overtime pay scale come about for hourly workers? What role did unions play in establishing overtime pay? (Chapter 7)

8. Do you think the infants displayed in the infant incubator exhibit at Coney Island's Luna Park were exploited for financial gain? (Chapter 8)

9. In her letter to Angie, Elsbeth Ferguson describes how an Ellis Island guard lent a twenty dollar bill to her husband during his hearing for the cost of one dollar. Do you think this happened often? (Chapter 7)

10. Many old world treatments that were passed down from generation to generation were highly effective and are still effective today. Do you know of any? Why have people forgotten them? How do federally-approved pharmaceuticals compare to natural treatments? (Chapter 8)

11. The settlement house played an important role in shaping a diverse community. How did it influence the lives of the immigrants? What impact did it have on the Americanization of the immigrants? Do you know of similar establishments in your neighborhood today? (Chapter 9)

12. As Angie walks uptown, she recalls Miss Elsie lecturing the nurses. Miss Elsie says: *Nurses are always caring for others, but never take the time to care for themselves. Remember to take care of yourself. Eat breakfast. Take your bathroom breaks. Step out into the fresh air at least once a day.* As a new mother, or someone caring for a parent or relative, what have you discovered about caring for

yourself while you care for others? How do you find the time to do this? (Chapter 11)

13. Many cultures have a version of the evil eye in which they believe hardship can be passed on to another. What do they call it in different countries? What protective measures do they use to ward it off? (Chapter 12)

14. Mr. Stewart changed his first-class ticket to a steerage ticket. First-and second-class steamship passengers were not required to go through Ellis Island screening. Do you feel it was fair that only steerage passengers, like Mr. Stewart, were required to go through the Ellis Island registration process? Do you think this policy fulfilled the screening criteria outlined in the law of the day? (Chapter 15)

15. In 1925, it was not ordinary to see a woman drive a car. Do you or your parents remember the days when women did not drive automobiles? Do you remember a jiggle you recited if you saw a *lady-driver*? Do you know that there are countries today where women are forbidden to drive? How does that make you feel? (Chapter 18, 25)

16. Frieda Kohl used an alias when she took the Moretti boy to the clinic. Do you think that happened often? Does it happen today? (Chapter 21)

17. Merta Flanagan delivered her baby and did not know to cut the umbilical cord. Can a baby live with the placenta attached? Some cultures refer to this as a *lotus birth*. (Chapter 22)

18. Do you think Merta should have been jailed for leaving her baby at the door of the Nativity Settlement House? What states in the United States have a law that allows a parent to

safely leave a baby at a hospital or health care facility? (Chapter 22)

19. Baby Henri was sleeping on his stomach when Madame Louise was caring for him. Why are new mothers now encouraged to position their newborns to sleep on their backs and not their stomachs? (Chapter 27)

20. As young adults, we were given the advice to, "Sleep on it!" Do things become clearer when you sleep on a decision? (Chapter 33).

Discussion Guide Two
For Nurses and Nursing Students

1. Miss Angie goes through an elaborate procedure to prepare a narcotic injection for her patient, Mrs. Mertens. Compare this to how an injection is prepared and given in a hospital setting today. (Chapter 2)

2. Sister Gwendolyn, Miss Elsie and Miss Angie discuss the qualities of a good nurse during supper. What characteristics do you appreciate and expect in a nursing colleague? (Chapter 3)

3. Have you ever been floated or transferred in a different department and expected to know what was going on? What would have helped to make the transition easier? (Chapter 4)

4. Angie writes a letter to Adeline. She says: *You often spoke of how frightened the immigrants became when they were taken ill. They avoid formal hospital and clinic settings for fear that they will be deported, or their children will be taken from them.* Do you think that immigrants in this country may still have some of these same fears today? (Chapter 5)

5. Have you ever experienced having the jitters before you were expected to do something important at work? How did you calm yourself? How did you feel afterward? (Chapter 6)

6. Sister Gwendolyn tells us that during the busiest registration years, the physicians had a mere six seconds to do a physical assessment on an immigrant walking past them in the Registry

Room. If you had the same six seconds to do a physical assessment on a patient, what would you look for? Try to list at least six symptoms that the physicians were on the alert for? (Chapter 7)

7. Sister Gwendolyn states in her journal that: *the old boys had a club meeting without me.* Have you ever observed or experienced a division between those who work in Hospital Administration and the Nursing Administrators in the Nursing Department? (Chapter 7)

8. Today, it is almost inconceivable to work overtime without getting paid appropriately for your extra work. When did an overtime pay scale come about? What role did nursing unions play in establishing overtime pay for nurses? (Chapter 7)

9. Do you think the infants displayed in the infant incubator exhibit at Coney Island were exploited for financial gain? Dr. Martin explains the premature infants have no fat to retain their body heat. What other challenges do they face? (Chapter 8)

10. Many old world treatments that were passed down from generation to generation were highly effective and are still effective today. Do you know of any old world treatments that work effectively? Can you explain why? Why have people forgotten them? How do federally-approved pharmaceuticals compare to natural treatments? (Chapter 10)

11. As Angie walks uptown, she recalls Miss Elsie lecturing the nurses. Miss Elsie says: *Nurses are always caring for others, but never take the time to care for themselves. Remember to take care of yourself. Eat breakfast. Take your bathroom breaks. Step out into the fresh air at least once a day.* What have you discovered about caring for

yourself while you are caring for others? How do you find the time to do this? (Chapter 11)

12. *For the smart visiting nurses knew that good health came from healthy living, fresh air, sunshine, and pristine hygiene. They discovered, early on, that improving the social aspects of the neighborhood, improved the health of its residents. The nurses not only provided nursing care, they fought for social reform as a means to improve the health of the community.* What role do social and economic pressures play in preventing illness and maintaining wellness in contemporary communities? (Chapter 11)

13. Lillian Wald advises Angie: *Start with prenatal classes. Always remember that a young mother's love will seek out wellness for her unborn child. The maternity link with healthcare is often the first link for families. After that link is made, the families attach and will come to trust you.* Do you think this is true for today's hospital systems? Do hospitals incorporate this concept into their marketing and advertising strategies? (Chapter 11)

14. The settlement house played an important role in shaping a diverse community. How did it influence the lives of the immigrants? What impact did it have on the Americanization of the immigrants? What does the Settlement House Concept and the current Affordable Care Act have in common? (Chapter 13)

15. Sister Gwendolyn chose to rotate the chief nurses to house supervision. Do you think it was a good idea for Sister Gwendolyn to postpone selecting a replacement for Miss Elsie? (Chapter 15)

16. Frieda Kohl used an alias when she took the Moretti boy to the clinic. Do you think that happened often? Does it happen

today? What precautions do hospitals take to avoid this when they register patients? (Chapter 21)

17. In modern day hospital deliveries, the placenta is delivered immediately after the birth of the baby. Why did the placenta take a half-hour to release after Merta's baby was delivered? Can a baby live with the placenta attached? In some cultures, this is referred to as a *Lotus Birth*. (Chapter 22)

18. Do you feel Merta Flanagan should be jailed for abandoning her baby? What states in the United States have a law that allows a parent to safely leave a baby at a hospital or health care facility? (Chapter 22)

19. Baby Henri was sleeping on his stomach when Madame Louise was caring for him. Why are new mothers now encouraged to position their newborns to sleep on their backs and not their stomachs? (Chapter 27)

20. If you were marketing a new program, such as a community education class, for a local hospital or health center, and there was no budget for formal advertising, how would you get the word out to the community by grassroots marketing?

ELLIS ANGELS:

The Nurses of Ellis Island Hospital

A Novel By Carole Lee Limata

Ellis Angels is a heartwarming story about the compassionate nurses of Ellis Island Hospital, the *ladies-in-white*, and the loving care they gave their immigrant patients. Ellis Island Hospital has been closed since 1954. When Superstorm Sandy bombards New York Harbor in 2012, Ellis Island is battered and flooded. During an extensive clean-up, a file cabinet is discovered in the long-abandoned hospital building. It was found to contain the files of a former Nursing Superintendent. Filled with documentation of nursing procedures, notes, schedules, and pages from her 1924 journal, the tender tale of Ellis Angels was inspired from these files.

Newly-arrived immigrants are facing enormous physical and emotional challenges. The Stanescu twins are separated from their mother, and admitted for favus scalp infections. Fabiana Morales, a beautiful young woman, comes to America to be married, and is rejected by her future husband because of her goiter. Mrs. Ryan, pregnant with her fifth child, is hospitalized for pregnancy complications. Mrs. Brunne and her newborn are facing deportation because of a new Quota Law, and a teenager has delivered a premature infant on the floor of the Women's Detention Dormitory.

During her orientation, Miss Angie, a nurse recruit, learns the routines of the Hospital. She meets handsome Dr. Goodwin who is searching for the nurse of his dreams. Miss Adeline, an experienced and spirited nurse, takes Angie under her wing. The Nursing Superintendent, Sister Gwendolyn, is keeping a watchful eye on all of her nursing staff.

Together, through their creativity and united efforts, the nurses and doctors of Ellis Island Hospital discover ways to help their patients follow their dreams, and in the process, they achieve their own American Dream as well.

Made in the USA
Middletown, DE
08 May 2015